Prai...

Cloche an...

"A delicious romp through my ... with a delightful new heroine."

—Deborah Crombie, *New York Times* bestselling author

"Brimming with McKinlay's trademark wit and snappy one-liners . . . Anglophiles will love this thoroughly entertaining new murder mystery series. A hat trick of love, laughter, and suspense, and another feather in [Jenn McKinlay's] cap."

—Hannah Dennison, author of
the Vicky Hill Exclusive! Mysteries

"Fancy hats and British aristocrats make this my sort of delicious cozy read."

—Rhys Bowen, *USA Today* bestselling author of
the Royal Spyness Mysteries

Praise for Jenn McKinlay's Library Lover's Mysteries

Book, Line, and Sinker

"Entertaining . . . An outstanding cozy mystery . . . featuring engaging characters and an intriguing story."

—*Lesa's Book Critiques*

"A great read . . . in this delightfully charming series."

—*Dru's Book Musings*

"Quickly paced, tightly plotted, intricately crafted . . . Action-packed."

—*The Season*

Due or Die

"[A] terrific addition to an intelligent, fun, and lively series."

—Miranda James, *New York Times* bestselling author of
the Cat in the Stacks Mysteries

continued . . .

"What a great read! . . . McKinlay has been a librarian, and her snappy story line, fun characters, and young library director with backbone make for a winning formula."

—*Library Journal*

"McKinlay's writing is well paced, her dialogue feels very authentic, and I found *Due or Die* almost impossible to put down."   —*CrimeSpree*

Books Can Be Deceiving

"A sparkling setting, lovely characters, books, knitting, and chowder! What more could any reader ask?"

—Lorna Barrett, *New York Times* bestselling author of the Booktown Mysteries

"With a remote coastal setting as memorable as Manderley and a kindhearted, loyal librarian as the novel's heroine, *Books Can Be Deceiving* is sure to charm cozy readers everywhere."

—Ellery Adams, *New York Times* bestselling author of the Books by the Bay Mysteries

"Fast-paced and fun, *Books Can Be Deceiving* is the first in Jenn McKinlay's appealing new mystery series featuring an endearing protagonist, delightful characters, a lovely New England setting, and a fascinating murder. Don't miss this charming new addition to the world of traditional mysteries."

—Kate Carlisle, *New York Times* bestselling author of the Bibliophile Mysteries

Praise for Jenn McKinlay's Cupcake Bakery Mysteries

Red Velvet Revenge

"You're in for a real treat with Jenn McKinlay's Cupcake Bakery Mystery. I gobbled it right up."

—Julie Hyzy, *New York Times* bestselling author of the Manor House Mysteries and White House Chef Mysteries

"Sure as shootin', *Red Velvet Revenge* pops with fun and great twists. Wrangle up some time to enjoy the atmosphere of a real rodeo as well as family drama. It's better than icing on the tastiest cupcake."   —Avery Aames, author of the Cheese Shop Mysteries

Death by the Dozen

"It's the best yet, with great characters, and a terrific, tightly written plot."   —*Lesa's Book Critiques*

"Like a great fairy tale, McKinlay transports readers into the world of cupcakes and all things sweet and frosted, minus the calories. Although . . . there are some pretty yummy recipes at the end."   —AnnArbor.com

Buttercream Bump Off

"A charmingly entertaining story paired with a luscious assortment of cupcake recipes that, when combined, make for a deliciously thrilling mystery."   —*Fresh Fiction*

"Another tasty entry, complete with cupcake recipes, into what is sure to grow into a perennial favorite series."
                                                      —*The Mystery Reader*

Sprinkle with Murder

"A tender cozy full of warm and likable characters and a refreshingly sympathetic murder victim. Readers will look forward to more of McKinlay's tasty concoctions."
                                          — *Publishers Weekly* (starred review)

"McKinlay's debut mystery flows as smoothly as Melanie Cooper's buttercream frosting. Her characters are delicious, and the dash of romance is just the icing on the cake."
                        —Sheila Connolly, *New York Times* bestselling author of
                                                            Scandal in Skibbereen

Berkley Prime Crime titles by Jenn McKinlay

Cupcake Bakery Mysteries

SPRINKLE WITH MURDER
BUTTERCREAM BUMP OFF
DEATH BY THE DOZEN
RED VELVET REVENGE
GOING, GOING, GANACHE
SUGAR AND ICED

Library Lover's Mysteries

BOOKS CAN BE DECEIVING
DUE OR DIE
BOOK, LINE, AND SINKER
READ IT AND WEEP

Hat Shop Mysteries

CLOCHE AND DAGGER
DEATH OF A MAD HATTER

DEATH OF A MAD HATTER

Jenn McKinlay

BERKLEY PRIME CRIME, NEW YORK

THE BERKLEY PUBLISHING GROUP
Published by the Penguin Group
Penguin Group (USA) LLC
375 Hudson Street, New York, New York 10014

USA • Canada • UK • Ireland • Australia • New Zealand • India • South Africa • China

penguin.com

A Penguin Random House Company

DEATH OF A MAD HATTER

A Berkley Prime Crime Book / published by arrangement with the author

Copyright © 2014 by Jennifer McKinlay Orf.
Excerpt from *On Borrowed Time* by Jenn McKinlay copyright © 2014 by
Jennifer McKinlay Orf.

Berkley Prime Crime Books are published by The Berkley Publishing Group.
BERKLEY® PRIME CRIME and the PRIME CRIME logo
are trademarks of Penguin Group (USA) LLC.

For information, address: The Berkley Publishing Group,
a division of Penguin Group (USA) LLC,
375 Hudson Street, New York, New York 10014.

ISBN: 978-0-425-25890-3

PUBLISHING HISTORY
Berkley Prime Crime mass-market edition / May 2014

PRINTED IN THE UNITED STATES OF AMERICA

10 9 8 7 6 5 4 3 2 1

Cover illustration by Robert Steele.
Cover design by Diana Kolsky.
Interior text design by Laura K. Corless.

For my mom, Susan N. McKinlay. From the moment I came to be, you have loved me unconditionally. It is the greatest gift a mother can give a child, and I am ever grateful that you're my mom. All that I am, I owe to you. I love you heaps and heaps, Mom!

Acknowledgments

Not only do I judge books by their covers, I judge them by their titles as well. And so, a grateful tip of the brim is due to my brilliant agent, Jessica Faust, for coming up with this spectacular title. You are a genius! Also, I want to thank my editor, Kate Seaver, for her invaluable input during the idea stage of this book. Your wisdom and patience never run out. You amaze me!

Big smooches to my husband, Chris Hansen Orf, for his constant support and encouragement. You never doubt me, Hub, which is a gift beyond measure. Thank you!

Lastly, a crusher hug of thanks for my travel buddies, Wowa and the Hooligans Beckett and Wyatt. Traipsing around London with the three of you will be one of my most cherished memories—forever and ever. Mind the gap!

Chapter 1

"Take it off, Scarlett. You look like a corpse."

My cousin Vivian Tremont stared at me in horror as if I had in fact just risen from the grave.

"Don't hold back," I said. "Tell me how you really feel."

"Sorry, love, but pale redheads like you should avoid any color that has gray tones in it," Viv said. Then because calling me a corpse wasn't clear enough, she shuddered.

I crossed the floor of our hat shop to the nearest freestanding mirror. Our grandmother, Mim, had passed away five years ago and left her shop, Mim's Whims, in London to the two of us. Viv was the creative genius behind the hats, having grown up in Notting Hill just down the street from the shop, while I was the people person—you know, the one who kept the clients from running away from Viv when she got that scary inspired look in her eye.

JENN McKINLAY

Having been raised in the States, I had chosen to go into the hospitality industry. Things had been going well until I discovered my rat-bastard boyfriend, whose family happened to own the hotel of which I was assistant manager, was still married. At Viv's urging, I escaped that fiasco and came here to take up my share of the business. So far London had done quite a lot to take my mind off of my troubles. Viv in particular kept me on my toes, making sure I didn't lose my people skills.

In fact, just the other day she'd gotten swept up in an artistic episode and tried to convince the very timid Mrs. Barker that wearing a hat with two enormous cherries the size of beach balls connected by the stems and with a leaf the size of a dinner plate would be brilliant. It was—just not on Mrs. Barker's head.

It had taken me an afternoon of plying Mrs. Barker with tea and biscuits and yanking Viv into the back room and threatening to put her in a headlock to get them to an accord. Finally, Mrs. Barker had agreed to a black trilby with cherries the size of golf balls nestled on the side and Viv had been satisfied to work her magic on a smaller scale.

I ignored my dear cousin's opinion of my complexion and stood in front of the mirror and tipped the lavender sun hat jauntily to one side. It was mid-May and summer was coming. I'd been looking for a hat to shade my fair skin from the sun and being a girly girl, I do love all things pink and purple.

"Oh, I can just see the headstone now," a chipper voice said from behind me. "Here lies Scarlett Parker, mistakenly buried alive when she wore an unfortunate color of sun hat."

2

I glared at the reflection of Fiona Fenton, Viv's lovely young apprentice, glancing over my shoulder in the mirror.

Viv laughed and said, "I can dig it."

"In spades," Fee quipped back.

"Fine," I said. I snatched the hat off of my head. "Obviously, the hat is a grave mistake."

They stopped laughing.

"Oh, come on, that was a very good quip," I said. They shook their heads in denial.

"You need to bury that one and back away," Viv said. They both chortled.

"I still think you're being a bit harsh," I said. I replaced the pretty hat on its stand and shook out my long auburn hair.

"No, harsh was that hat on your head," Fee said. She smiled at me, her teeth very white against her cocoa-colored skin. Her corkscrew bob was streaked with blue, she was always changing the color, and one curl fell over her right eye. She blew it out of her face with a puff of her lower lip.

"But I need a sun hat," I complained.

"Plain straw would look very nice," Viv said. "Perhaps with a nice emerald-green ribbon around the crown."

"I'm tired of plain and I'm sick of green."

I knew I sounded a tad whiny, but I didn't care. I was jealous of Fee and Viv. Fee's dark coloring looked good with everything and so did Viv's long blonde curls and big blue eyes, both of which she had inherited directly from Mim. I only got the eyes. So unfair!

The front door opened and I glanced up with my greet-the-customer smile firmly in place. It fell as soon as I recognized the man who walked into the shop.

"Oh, it's you, Harry," I said with a sigh.

Harrison Wentworth, our business manager, raised an eyebrow at my unenthusiastic greeting.

"Harrison," he corrected me. "Pleasure to see you, too, Ginger."

I felt my face get warm at the childhood nickname. Yes, Harry and I had a history, one in which I did not come out very well.

"Sorry. I didn't mean anything by it," I said. "I was just hoping you were a customer so everyone could stop telling me how gruesome I look in lavender."

"I didn't say you were gruesome," Viv corrected me as she rearranged the hats on one of the display shelves. "I said you looked like a corpse. Good morning, Harrison."

She stood on her tiptoes and kissed his cheek.

"Now that's a proper greeting," Harrison said, giving me a meaningful look.

"Hello, Harrison," Fee said. She also kissed his cheek and smiled at him. He returned the grin. I glanced between them. They seemed awfully happy to see each other.

Harrison was Viv's age, two years older than my modest twenty-seven, but Fee was only twenty, entirely too young to be considering a man in his advanced years, in my opinion. And no, it had nothing to do with the fact that Harry and I had a history, if you consider me standing him up for an ice-cream date when I was ten and he was twelve and breaking his adolescent heart a history. I did mention that I didn't come out very well in it, didn't I?

As Fee stepped back, Harrison looked at me expectantly. Before I could stop myself, I found myself looking at him from beneath my lashes and giving him my very practiced, secretive half smile. Sure enough, the man looked as riveted as if I had just propositioned him.

Ugh! Honestly, I am a dreadful flirt. It's like breathing to me and I don't discriminate. I flirt with everyone—kids, pets, old ladies, men, you name it. Probably, that's why the hospitality industry was such a natural fit for me. I am very good at managing people.

I blame my mother. After thirty years of marriage, she still has my dad wrapped around her pinky, and it's not just because of her charming British accent either. My mother is an incorrigible flirt and my dad a complete sucker.

After my last relationship disaster, I made a promise to myself that I would go one whole year without a boyfriend. So far it had been two months. Prior to that the longest I'd gone was two weeks. Shameful, I know.

I shook my head and forced myself to give Harrison my most bland expression. He looked confused. I really couldn't blame him. I was probably giving him emotional whiplash.

Mercifully, the front door opened again and this time two ladies entered. I charged forward, relieved to escape the awkward moment.

"Good afternoon, how may I help you?" I asked.

"You're not Ginny." The older of the two women frowned at me.

"No, I'm Scarlett, and this is my cousin Vi—"

"Ginny!" The older lady shot forward with surprising speed and hugged my cousin close.

Viv looked startled, but she hugged the woman back, obviously not wanting to offend her.

5

I quickly examined the two ladies. The older one had gray hair and wore a conservative print dress that had Marks & Spencer all over it, while the younger woman, a pretty brunette who looked to be somewhere in her twenties, was much more fashion forward, wearing a tailored Alexander McQueen chemise.

"You haven't aged a day," the older woman exclaimed. She cupped Vivian's face and examined her closely. "How have you managed that?"

Viv gave an awkward laugh as if she was quite sure the woman was teasing her, but the woman frowned. "No, really, how have you managed it?"

"Um, my name is Vivian," she said. "I think you might be confusing me with my grandmother Eugenia; everyone called her Ginny."

The older woman stared at her for a moment and then she laughed and said, "Oh, Ginny, always such a joker. Didn't I tell you, Tina?"

"You did at that, Dotty," the other woman said as she stood watching.

"Oh heavens, where are my manners?" Dotty said. "Ginny, this is my daughter-in-law Tina Grisby. Tina, this is my friend the owner of Mim's Whims, Gi—"

"Everyone calls me Viv," Vivian interrupted as she extended her hand to Tina. "This is my cousin Scarlett; our apprentice, Fiona; and our man of business, Harrison."

"You changed your name?" Dotty asked Viv. "How extraordinary."

Viv stared at her for a second and then clearly decided that it did no good to insist she wasn't Mim.

"Yes, I feel more like a Viv than a Ginny," she said.

"Huh." Dotty patted an errant gray curl by her temple. "Maybe I'll change my name. I always fancied myself a Catriona."

Tina gave her mother-in-law an alarmed look. "Dotty, we really should explain our purpose so that we don't keep these kind ladies from their business."

"Yes, you're right," Dotty said. "But I do love the idea of a new name."

"Are you in need of a hat for a specific occasion?" I asked, thinking to get the conversation on track. "Fee, would you bring us some tea?"

"Right away," she agreed.

"I'll just go and attend the books," Harrison said. "If you'll excuse me, ladies."

I watched as he and Fee shared a laugh as they left the room and wondered what they could be discussing that was so amusing. I suspected it was me in my lavender hat.

"Don't you agree, Scarlett?" Viv asked. She was seated in our cozy sitting area with the Grisbys and all three of them were watching me.

"Um," I stalled and when I glanced at my cousin, she had her lips pressed together as if she was trying not to smile. I quickly sat down.

"The Grisby family is hosting a tea in honor of Dotty's late husband and they are planning to have an *Alice in Wonderland* theme," Viv said.

"Oh, I like that idea," I said. "How can we help?"

"Well, it's to be a fund-raiser so that we can name a wing of the hospital after my husband," Dotty said. "Each family member will host a table, and we'd like them to wear hats that can be tied to characters from the book."

I glanced at Viv. Being the creative quotient in the business, this was really her call.

"When would you need these by?" she asked.

"We're hoping to have the tea in late June," Tina said. She gave us an apologetic look. "I know it is short notice."

"Ginny doesn't mind, do you, dear?" Dotty asked. She patted Viv's hand as if they were old friends.

I tried to remember Mim mentioning Dotty Grisby, but I couldn't bring the name up in any of my memories. Of course, given that I was only here on school holidays, I wouldn't have as broad a frame of reference as Viv would. Judging by Viv's surprised expression when Dotty had hugged her, however, I was betting Viv didn't remember her either.

Fee came out with a tray loaded with tea, biscuits, cheese, and fruits. The Grisby ladies enjoyed a cup each and nibbled some of the food. It was agreed that Viv would work up some sketches and they would come in to see them next week.

Dotty took Viv's arm as we walked them to the door. The older lady looked so happy to see her dear friend that I was glad Viv had decided to go along with Dotty's faulty memory. I fell into step beside Tina.

"Your cousin is being very kind," Tina said. "Please tell her that I appreciate it."

"I will," I said. "It must be hard to watch Dotty struggle with her memory."

"Honestly, she's been like this since her husband left her

thirty years ago. Her reality is different from everyone else's and, as my husband explained it to me, it is just better if we go along with her."

"Thirty years ago?" I asked. "I'm sorry, but did I understand that she wants the wing of a hospital named after him?"

"Yes, well," Tina lowered her voice. "They never divorced. He lived in Tuscany with his mistress until he died a month ago. She always told everyone that he was away on business, and I think she managed to convince herself that was the truth. One does wonder, though . . ."

"What?" I asked.

"If that's why she is slightly addled," Tina said. "She never got over him leaving her."

A driver was outside waiting for them and Viv and I waved as they drove away.

Harrison came out from the back room. "The books are done for this week and I'm pleased to announce you're still in business. How did it go with the madames Grisby?"

"They want a tea party à la *Alice in Wonderland*," Viv said. "It'll be tight, but I think I can get it done."

Harrison made a face.

"What? I think it will be great fun," I said.

"You would," he retorted. I was pretty sure this was an insult, but I didn't press it.

"What about you, Viv?" Harrison asked. "How do you feel about it?"

She was quiet for a moment, staring out the window as if contemplating something. When she turned around, she gave us a wicked smile.

"If it's a mad hatter that they want, then it's a mad hatter that they'll get," she declared.

I exchanged an alarmed glance with Harrison. Between Mrs. Grisby's dottiness and Viv's Cheshire cat grin, I was beginning to feel as nonplussed as Alice when she fell down the rabbit hole. Oh dear.

Chapter 2

"No, no, no, oh goodness, no!" Marilyn Tofts, the posh event planner that the Grisby family had hired to pull off their *Alice in Wonderland* tea, was flipping through Viv's sketches. So far, there was a whole lot of "no"s happening and not much else.

Viv was hand stitching several white silk roses and a cluster of berries onto the outside of a sweatband on a periwinkle-blue wide-brimmed sinamay hat. I watched her fingers nimbly move over the fabric. She didn't even seem to notice or care that Marilyn Tofts was rejecting every one of her sketches.

I glanced at the Grisby ladies. Today Dotty had returned with Tina, as well as two of her daughters, Daphne and Rose. Daphne was pacing across the front of the shop. So far she had spent all of her time on her phone haggling with her son over attending the tea party in a way that reminded me of a carnival hustler trying to get suckers to come knock over the bottles at his booth.

"I'm afraid these are not up to my standards," Marilyn announced with a sniff. She waved her hand dismissively at the sketches.

I narrowed my eyes at her. When I'd heard the Grisbys had hired Ms. Tofts, I had done some research. She was a very ambitious event planner and was making a name for herself in London as one of the go-to party planners for the elite.

She certainly looked the part. She wore a flirty little floral skirt under a tailored jacket with the very latest in shoes by Stella McCartney. Her long honey-colored hair was done in an old-Hollywood-starlet style that swooped over one of her eyes and I imagined was supposed to be sexy but made me wonder if she was just hiding an advanced case of pinkeye. Not nice of me, I know.

Her makeup consisted of a heavy hand on the mascara and eyeliner and a bold red lipstick that matched her finger- and toenails.

I didn't like her. Maybe it was the fact that she was dissing my cousin's work, maybe it was the dimple in her cheek when she smiled—a smile without humor—or maybe it was just the overall feeling of poseur that I got off of her. She struck me as one of those people who, lacking their own creative gifts, liked to diminish the genius of others while pretending to hold some high ideal that could not be met.

Petty. That's the word I was looking for to describe her. She struck me as someone who kept score, and the score always had to be in her favor. Mercifully, she was not our client—the Grisbys were, so I really didn't give two hoots whether she liked Viv's designs or not.

It was time for a power play. I crossed the small sitting area and gathered up Viv's sketches. Then I sat beside Dotty and Tina.

"So, here they are," I said. "Have a look and see what you think."

"I beg your pardon," Marilyn said. "I've already said these won't do."

Her lips were puckered as if she'd tasted something sour.

"And we absolutely value your opinion," I said. This was my tactic for telling people what they want to hear while completely ignoring them. Works like a charm.

Viv kept sewing but I saw the corner of her mouth twitch.

"Well, I should think so. I am the event planner," Marilyn said as if this were news.

"And as such, I'm sure you'll want the input of the people whose party you are planning," I said.

I turned my back on her and held out the sketches to Dotty.

"Oh, thank you, dear," Dotty said. She perched her reading glasses on the end of her nose and studied Viv's sketches. "Oh, I like that."

I glanced at the paper. They were looking at Viv's sketch for the Mad Hatter's hat. It was the standard top hat that the Mad Hatter always wore, but Viv had made it bold in bright-blue fabric with white polka dots. The hat band was contrasting red and tucked into it was the *In this style 10/6* note, which was how the original illustrator of the book *Alice's Adventures in Wonderland* and its sequel, *Through the Looking Glass,* Sir John Tenniel, had depicted the hat.

"What does that mean?" Tina asked. "The ten and six?"

"It means the cost of the hat is ten shillings and six pence," Viv said.

"Nice detail. I'm impressed," Tina said.

"Don't be. I looked it up," Viv said with a smile.

She checked the flowers on the hat to see that they were securely fastened and then she tied off her thread, snipping the end with a pair of embroidery scissors that were in the shape of a stork. I remembered they were Mim's old scissors, and it made me feel nostalgic to see Viv use them.

"Ginny, I just love how you've livened up the idea," Dotty said. She reached over and patted Viv's hand. "I think these will do very well."

"I thought her name was V—" Rose began, but Tina shook her head.

The two of them looked at one another, and I saw Rose give Tina a slow nod as if understanding a secret message. They were two of a kind: both brunettes with stylish cuts and clothes that looked casual but were exquisitely made and came with a matching price tag.

"Well, I can see that my services won't be needed for this party, since my opinion is obviously of no interest. I am sure there are other events I can be attending to," Marilyn huffed.

"Here now, what's this?" Daphne asked as she tucked her phone back into her clutch purse and joined the group.

"Apparently, my opinion of the hat designs is of no importance," Marilyn said. "So I am assuming that my services as the event planner are not required either."

"Oh no!" Daphne cried. "You simply have to work on the tea party. Tell her, Mother."

Dotty didn't look up. Instead she shuffled the sketches until she got to the next one.

I glanced at Daphne. She was in full-on middle age, with thick hips and hair beginning to go gray, not that she was letting it win that battle. I imagined her colorist was making a fortune off of her trying to keep her chin-length hair the shade of ash blonde she had going. Given how enamored she was with Marilyn, I assumed she was the type to buy into the other's pretentions.

"Mother, are you listening?" Daphne asked.

Dotty glanced up. "Don't worry, dear," she said. "I'm sure it won't make any difference to Brenda whether Ms. Tofts or someone else plans the tea."

Marilyn and Daphne looked at one another and gasped.

"You never said!" Marilyn accused Daphne.

"I didn't know!" Daphne protested.

"Mrs. Grisby, under the circumstance, I'll be more than happy to plan the tea party," Marilyn said. Her tone was clearly groveling.

I frowned. Obviously, I was missing something, like who the heck was Brenda?

"Well, that's excellent news," Dotty said. "Perhaps you should go see to the caterers, then; I do think my friend Ginny has the hats in hand."

"Of course, my pleasure," Marilyn said, all but bowing as she made her way to the door.

Daphne walked her out and I could hear the two of them whispering excitedly as they went.

"Mum, what are you playing at?" Rose asked. She pushed her black-framed glasses up her nose.

"Why nothing," Dotty said. "My friend Brenda is coming up from Brighton for the tea, and I'm sure she doesn't care who does the planning."

Viv and Tina both burst out laughing, while Rose shook her head and looked nervous.

"All right, catch me up," I whispered to Viv. "What's the inside joke?"

"My friend Dotty just pulled one over on Ms. Tofts," Viv said. "Brenda is the queen's nickname amongst her staff, so she made it sound like—"

"The queen would be attending the tea," I finished for her with a smile. "Very clever."

"Until Daphne figures it out," Rose said worriedly. "Then she's going to have a fit."

Although I had only just met her, I got the distinct impression that Rose was the peacemaker in the family. As the youngest, she was very quiet, almost timid, and seemed to get agitated if anyone showed any sort of upset.

"She'll be fine," Dotty said dismissively. "Now, how are we going to decide who will wear which hat?"

I glanced at Viv. I had no idea if she'd put any thought into this or not. Things could get dicey if family members wanted the same hat.

"Geoffrey asked to be the Mad Hatter," Tina said.

"Of course he did. Whatever Geoffrey wants Geoffrey gets," Daphne said as she rejoined the group. She looked grumpy at the mention of her brother, and I exchanged a glance with Viv.

"Lily has to be the rabbit," Dotty said. "She's always late. It's perfect."

Rose nodded, but Daphne looked even more sour.

"Tina, I think you should be Alice," Dotty said.

"What?" Daphne snapped. "Why her? She's not even a Grisby, not really."

"She is your brother's wife, and since he is the sole heir to his father's fortune, she is the lady of the house, so it is only fitting that she be Alice."

"Just because darling Daddy forgot that he had three other children—" Daphne sniped, but Dotty held up her hand.

"That's enough," she said. "Do not speak ill of your father to me."

Both Tina and Rose looked tense while Daphne visibly seethed. "Fine. Just make me Tweedledee or Tweedledum. I couldn't care less."

With that, Daphne stormed out of the hat shop, slamming the door so hard in her wake that the glass rattled.

Dotty glanced after her daughter. "All right, then. Tweedledum it is."

Chapter 3

Viv and I waved through the glass when the Grisby family finally departed. I was not sorry to see them go. Tina was nice, but Dotty was definitely not all there. Daphne, I wanted to hand a large Pimm's Cup and tell her to calm down, and Rose was so meek, I just wanted to kick her.

That's horrible of me, I know. I am usually excellent with people, all people, but I discovered when I was working in the hospitality industry back in the States that the one sort of person I really struggle with is the helpless whiner. Ironic, yes?

You would think that since I am such a pleaser, the high-maintenance, needy type would be my favorite, but no. The martyr thing just irritates me. If the light in your bathroom is out, call the front desk; we're happy to fix it. Don't wait until the end of a five-day stay to mention it and act all put out because we didn't know. How could we know, since you didn't call and you refused maid service? Argh! Sorry, old issues. But Rose Grisby was definitely one of those martyr types and I just wanted to slap a backbone into the girl before she wilted into a helpless heap of boo-hoo-hoo.

"So, I'm thinking Rose could be the Cheshire cat," Viv said.

"Really?"

"It would force her to have some oomph, don't you think?"

"Maybe," I said, which was my polite way of saying no. "I really thought Dotty should be the Mad Hatter, you know, because she's nuts."

"No, that would be much too obvious." Viv laughed. She turned away from the door and looped her arm through mine. Together we walked into the workroom at the back of the shop.

Fee was there working at the large wooden table in the center of the room. She was brushing fabric stiffener onto a wooden hat form that had a red straw fabric stretched and pinned to it.

She glanced up when we entered. Her face lit with a smile but then dimmed as she recognized us.

I glanced at Viv. "I don't know about you, but that felt like a snub."

"No question," Viv said. "She absolutely snubbed us."

"No!" Fee cried and shook her head. "I'm sorry. I just thought you were someone else."

Again Viv and I exchanged a glance. "Do tell," I said. "Who were you expecting?"

"Oh, no one," Fee said. She turned away.

Viv raised one eyebrow whispered, "Do we press her or let it lie?"

"Let it lie," I said. "This time."

Viv looked reluctant but then shrugged. "Tea, then?"

"Sounds good," I said.

Viv went to fill the kettle while I foraged in the cupboards for something to snack on. I glanced at Fee out of the corner of my eye. The truth was I didn't want to press her because I had a feeling she'd been hoping that we were Harrison and I did not want my suspicion confirmed.

The thought that she might be crushing on our man of business bothered me, but I wasn't sure why and I really didn't want to talk about it and be forced to acknowledge something I wasn't prepared to deal with.

"So, how are things shaping up for the Wonderland tea?" Fee asked.

"Once we got rid of Tofts the event planner, it went very well," Viv said. "I'll need your help with the hats, of course."

Fee looked delighted, and I felt the teensiest bit left out. Then I remembered how many times I had stuck myself with pins while trying to attach a bit of fabric to a hat form and I got over it. Millinery just wasn't my gift.

"Hello?" a man's voice called out from the front of the shop.

Fee sat up straight and gazed at the door, looking hopeful.

"We're back here!" I called out.

I knew that voice. It was low and deep and rumbled through my chest like a freight train. I hoped I didn't look as giddy as Fee to hear it. I watched Fee as the man entered through the narrow doorway. Her reaction to seeing him would be very telling. She beamed. Damn.

"Are you closing up early today?" Harrison asked.

Fee sat grinning at him and he smiled in return, looking equally delighted to see her before turning to me and Viv.

"No," I snapped. "Why would you think that?"

"Well, because no one is minding the store," he said. Then he frowned at me. "And because we're supposed to go over to Andre's gallery and help him and Nick set up for his opening show. You do remember that his big art show is coming up, and you made us all promise to help."

I had met Andre Eisel, a photographer, and his life partner, Nick Carroll, a dentist, when I had moved back to London a few months before. I had convinced Andre to photograph Lady Ellis wearing one of Viv's hats and, well, let's just say we bonded over the traumatic event and we have been BFF ever since.

"Oh yeah," I said.

"You forgot!" he accused.

"No, I didn't," I said. Yes, big fat lie. "I'm merely preoccupied with the very large order of hats we have to make for the Grisby family."

"Is that so?" he asked.

Harrison tilted his head and studied me. He was wearing well-worn jeans and a Mansfield United sweatshirt. He looked annoyingly handsome in more casual clothes than I was used to seeing him in, like he was the sort of guy who knew what each end of a hammer was for and knew how to use one. Handiness is always attractive.

I could tell he didn't believe that I was thinking about the Grisbys, so naturally I had to prove him wrong by talking about them.

"What did Daphne mean that their father had forgotten that he had three other children?" I asked Viv.

I grabbed a package of rye Finn Crisps out of the cupboard and placed some on a plate. In the small refrigerator, I found a tube of Primula cheese spread with chives. I loaded up a crisp and took a bite. This would hold us over until we finished helping Andre and Nick.

"Well, it's complicated," Viv said. "But in a nutshell, because Geoffrey is the only boy born into the family, he inherits the entire Grisby fortune."

"That's barbaric!" I said. "No wonder Daphne is so cross."

Fee and Viv helped themselves to the crackers.

"It's called male primogeniture," Harrison said. He stirred sugar into his tea. "It's been the custom for centuries."

"I thought the Act of Succession was changed," I said. I sipped my own tea. I hoped it was high-octane in the caffeine department, because I was feeling the late-afternoon blahs catch up to me.

"It was adjusted before the arrival of Prince George, in case he was a Georgette," Fee said. "The royal primogeniture is now firstborn, first rule."

"But apparently, in the Grisby family, Geoffrey senior did not make this provision, or any provision, in fact, for his daughters," Viv said. She washed down a bite of cracker with some tea.

"I'm surprised the daughters even want to participate in the hospital wing fund-raiser," I said. "I'd boycott."

"And have the family cut you off?" Harrison asked.

DEATH OF A MAD HATTER

"It seems like they already have cut the daughters off—at the financial kneecaps," I said.

Every feminist cell in my body made me irritated on the Grisby daughters' behalf. I still thought Daphne was a pill, but at least now it made sense to me. I couldn't help but wonder what sort of brother would be okay with gaining his family's entire fortune while his sisters were cut out entirely.

"Has that tape touched anyone else?" Geoffrey Grisby asked as he ducked away from the measuring tape in Viv's hands.

"Beg pardon?" she asked.

"That!" He pointed at the measuring tape. "Have you used that on anyone else's head?"

Viv stared at him.

"I could get lice or bedbugs or a horrible infection!" he cried. "I can't have anything touching my head that may have touched someone else's."

"Don't be silly, darling," Tina Grisby said. She was standing in front of one of the smaller mirrors. "It's just a tape measure. I'm sure they've never had an outbreak of lice here."

Viv looked like she wanted to wrap the tape measure around Geoffrey Grisby's germ-phobic neck. I took the tape measure out of her hands and put it away.

"I'm sure I have a new one in the back," I said. "I'll just go get it."

"Tina, please stop trying on the hats," Geoffrey said. "You don't know where they've been."

I saw Viv's eyes narrow into slits. And I knew she was

23

not appreciating the insinuation that her hats might harbor an infestation of some sort.

"Viv, how about you show Mr. Grisby what the finished hat will look like?" I suggested in a tone that signaled it wasn't really a suggestion.

"Right," she said. She sat down next to Mr. Grisby and picked up her stack of sketches off of the table.

I glanced over at Tina and tipped my head in their direction. She hastily took off the hat she'd been trying on and joined them in the seating area. I figured Viv would be fine, but it never hurt to have a mediator if Geoffrey Grisby decided to put his foot in it again.

I hurried to the workroom in back and opened the supply cupboard shelves. Surely, we had to have a backup tape measure. I scouted around until I found a paper one that looked like it was a throwaway from a furniture store. Good enough. I carefully folded it up and wrapped it in some crinkly cellophane that Viv used to wrap hats that she shipped.

It looked like new packaging if you didn't look too closely. Satisfied, I went back into the front of the shop.

"You don't like it?" Viv asked. She didn't sound happy.

"It's blue with polka dots," he said. "I pictured the plush velvety hat with the wide orange band, you know, like Johnny Depp in the movie."

Viv opened her mouth and I had a feeling that whatever was going to come out would scorch Geoffrey Grisby to a pile of smoking ash.

"Found it!" I cried. I hurried across the room and handed the cellophane measuring tape to Viv. "Go ahead, you can get his measurements now."

Viv slowly closed her mouth and stood, taking the tape from me.

"You agree with me, don't you?" Geoffrey asked his wife Tina. "I think I have the same jawline as Johnny Depp. I'm sure I could carry off his look."

Tina glanced at her husband and then at us. I gave her major props for not cracking up.

I then glanced at Geoffrey Grisby. He was in the peak of middle age with a round belly, a sad comb-over and two chins that wobbled when he talked. The only resemblance he bore to Johnny Depp resided in his own imagination.

"What's my hat size?" Geoffrey asked.

"The average head size in the UK is seven and one-eighth," Viv said. "Or fifty-eight centimeters."

"I am quite certain I'm above average," Geoffrey said.

Viv was standing behind him, so mercifully only I saw her stick her tongue out at him. I gave her a look, but she ignored me, placing the measuring tape around his head just above his ears.

"Well?" he asked.

"Average," Viv said. "No, wait, I was wrong."

Geoffrey Grisby looked up as if his eyes could roll into the back of his head and he could see Viv.

"Smaller than average," she said. "By a half centimeter."

"You're quite sure?" he asked.

"Quite," she confirmed.

"I still want a plush hat," he said. His voice sounded petulant. I imagined being told he was below average was not sitting well with him.

"Oh, I'll make it plush," Viv promised.

I did not like the look in her eye, and if Geoffrey Grisby had a brain in his head, he would take note of it as well. Of course, he did not.

"Good," he said. "I know you hat people are all a bit daft, but I won't be made a laughingstock because of your whims."

Viv still held the measuring tape in her hands. Not that she would cause Geoffrey Grisby any harm, but it occurred to me that the tape would make an excellent tool with which to strangle a person. Thank goodness this one was paper.

I nudged Viv and took the tape out of her hands. "You should probably write down those measurements, don't you think?"

"Certainly," she said. She picked up a pencil and jotted the size down on the sketch of the Mad Hatter's hat.

"They aren't mad, you know," she said.

"Who?" I asked.

"I was talking to Mr. Grisby," she said.

"Oh, what's that?" Geoffrey looked up from his cell phone at Viv.

"You said hat people are daft," she said. "We're not."

I fleetingly thought of how she went missing just a few months ago and had to bite back the urge to point out the episode.

"Is that so?" Geoffrey Grisby asked. He glanced quickly down at his phone, making it clear he couldn't care less.

"Yes that's so," Viv said. Her voice was shrill, enough so that even Grisby picked up on it.

He blinked at her. "Still, you are an odd lot, aren't you?"

"Geoffrey!" Tina chastised.

"What? It's true," he protested. "Have you seen some of

the hats my sisters have worn over the years? They look ridiculous, and they don't come cheap, now, do they? Nothing like paying a fortune to let someone make you look like an idiot."

"Some people could use a hat to make them look more attractive—a very large hat," Viv said.

I didn't like the way that was going.

"Why don't you see if you have some plush materials that Mr. Grisby might like for the hat?" I asked.

Viv rose from her seat. She was wearing a pretty floral dress that reached almost to the floor. Her long blonde curls were loose and she tossed them over her shoulder as she left the room. Even though she was my cousin and I loved her, when I observed her out of the Grisbys' eyes, I had to acknowledge, she did seem a bit different.

The front door opened and another customer strolled in. It was just me in the shop now, so I excused myself and went to greet the woman. She went straight to the rack of wide-brimmed sun hats, so I figured this would be a quick sale. It was.

A tourist from Belgium, she was spending the next day in the Kew Gardens and wanted to purchase a hat to shield her eyes and prevent a sunburn while outside. She chose the lavender hat I had admired, and I tried not to sigh as I rang it up for her. It occurred to me that we probably needed to move this rack closer to the door for upcoming summer purchases.

I waved her out and went to return to the Grisbys. They had moved into a corner of the shop and were having a heated conversation. I didn't intend to eavesdrop, but their hissing voices carried across the empty room.

"Why aren't you pregnant yet?" Geoffrey asked. "What's wrong with you?"

"I've told you the doctor says I'm fine," Tina responded. Her voice sounded weary, as if this was an argument she knew by heart. "Maybe if you would go in and get checked—"

"There is nothing wrong with me," Geoffrey interrupted. His voice sounded menacing. "You're the defective one. I thought if I married someone young, she would be sure to produce an heir, but instead you've proven useless to me."

"I'm not useless," Tina said. Again, her voice sounded exhausted.

"I'm sure your lover has many uses for you," he said. His tone was nasty.

"I've told you I do not have a lover," she said. "Not like you and your secretary, at any rate. Tell me, have you called things off with the tart?"

Geoffrey raised his hand, looking as if he'd strike her.

"Hey, there!" I cried as I shot forward across the room. "How about some tea and biscuits?"

Tina glanced at me with relief while Geoffrey turned his raised hand into an awkward stretch. I decided right then and there that I loathed him. Any man who would strike his wife was no man to me.

"Sadly, I can't stay," Geoffrey said. "I have an engagement."

He snarled the last few words at his wife and I suspected this was code for saying he was going to go visit his secretary. If I were Tina, I'd send the poor woman flowers and a thank-you note, but that's just me.

He grabbed Tina's chin between his thumb and index

finger and held her still while he pressed his fleshy lips to hers. I glanced away and suppressed a shudder.

"Oversee the details of my hat," he said. "And try not to muck it up."

Tina waited until he was gone before she pressed her fingers to her mouth as if to check for bruises.

Fee came out from the workroom with a tray of tea and I could have kissed her. I knew I needed a bracing cup of something and I was pretty sure Tina could use one as well.

"Here are some plush samples," Viv said. She was carrying several rolls of fabric, which she dumped on the seat Geoffrey had vacated.

"Don't trouble yourself," Tina said as she dropped some sugar into her tea. "Unless, of course, you have something in a hideous pink with orange polka dots."

Viv blinked at her, but I laughed. Tina Grisby had style.

Chapter 4

"Do you think Tina's having an affair?" Viv asked.

"No idea," I said. "But I don't blame her if she is. Geoffrey Grisby is an awful man."

"Agreed," Viv said. "A right tosser, in fact."

It was early the next morning and we were bracing ourselves for more of the Grisby family to arrive to be measured.

Dotty Grisby was coming with all three daughters as well as Daphne's sons. Given Daphne's sour nature, I was really looking forward to the appointment. Really.

I wondered if Tina and Geoffrey had purposefully made their appointment when the others weren't there so they could avoid any unpleasantness. Of course, Geoffrey seemed to bring his own brand of unpleasantness, so really, how much worse could it be?

Despite Daphne's volunteering to be Tweedledum at their

last visit to the shop, Viv had pointed out that those characters don't appear until Lewis Carroll's second book, *Through the Looking Glass*. Dotty was a bit put out by that, but Viv had promised to come up with a suitable character for Daphne.

It was just before midday when the Grisbys arrived. I had already made up a tea tray and signaled to Fee to put the kettle on. Dotty came in on the arm of a woman I didn't recognize, but judging by her resemblance to Daphne and Rose, who walked behind her, I figured this had to be Lily, the artist sister who lived in Paris.

Rose looked as meek as ever while Daphne seemed resigned. Bringing up the tail end of the group were two handsome men who looked to be in their early twenties. Viv and I exchanged a glance. They had to be Daphne's sons, and one thing was for certain: they did not get their good looks from their mother.

"Ginny." Dotty greeted Viv with a warm hug. I glanced over their heads to see a bemused look on Dotty's grandsons' faces.

The older one had jet-black hair and bright-blue eyes, and when he met my gaze there was a decided twinkle in his eye.

"Ginny," Dotty said. "I am just never going to get used to calling you Viv. This is my daughter Lily and my grandsons, Liam and George. And you've already met Daphne and Rose."

"How do you do?" Viv said and she shook their hands. She gestured to me and said, "This is my cousin Scarlett Parker."

I stepped forward and shook hands with everyone as well. Lily was definitely the looker of the three sisters. Where

Daphne's face was sallow and wrinkled and looked tight with tension and Rose's face was pasty and pinched with worry, Lily had a square jaw, flawless skin and warm brown eyes. When she smiled, deep dimples appeared on either side of her full lips, and she had a serenity about her that soothed.

"It's a pleasure to meet you, Viv," she said. "And I do think the name Viv suits you much more than Ginny."

Viv grinned at her and Lily turned to me. "Scarlett, I hear you hail from the States. It's so nice not to be the only one from afar."

"Paris is only three hundred and forty kilometers away," Daphne said. "Hardly far at all."

"And yet you never come to visit," Lily countered. "Why is that?"

"I am busy raising my sons," Daphne said. "Of course, an unmarried woman like you would never understand the sacrifice."

"I'm quite certain I'm no longer in nappies," Liam, the older brother, said with a mischievous grin. "So, it must be you, George, who is keeping Mum tied up in her apron strings."

"Don't be a prat," George said. "Everyone knows you still need your nightly tuck-in. If it's anyone, it's you holding her back."

George was smirking at his brother good-naturedly and Liam laughed at his joke. I decided that I liked these Grisbys. Unlike Liam, George had light-brown hair and hazel eyes, but they shared the same strong features of a high forehead, blunt nose and rough-hewn jaw. They were both tall and seemed to fill the shop with their broad shoulders.

"Boys, that's enough," Daphne said but there was affection

in her tone. It was the first time I had seen her face soften, and it transformed her look into one of faded beauty. So maybe Lily wasn't the only looker.

"This won't take very long," Viv said. "I really just need to get measurements and make sure you each approve of the hat we'll be creating for you."

"I can help," I volunteered. "I've no talent at millinery, but I wield a mean measuring tape."

"Excellent," Viv said, and she handed me a tape. I wondered if any of the other Grisbys were as germ-phobic as Geoffrey, but no one darted away at the tape, so I assumed not.

"I'll go first," Liam volunteered, and he sat down right in front of Viv and gave her a charming smile.

When I had first arrived in London, I had thought that maybe Viv and Harrison had a thing going. Having spent an awful lot of time with them over the past few months, I could see that they shared a deep affection, but that was about it.

I realized now that I hadn't seen Viv show an interest in any man. Come to think of it, in all the years I'd known her, she had never really had a real relationship. She dated, but it was always kept casual. She said she was caught up in her art and the business, but I wondered, was she pining for someone she couldn't have?

I didn't like that. Viv was a beautiful woman with long, curly blonde hair and big blue eyes. She had a ripe figure with long legs and a laugh that was deep and throaty. A man would be damn lucky to have Viv. So why was she single?

A glance at the look on Liam's face and I could tell he was halfway to smitten. Viv was nothing but professional as she took his measurements. I heard her say something about being above average, and Liam made a few teasing remarks that made her smile.

"My head awaits you, my lady," George said to me and executed a fabulous bow.

I shifted my gaze to him and smiled. I lifted up my tape measure and said, "Please sit."

George sat on the small blue chair beside me. I gently put the tape around his head. He, too, was slightly above average.

"So, go on, tell me the bad news," he said.

"Excuse me?" I asked.

"Will I live, doctor?" he asked. He gave me a pitifully earnest look.

"Well, that depends," I said. I glanced at Viv's sketchbook. "How do you feel about being dressed as a caterpillar?"

He frowned. "What part did Liam get?"

I glanced back at the pad. "He's the knave of hearts."

"Which would you say is the bigger part?" George asked.

"Are you in competition?" I asked.

"Always," he said, drily. "He is the heir apparent, after Uncle Geoffrey, of course, so I must keep my wits about me lest I get shafted."

I glanced over to where Liam was teasing his grandmother Dotty while Viv measured her head.

"I doubt your brother would leave you penniless," I said. "He seems the caring sort."

"Ack, then he has you good and truly fooled," George said. "My brother is as greedy and avaricious a bastard as ever lived. Why, he'd sell out Gram for a new pair of shoelaces." His face was set in severe lines and I wondered if I had wandered into a conversation that was going to be awkward at best.

"Fine weather out there today," I said. "Warm sun, cool breeze, quite nice."

George's serious face split into a wide grin and he laughed.

"Got you, didn't I?" he asked.

"You were teasing me!" I cried.

"Of course," he said. "And you brought up the weather just to keep it cordial. Are you really American?"

"Half," I said. "My mother is British."

"No wonder you were so shocked at my candor," he said.

"Dear brother, what are you playing at now?" Liam asked as he joined us.

"I was teasing Ms. Scarlett by telling her you're a selfish git," George admitted. "I couldn't resist."

"Please forgive him," Liam said to me. "I'm quite sure he's adopted."

I laughed. "I believe he called you a greedy, avaricious bastard."

"Oh, so you were bragging about me again, eh, little brother?" Liam asked, and the two laughed. "Don't believe a word he says. He exaggerates."

"Only the good qualities," George remarked.

"Hmm," Liam hummed. He smiled at me and said, "I imagine Vivian's husband must be quite proud of her achievements in the fashion world."

"Of all the ham-fisted, clumsy attempts to find out if a woman is available, that has to be the worst I've ever seen," George cried. "Good grief, I think it left an odor behind."

George looked so affronted at his brother that I had to laugh.

"I suppose *you* could have finagled the information more gracefully?" Liam asked.

"I could perform ballet in combat boots more gracefully than that," George said. "But then, so could an elephant, so that's not really saying much, now, is it?"

I took pity on Liam and said, "Vivian is single, but—"

"But what?" Liam asked. "Is she pining for someone?"

"No—at least, I don't think so," I said. I wasn't really sure how to say what I had to without offending him, and given that he was a customer, it went against my nature to be less than helpful. Still, it had to be said. "She's a bit older than you."

George burst out laughing but Liam just shrugged and said, "Age is merely a number and the heart won't be denied."

At this, George rolled his eyes and made a gagging noise. I couldn't help it. I laughed.

I liked the brothers. They were funny and charming and I suspected took after their father.

"I can't really argue with that, now, can I?" I asked George.

"No, like me, you'll just have to grab a bucket of water and prepare to put the poor bugger out when he crashes and burns," George said.

"Perhaps," Liam said. "Or maybe she'll shock you right out of your knickers by saying yes to a night on the town with me."

"Scarlett," Viv called me. "Could you get the swatches I left in the workroom?"

"On it," I said. "Excuse me."

Both George and Liam inclined their heads as I left. I wondered what Viv would make of Liam's interest in her. My guess was that he was in his early twenties, maybe twenty-two or -three. That would make him six years younger than her, which would be the equivalent of me dating his younger brother George, who, while charming, still had the scent of his college years about him, making him entirely too immature for me. I supposed Viv might feel differently, but I couldn't imagine it.

Then again, she hadn't dated anyone in so long, at least no one she'd told me about, that maybe she'd just be happy to have a date.

Back in the workroom, Fee was fastening a fat pink ribbon onto the crown of a wide-brimmed white hat. The ribbon was shaped into a large flower in the back, and it made me think of the taste of sun-ripened raspberries and sand between my toes.

"That says summer to me," I said.

"It does?" Fee asked. She looked nervous. "It's one of the hats I'm designing for the bride for the Butler-Coates wedding. She wanted casual but elegant, something that said an afternoon picnic in the park, because that's what they're doing for their wedding."

"Oh, that should be lovely," I said. "I like the pink ribbon. It's very feminine."

"It's to match her gown," Fee said. "She's wearing a pink gown by Sarah Burton."

"The designer of the Duchess of Cambridge's wedding dress?"

"That's the one," Fee said.

"And you're nervous about being in charge of the hat?" I asked.

"Terrified," Fee said.

"Don't worry," I said. "It looks amazing. She'll love it."

Fee gave me a half smile and I picked up the stack of fabric Viv had left on the table. I turned to head back to the shop when I stopped. Fee had been working with Viv very closely over the past year; maybe she knew if there was someone special in Viv's life.

"Fee, when was the last time Viv had a boyfriend?" I asked.

Fee glanced up from the hat. She frowned at me. "As far as I know she hasn't had one, at least not since I've been working here. Unless she's really keeping it hush-hush."

"Thanks," I said. I went back into the front of the shop to find Liam orbiting around Viv while his brother watched with a smile.

I handed Viv the swatches and moved to stand beside George.

"Has he made his move yet?" I asked.

"Hard to do under the watchful eye of Mama Hen," George said as he gestured toward Daphne. "No one is good enough for her darling firstborn."

"You should help him out with a distraction," I suggested.

"But then I'd miss the show," he protested. "You do it."

"Well, I don't want to miss it either," I said. "Besides, I thought I was supposed to man the bucket if he went down in flames."

"Would she be that cruel?" George asked.

I shrugged. I had no idea how Viv would handle the request for a date.

"All right, you two, whatever are you up to?" Lily asked from behind us, causing both George and me to jump. "Because I have to tell you that your whispering looks very suspicious."

Chapter 5

"We're watching Liam stalk his prey like a mighty hunter," George said. "Scarlett, here, thinks I should offer myself up as bait to draw off the protective mama, but I don't want to miss Ms. Vivian sending the boy down in a blaze of humiliation."

Lily gazed past us to where Viv was showing Dotty, Daphne and Rose the different sorts of fabric that could be used for their hats. Liam glanced up at the three of us watching and wiggled his eyebrows.

"I know just the ticket," Lily said. She joined the group on the sofa and as Viv worked her way through the samples, Lily pointed to a pretty rose-colored shade and said, "That one. Oh, I simply must have that one."

"What?" Daphne squawked. "You can't just sashay forward and take the best one. What if Mum or Rose had their eye on it?"

"Oh, I didn't, dear," Dotty said. "That color makes me look peaky."

Rose nodded in agreement. "I like a quieter color."

I glanced over to see Liam taking advantage of the ker-fuffle and whispering something in Viv's ear. She turned and gave him an amused smile and then she laughed.

He flashed the rest of us a triumphant grin.

"Well, he's certainly not letting any grass grow under his feet," I said to George.

"Good thing, too," George hissed. "I think Aunt Lily's dis-traction might work too well and if I'm right, Mum is about to throw a wobbler."

I knew from my years on vacation over here that he meant she was about to pitch a hissy fit. He was right.

"Oh, of course, the ever-favored Lily gets to pick her fabric first," Daphne snapped. "I am the oldest. Did it never occur to anyone that maybe I should get to pick first? Oh, no. Why would it when being born a man, even the fourth born in a family, means he gets to inherit it all?"

"Oh goodness, not again, Daphne," Dotty said. "Your father's will is what it is. There is no changing it and pouting about it certainly isn't going to make a bit of difference."

"No, but Geoffrey could make a difference if he wanted to," Daphne snapped. Two bright spots of red blazed on her cheeks and her nostrils flared in and out with every breath.

"Uh-oh," George said. "She's winding up."

"Is there something I can do?" I asked.

"No, she's not been right since the reading of the will," he said. "Given Gram's eccentricities, Mum assumed that as the oldest she would be the executor of our father's estate and would take care of Gram and parcel out a quarter of the family fortune among the four siblings. Well, when we discovered Uncle Geoffrey was the sole heir, it didn't sit well, and when he refused to parcel out the estate, it sat even less well."

"I've met Geoffrey," I said.

"Lovely chap, isn't he?" George asked.

"Is there any way I can answer that respectfully?" I asked.

"No," he said. "I don't believe there is."

"I do like his wife," I said. "Tina seems very nice."

"Awfully young for him, though, wouldn't you say?" George asked.

"I refuse to answer on the grounds that my answer might concur with your observation and make it appear that I am gossiping about a client, which would be very wrong," I said.

"You know, I've always been partial to redheads, but you're more than that. There's much more to you than a fiery mane, isn't there?" George smiled at me. "I like you."

I inclined my head. "The feeling is mutual."

"Would you go out with me?" he asked.

"No, but I appreciate the offer," I said.

"I'm too young for you," he said.

"By a year or five," I said. "Plus I've taken a year off from dating."

"Oh, I definitely want to hear the story behind that, but first let's see if your cousin is as stodgy as you," he said. He smiled so I knew he was teasing. We glanced back at Viv to find Liam still hovering and whispering.

"Daphne, you have to give Geoffrey some time," Lily said. "Dad only passed away a month ago, and he's still figuring it all out."

"Oh, you think so? Is that why he's transferring all of the family fortune into new accounts with just his name on them?" Daphne asked. Her voice cracked like a whip and Rose looked as if she'd like to cower under the furniture to get away from her sister, while Lily appeared completely unruffled.

"Daphne, can we not speak of this now?" Rose asked. She cast Dotty a worried glance as if afraid Daphne's outburst would upset their mother.

"Do you really think our brother isn't out to take everything that is rightfully ours?" Daphne asked.

"What do you care?" Lily asked. "You're married to Tom Mercer, a wealthy man in his own right."

"Yes, he is, and he's worked for every penny," Daphne said. "Why if he were here instead of in the States, working on a merger for his company, he would agree with me completely."

"Oh, come off it," Lily said. "You and Tom aren't hurting for money; what do you care if Geoffrey is in charge of the estate?"

"It's the principle of the thing," Daphne snapped. "It wasn't just Mum that he le—"

"No!" Rose jumped up and shoved into Daphne, cutting off her words. "Do not say it!"

"Smooth move, Aunt Rose," George said. "That could have gotten nasty. Gram always goes a bit sideways when

43

there's any talk of Gramps leaving her for his mistress. Still, Aunt Lily is my favorite."

"Girls, this unacceptable behavior," Dotty said. She frowned at Viv. "Ginny, I am so sorry about this. Liam, stop pestering my friend in her place of business."

George and I turned away together to hide our grins.

"You know the fact that your grandmother thinks that Viv is her age adds quite a twist to Liam asking Viv out, doesn't it?" I giggled.

"Can you imagine her at Sunday dinner with Gram thinking she's shagging her grandson?" George chortled.

"Awkward," I said out of the side of my mouth.

"Fine, if we can't discuss the brass tacks of what's happening in our own family, then I suggest we don't speak at all. George, Liam, we're leaving," Daphne announced.

"And that's that," George said. "It's been a pleasure, Scarlett."

"Likewise," I said. He gave me a half bow and walked over to his mother. She still looked angry enough to spit nails, primarily at her sister.

Liam seemed more reluctant to leave Viv, which made me think he had not yet sealed the deal on a date.

Daphne, oblivious to her son's reluctance to depart, stomped toward the door.

"Daphne, what are we to do with your hat?" Lily called after her.

"I don't care," she said. "I'm sick to the back teeth of the whole bloody situation."

With that she shoved out the door. George paused to kiss

Dotty on the cheek and wink at his aunts, while Liam heaved a sigh and did the same. He waved at Viv, looking like a lovesick schoolboy as he exited the shop after his brother.

Viv glanced at the three remaining ladies. "Don't worry. I have her measurements and will manage a perfect hat for her."

"Oh, thank you, Ginny. Whatever would we do without you?" Dotty asked. "Now, you and Scarlett will be coming to the tea, won't you?"

"Uh," I stammered. I really couldn't imagine willingly spending any more time with this family.

"Oh, do say you'll come," Lily chimed in. "It will be such fun. I promise we'll all be on our best behavior."

Dotty reached over and patted Viv's hand. "For me?" she asked.

Suddenly, the scent of lily of the valley tickled my nose. I frowned and looked at Viv. I saw her nose twitch and then she glanced at Mim's old wardrobe in the corner, the one with the carved bird on top, a bird I had nicknamed Ferd.

I knew what she was thinking. Lily of the valley was Mim's scent, and it wafted through the shop with no discernible point of origin. We had not discussed it, but I was pretty sure Viv believed that Mim, or the essence of Mim, appeared in the shop at moments of great importance.

Viv patted Dotty's hand and said, "Of course, we'd love to come."

It took me a moment to identify the feeling that swirled in the pit of my stomach, but there it was—dread. Where Viv had taken Mim's scent as a sign of encouragement, I had taken it as a warning. I supposed only time would tell which of us had been right.

"Do you really think this is wise?" I asked Viv as soon as the door shut behind the last of the Grisbys. "I mean they're all a bit crazy, don't you think?"

"What did you expect me to say?" Viv asked. "I was all at sixes and sevens when she asked and then—"

"Lily of the valley," I said. "I smelled it, too."

"I think it was Mim telling us to go," she said.

"Maybe she was telling us *not* to go," I said.

Viv looked worried. "Maybe."

"Viv, you have to be straight with me," I said. "Do you think Mim is haunting the shop?"

"No!" Viv said immediately and then added, "Perhaps."

We looked at each other and then we both glanced around the shop. Mim was still very much a part of this place. It wasn't hard to imagine her hanging on even from the beyond. And as much as it alarmed me, it also comforted me.

Viv began gathering the materials she'd been going over with the Grisbys. She had finally nailed down all of their hats and needed to get to work on them immediately, as the Wonderland tea was just a month away.

"What if it was just someone's perfume that we caught a whiff of?" I asked.

Viv shook her head.

"I've only noticed that particular scent a few times over the past five years," she said. "I thought when you came and joined the business, it might stop."

"Is that why you invited me?" I asked. I can admit my feelings were a teeny bit hurt.

"Don't be thick," Viv said. She handed me the fabric samples to carry to the back room while she gathered her sketches. "You know I've wanted you here for years."

I glanced at her and she gave me a level stare. I knew she was telling me the truth, and then I felt bad that it had taken a personal crisis to get me here.

"Okay," I said. "So, are we talking Mim's ghost or just an essence?"

"I'd say an essence, leastways I haven't seen a ghost, have you?" Viv asked.

"No," I said. "But I'm suddenly thinking I need to watch my language a bit more carefully."

"And no bringing any boys home," Viv said with a laugh. "I don't want to be smelling lily of the valley when I'm snogging a date."

"Oh, horror," I agreed.

Viv led the way as we carried our things to the workroom. Since we seemed to be in such a sharing place, I figured this was as good an opportunity as any to find out about Viv's personal life.

"So, young Liam seemed pretty taken with you," I said.

"Really? I didn't notice."

Fee was sitting cross-legged on the big wooden table, fashioning a very large silk peony flower out of a wide blue ribbon.

"Didn't notice?" I asked. "How could you not notice? He was following you as closely as a shadow."

47

Viv put down her sketches and I offloaded my armful of fabric.

"Who's this?" Fee asked.

"Scarlett seems to think Liam, the older of Daphne Grisby-Mercer's sons, fancies me," Viv said with a laugh.

"I don't think it I know it," I said. "He said as much to me and his brother George."

"Oh, was he the one with the dark hair? He was quite good-looking," Fee said. We both looked at her and she shrugged. "I heard male voices, so I took a little peek. It's not like we get than many men in here, yeah?"

"So what did you think of him?" I asked Viv.

"He had a nicely shaped head," Viv said.

"That's it?" I asked. "He is going to be so disappointed."

"I expect he'll live," Viv said.

"Well, now that we're going to the tea, I'm sure he'll try to charm you senseless," I teased. "Unless, of course, your interest is elsewhere?"

Viv didn't say anything to this—very annoying of her. Instead, she headed over to the kitchenette and took a sparkling water out of the minifridge.

"You're not going to talk about your personal life, are you?" I asked.

"There's a reason it's called a personal life," she replied.

"Oh, come on," I insisted. "How many hours did I spend listening to you try to decide which Backstreet Boy was your favorite?"

"Shaming me will not get you into my confidence," Viv said. "Besides, I listened to you, too."

"That's because I was going to be Mrs. Nick Carter," I said.

"Who?" Fee asked.

"Please do not tell me you've never heard of the Backstreet Boys," I said.

"Sorry, I'm more of a Jonas Brothers girl," Fee said.

Viv and I exchanged a look. It was a horrible thing to be age-stamped by the boy band of your heart.

"Back to the topic at hand," I said. "I realize that due to my own selfish neglect, I have no idea what's been going on in your personal life, so is there someone special that you haven't told me about?"

"If I haven't told you before, what makes you think I suddenly will now?" she asked.

"Because I'm asking," I said. This seemed pretty obvious to me.

Viv tipped her head and studied me. "Sometimes you are such an American."

"That sounded like an insult," I said. I looked at Fee. "Did that sound like an insult to you?"

She raised her hands as if to show she was unarmed. "Impartial apprentice here."

"It's not an insult," Viv said. "Just an observation. Americans tend to be more—how do I say it?"

"In-your-face?" I suggested.

"Yes," she cried. "You have fewer boundaries."

"So you're telling me that you have a boundary around your personal life and I am to butt out," I said.

Viv tossed her long blonde curls over her shoulder. "Yes, I'd say that's about right."

"And you really think that's going to work with me?" I asked.

To her credit, Viv looked at me and laughed. "Right. Whatever was I thinking?"

Chapter 6

Apparently, Viv wasn't just thinking it. Much to my surprise, she evaded my every attempt to get information of the relationship sort out of her. Obviously, she underestimated my staying power.

I decided my best chance for information would be to observe her at the tea and see how she responded to Liam now that she knew he was interested in her. This at least made the idea of an afternoon of awkward conversation and finger sandwiches seem bearable.

In the days before the tea, the Grisbys were in and out of the shop to pick up their hats. Geoffrey Grisby even said his hat had turned out better than he had anticipated, which Viv and I took as high praise from him. Unfortunately, he also used his handkerchief to touch the doorknob on the way in and out of the shop, as if we were unclean somehow. I still didn't like him and could not imagine why Tina was married to him. I supposed it was none of my business, not that that stopped me from pondering the situation.

On the day of the tea, I was riddled with doubt as to what to wear, but Viv helped me pick a pretty ecru dress with bunches of blue hydrangea blossoms on it. I chose a matching blue sun hat with an ecru ribbon from the shop's display to advertise Mim's Whims and wore a strappy pair of navy sandals to complete the look.

Viv looked amazing in a pale-rose-colored dress with white eyelet trim and a white cap that sported a burst of rose-colored eyelash feathers on the right side. She wore taupe sandals that kept us about the same height.

"Think we'll do?" she asked Fee as we prepared to leave.

"I think hearts will be breaking all over Wonderland when they get a load of you two, yeah?" Fee said.

"We should give her a raise," I said to Viv.

"Agreed. I have my mobile," Viv said to Fee. "Call me if you need me."

"Right," Fee said.

I had convinced the Grisby family to hire my friend Andre to take pictures of the event. He met us in front of the shop with his equipment loaded into his car and ready to ride.

"Well, look what dropped down from heaven," he said when he saw us. Andre was looking very dapper himself in black slacks and a cream-colored shirt that complemented the rich brown color of his skin.

"Flattery will get you anywhere," I said and kissed his cheek.

He grinned. "You're only saying that because you know I'm already taken."

He opened the doors for Viv and me, I sat in front and we shot out into the midafternoon traffic. The Grisby estate wasn't far, and Andre gave a quick history lesson along the way.

"The Grisby estate is called Grisby Hall and it's located on Bishops Avenue," Andre said.

"Where all the posh reside," Viv said from the backseat.

"Indeed," Andre agreed. "Grisby Hall was built in the eighteen twenties by a steel industrialist, Charles Brady. Unfortunately, his wife spent him into poverty and Geoffrey Grisby Senior's grandfather, Malcolm Grisby, who was a business associate of Brady's, picked it up for a song."

"He must have had quite a voice," I quipped. Both Andre and Viv rolled their eyes.

"Safe to say he knew how to sing for his supper," Viv said. They both chuckled, and this time I rolled my eyes.

Andre drove past Hampstead Heath on Spaniards Road toward the exclusive addresses on Bishops Avenue.

"Where did the Grisbys get their fortune?" I asked.

"Malcolm Grisby was also an industrialist. He was what I believe you Americans call a robber baron," Andre said. "His money came mostly from paying low wages, having good friends in parliament, and crushing his competition by buying them out."

"Ruthless," I said.

"Utterly," Andre agreed.

"It seems the Grisby men like to make money," Viv said. "I think they consider it quite macho."

"Do you suppose they're compensating for something?" I asked. I thought of Geoffrey's inability to father a child. "Or perhaps for the lack of something?"

Andre laughed. "That's certainly a theory."

He turned onto Bishops Avenue and I felt my jaw drop. I had heard it was an exclusive area, but until I saw the tree-lined street with gated mansions, I'd had no idea.

We drove past several huge houses, when Andre put on his signal to turn.

Two large wrought iron gates embellished with gold were open and he pulled right through. In front of us sat a sprawling Greek Revival mansion with a green metal roof and six wide white columns supporting the portico. Painted a bright, blinding white, it was breathtaking.

"So, let me get this straight," I said. "Geoffrey Grisby Sr. left all of this to go live in Italy for thirty years with his mistress?"

"That's about the size of it," Andre said as he stepped out of the car. He popped the trunk in back and grabbed his gear and then handed his keys to a waiting valet.

"Did he have children with his mistress?" Viv asked.

"It's my understanding that his plumbing had been rerouted, so that wasn't really an option," Andre said.

"So he had a kink in his pipe." Viv chortled.

"I would think a good plunging would take care of that," I joked.

They both looked at me and Andre shook his head and gave me a pained look.

"Fine, be that way," I said, knowing full well that they enjoyed teasing me. "Still, I suppose that makes things less complicated. Daphne's already furious that everything was left to her brother Geoffrey, can you imagine what would have happened if their father had a whole other family that he actually remembered to provide for?"

"I heard he didn't even think to leave anything to his mistress, Cara Whittles. Not even a measly five quid," Andre said. "She was with him for thirty years. Can you imagine?"

"Did he think he was going to live forever?" I asked.

"Apparently," Viv said.

Andre was traveling light with just one camera bag, so he shouldered the bag and the three of us walked up the steps toward the main entrance. I felt as if I should be wearing a toga and sandals as we walked through the large, imposing columns into the house.

A butler in a dark suit stood just inside the door in the center of a highly polished foyer. My eyes were dazzled by the enormous chandelier that hung overhead, which sparkled as light shone through each and every glass crystal.

"Good afternoon, Ms. Tremont, Ms. Parker and Mr. Eisel," the butler greeted us.

I was a little taken aback that he knew our names, and it must have shown on my face, because he gave me a small smile.

"You are the last three names on my guest list," he explained. "Marilyn Tofts, the event planner, has been anticipating your arrival. I'm Buckley. If you'll follow me . . ."

We fell into step behind him. I quickly pulled my cell phone out of my clutch purse. Surely, we weren't that late. No, we were only off by fifteen minutes. I hoped we hadn't committed some huge social gaffe by being a few minutes late for an afternoon tea. Then again, I suspected Marilyn was being her micromanaging self and had stirred up the dust about our tardiness.

Buckley led us down a narrow hall that boasted large portraits of what I assumed were deceased members of the Grisby family. My suspicion was confirmed when I saw a wedding portrait of Daphne, looking lovely in a gorgeous white dress standing next to a handsome man, who had the same ruggedly handsome features as her sons.

Since Daphne's father had been gone for thirty years, I wondered if he had given her away or if he had even shown up for the wedding. It seemed horribly selfish to me for him to have left his wife to raise the children and manage their home while he was off in Italy whooping it up with his girlfriend.

It made me think of my last unfortunate relationship with a man who'd not only still been married when he told me he wasn't, but had also had me and several other women on the side. Suddenly, I had an urge to kick someone, a man, any man, really hard in the posterior. Irrational, I suppose, but there it was.

Buckley led us into a great room with large floor-to-ceiling windows that looked out onto a large sweeping veranda, which was decorated very festively with many tables in bright colors all set for tea.

Beyond the tables, a gorgeous garden filled the yard. I could see people wandering among the gravel paths admiring the statuary and fountains as well as the sculpted bushes.

"This is fantastic," Andre gasped.

Buckley gave him an approving nod. He opened a large French door and escorted us out.

Dotty was the first to spot us. She stood under a rose-covered portcullis, talking to a group of ladies. When she saw Viv, she raised her hand in greeting and waved us over.

Viv had done a spectacular job on Dotty's hat. She had decided to go as the March Hare, the Mad Hatter's tea party companion who enjoys annoying Alice.

"Ginny, don't you look lovely," Dotty said. She wore a pale-yellow dress, which matched the ribbon that had been fashioned into a bow tie on the crown of her straw bowler hat, which was a lovely nut-brown color to represent rabbit fur.

"Thank you, Dotty," Viv said. "You look lovely as well."

Dotty introduced us to her friends and we introduced Andre. Dotty was delighted that he was here to take pictures and she immediately sent him off into the garden to snap pictures of the guests.

I saw Tina Grisby standing alone by a large fountain and I made my excuses to the others as I went to check on her. I hadn't been able to forget the scene at the shop between her and Geoffrey. I couldn't help but think that it must be truly awful to be trapped in a marriage to a bully.

Tina's hat represented Alice. Viv had created a wide-brimmed white sun hat with pretty blue ribbons trailing down the back, which matched her blue dress. The outfit made her appear even younger, and I couldn't help but wonder if she was happy.

"Hello, Tina," I said.

She turned away from the fountain and glanced at me. She looked distracted and I noticed it took her a moment to focus on me.

"Scarlett," she said. She smiled at me. "How good to see you. You look lovely."

"As do you," I said. "You make a fine Alice."

She gave me a rueful glance and it said more than words that the family fallout continued. I knew without asking that Daphne was undoubtedly still in a snit over Tina being Alice.

"How are you?" I asked.

"Fine," she said. "Just fine."

"You do realize I don't believe you, right?" I asked.

This time when she smiled it reached her eyes.

"You caught me," she said. "Things have been rather stressful."

I glanced over my shoulder to make sure we were out of earshot of the other guests. "Geoffrey?"

"Oh, I know what you're thinking," she said. "He was terrible that day in the shop, but truly, he isn't always like that."

I gave her a dubious look, but I understood from her tone that she wasn't going to discuss it further.

"Well, the party looks amazing," I said. "Very festive, and it's quite a full house."

"I expect Dotty will be well on her way to getting that wing at the hospital," Tina said. "Each family member is hosting a table. I had them put you and Viv at my table so I could put the squeeze on you."

I gave her an alarmed look. Tina laughed a bright, musical chuckle, and I smiled at her as I realized she was teasing me.

"Don't worry," she said. "I actually had them put you at my table so that Liam and George don't monopolize you. I heard from Rose and Lily that they were quite taken with the milliners."

58

"Well, Liam for certain with Viv," I said. "I believe George understands that I am too old for him."

I glanced across the crowd, trying to spot the brothers. I could see several of the hats Viv had made. Lily was the White Rabbit; Daphne, the Dormouse; and, true to her word, Viv had made Rose the Cheshire cat. Their hats stood out among the others with whimsical details like a ticking clock on Lily's and glittery black fronds fashioned to look like whiskers on Daphne's and orange-and-yellow-striped feathers on Rose's. Viv really had done an amazing job.

A bell rang and Tina and I glanced up to see Marilyn Tofts, wearing a puffy white blouse over a purple skirt topped by an ostentatious, glittery purple hat that had deep-purple ostrich plumes launching off of it in all directions. She resembled a musketeer that had been electrocuted as she waved everyone forward into a large white tent that had been erected on the side lawn.

"That's the call to start the silent auction." Tina scanned the crowd and then frowned. "I don't see Geoffrey, do you?"

"No, I haven't seen him," I said. "And his hat is hard to miss."

Viv had outdone herself on Geoffrey's hat. She had made an extralarge top hat in a plush electric blue. As a compromise, she had kept the polka dots to the wide ribbon around the crown. She had chosen the color perfectly, as Geoffrey's usual sallow skin appeared robust under the brim of blue and even he had noted it when he came in to pick it up. Since we had been bracing ourselves for him to pitch a fit, it was a pleasant surprise that he had been agreeable.

"It really is a spectacular hat," Tina agreed. "He has quite embraced the role of the Mad Hatter."

I thought about the moment in the shop where he looked as if he was going to hit her. I didn't care what sort of personal crisis he was dealing with; that was unacceptable.

"Just so long as none of his madness is directed at you," I said.

Tina gave me a small smile. "Very diplomatic of you, but don't worry, I wouldn't tolerate any sort of abuse."

"Glad to hear it," I said. I glanced up at the terrace and saw Marilyn scanning the crowd. "Marilyn's looking irritated. Should we split up and look for Geoffrey?"

"We'd better," Tina said. "Marilyn will get Dotty all riled if he's late."

"I'll go this way," I said, pointing toward the garden. Tina nodded and headed in the opposite direction.

I took the first graveled path that led through the tall, shapely hedges. It went straight and then opened up around a large rectangular fishpond.

I tried not to get sidetracked but there were some lovely long-finned koi swimming under the lily pads that caught my eye, and I promised myself I'd come back later if I had time.

The path led onward through a vine-covered portico where colorful rosebushes lined each side of the path. The smell was heavenly. Beyond that the garden opened up to a large section full of shallow garden beds. Hand-painted wooden signs labeled each one and I saw dill, thyme, rosemary, and my favorite, lavender.

The rich scent of earth and newly mown grass seasoned with the scent of the herb garden made me take in great big gulping breaths as if I could suck in enough to keep those lovely smells inside of me.

A giggle interrupted my moment, and I frowned. I turned and realized how easy it would be to get lost in this garden, as the large hedges separated each section, making every twist and turn a new treasure to be discovered.

Focus, Scarlett, focus, I chastised myself. The giggle sounded again and I had a bad feeling that I might be interrupting some lovey-dovey couple amidst the forsythia. Ah well, I was doing them a favor if they were going to miss the tea, right? Per usual, I was dead wrong.

Chapter 7

I left the herb garden and made my way around a large statue of a lady in a toga with her hair swept up at the crown of her head and carrying a large basket of flowers. She had a serene expression and seemed content with her lot to oversee the gardens.

Past a trellis supporting pink roses, I rounded another corner and saw a familiar bright-blue top hat. The head underneath it was nuzzling the neck of a woman dressed in an exotic sheath in hues of orange and yellow with a sweep of jet-black hair topped by a bright-orange fascinator that looked askew.

Well, I'd found Geoffrey, but that was not his wife. I wondered if this was the secretary I had heard Tina mention. I quickly stepped back out of sight.

The idea of toppling the large female statue nearby on

them was sorely tempting, but I decided to channel my better nature. Given our location, I figured an allergy-driven sneezing fit would alert them to my presence, and then I could announce the beginning of the festivities.

Achoo! Achoo! Achoo! I faked three quick sneezes and waited three seconds before I stepped forward. When I did, I found Geoffrey proselytizing on the importance of a good head gardener.

"As you can see, you must maintain stringent standards for your gardeners," he said. The woman with him was nodding as she tried to straighten her dress and fix her hat.

"Oh, hello there," I said. I hoped I looked the picture of innocence. It was very hard to squelch the urge to blast him with a good shot of stink eye. "Mr. Grisby, I do believe the festivities are about to start and they need you to host the auction."

He made a great show of checking the ultraslim gold watch on his wrist. "Oh, would you look at that. Excuse me, ladies, I must be off."

He left us in a streak of blue hat and orange wig. Yes, he had insisted upon wearing a wig like Johnny Depp's despite our attempts to stop him. I was, however, quite impressed with the speed he managed in his escape from us.

I smiled at the lady who looked very guilt ridden as she hurried after him. Of course, that could just be my imagination but it made me feel better to think she was shame filled. In a fair world, she'd trip and land in a stinky compost pile. Sadly, these gardens seemed too well kept for that sort of thing.

I made my way back to the terrace, sad to leave the serenity of the garden behind. As I soaked in the beauty, again, I marveled at the idea that anyone would willingly leave such a beautiful home.

I took my time getting back to the party. Partly because I just wanted to see more of the garden and partly because I really didn't want to watch Geoffrey posing as a benevolent host and all-around good guy when I knew how badly he was treating his wife.

Yes, it was all very personal for me, having inadvertently been the other woman. At least I didn't know that the rat bastard I was seeing was still married. This woman had no excuse.

By the time I rejoined the party, I found Viv standing in the shade of a leafy red maple on the perimeter of the festivities and I wondered if she was hiding from Liam or if she was assessing the hats of the assembled guests.

"Whoever let that woman walk out of her house in that hideous yellow, well, 'kayak' is the only word that comes to mind, did not do her a kindness," Viv said when she saw me.

So, it was the hats. I didn't have to scan far to see the woman she was talking about. Wearing a bright-yellow hat that came to narrow points in front and back, she was hard to miss.

"I think it looks more like a banana," I said.

Viv snorted.

A great cheer went up in the tent as Geoffrey announced the winner of the first auction item, a sweet Rolls-Royce. Now I was glad I hadn't gone to look at the items in the tent because not being able to afford anything would have depressed me. Not that I wanted any of the trappings of the superwealthy, but still.

I had noted while working in the hotel industry that the ultra-affluent were seldom happy and in fact because their money couldn't buy them happiness, they were crankier than most. Given how much they could have done to alleviate poverty worldwide and maybe find happiness in a greater purpose, I found the uber-rich pretty pathetic, actually.

"Strike a pose, ladies," a voice instructed.

I glanced up to see Andre approaching with his camera at the ready. Viv went into a perfect starlet pose while I floundered, not knowing what to do with my hands and feet. Have I mentioned that I am the most unphotogenic person in the world? Honestly, I look in the mirror and I see a fairly pretty redhead then I see a picture of myself and I look like a pasty, apple-cheeked dork whose eyes are too close together.

"Scarlett, what are you doing, some sort of tribal dance?" Andre asked. He was laughing at me.

"I don't know." I waved my hands. "I'm much better when I don't know a picture is being taken. Still not attractive, but at least I'm not awkward."

"Look at Viv," he said. "Lean in like you're whispering some gossip."

"Oh, I do have gossip," I said.

Viv turned her head and raised one eyebrow in a perfect arch. I leaned in and blocked my mouth with my hand.

"I just caught Geoffrey canoodling his secretary," I said. I could hear Andre taking pictures but I was too focused on Viv's reaction to pay attention.

"That sounds very dirty," Viv whispered.

"It's like snogging," I said.

"Oh." She sounded disappointed.

"Well, it's not like I wanted to see him with his pants down," I said.

Andre had joined us and he looked at me and asked, "You're talking about me, aren't you?"

I started to laugh. "No! I'll tell you later when we're out of the crowd. I promise."

The noise from the tent had ceased. It took me a second to notice but when I did my attention turned toward the area and I saw that the people between us and the tent were standing on their tiptoes and craning their necks to get a look at someone.

"Uh-oh, do you suppose Daphne is clashing with Geoffrey?" I asked.

"No." Viv shook her head. "Daphne is over there with Liam."

I followed the direction of her gaze and saw the mother and son standing off to the side. They had a perfect view of the tent and their heads were bent together as Daphne whispered something to Liam, who frowned.

"Stop! You have no right to auction off my property!" a voice, female, shrieked.

Andre jumped up, springing up and down like a kangaroo, trying to see over the heads of the people between us and the tent.

"Bloody hats!" he cried. "I can't see!"

He jumped three more times and then landed with a gasp of surprise.

"What is it?" I asked. "What did you see?"

"A woman in pink who I swear is Cara Whittles," he said.

"The deceased Grisby's mistress!" I said.

"Well, that's bad form," Viv said. Then she frowned. "I don't think Dotty is up to that."

She began to push her way through the crowd. Viv has some talented elbows because despite everyone's obvious interest in the scene unfolding before us, they moved aside to let her through. Andre and I quickly followed in her wake.

Once we arrived at the tent, it was to see Buckley and several uniformed men, approaching the hysterical woman in pink with their hands out as if they intended no harm but were quite determined to get her out of there.

"You're not his widow," the woman in pink shrieked, pointing at Dotty. "I am his one true love, me and me alone."

"I'm sorry, dear, who are you?" Dotty asked. She looked genuinely bewildered.

"I am your husband's mistress," Cara declared.

A gasp went through the crowd. I stared at Dotty, worried about her reaction. She could pretend her husband had been away on business all she liked, but when confronted with the woman he'd actually been living with for the past thirty years, could she deny the truth any longer?

"Oh my, is there a performance of which I am unaware?" Dotty asked Geoffrey. "I didn't think we were having anything more than music. Did you plan a show as well?"

Geoffrey gave his mother a small sad smile and it occurred to me that no matter how beastly he was to his wife, he seemed to care about Dotty very much.

"No, Mother, this is just someone who has obviously turned up at the wrong address," Geoffrey said gently. "Lily, take Mum for some refreshments whilst I get this sorted."

Lily and Rose flanked their mother and led her out of the tent. Dotty looked wary until Viv stepped up and joined them. Viv smiled at Dotty to reassure her that all was well. Dotty returned her grin, and I saw Lily shoot Viv a look of gratitude.

As soon as they were out of earshot, Geoffrey turned on Cara Whittles with a snarl. "What are you doing here?"

"I've come to demand what is mine," she said with a dramatic head toss. "I am the rightful heir to the estate, not you or your sisters, and you have no right to sell off what is mine."

"How did you get in here without an invitation?" Geoffrey asked.

His hat was askew and his eyes were mere slits. The menace coming off of him was as tangible as the scent of the flowers from the garden.

"What does it matter?" Cara asked. "I want what I deserve and I am not leaving until I get it."

She was a beautiful woman, not much older than Geoffrey, with long auburn hair, large brown eyes and a figure that retained a perfect hourglass shape.

Geoffrey was visibly trying to control his temper. "This

is neither the time nor the place to have this discussion, Cara. You will leave now or I will have you arrested."

She strode forward, swiveling her hips as she went, with an air of oversexed she-devil in every step she took.

Geoffrey was riveted, watching her stalk him. She stopped right in front of him and leaned forward, giving him quite the front-row seat to her cleavage.

"Do it," she whispered. Her mouth was a lipsticked invitation to utter debauchery, and Geoffrey had to visibly shake himself loose.

He stepped back and gave a jerky nod to Buckley, who took the woman by the elbow and began to lead her away.

"Turn her over to the police," Geoffrey said.

I glanced at the crowd, everyone was watching the scene before them as if it was a reality show on TV.

Cara dug her heels into the grass, yanked her arm out of Buckley's grip and turned to hiss at Geoffrey.

"I was your father's real wife. I took care of him right up until he drew his last breath. I deserve more than to be cast aside with nothing, not even a home to call my own."

She sobbed, obviously going for the sympathy play. It didn't work. Geoffrey merely glared at her. She glanced at him from under her long eyelashes. When she realized that pity wasn't in Geoffrey's personal makeup, she lashed out.

"I'll have what's mine!" she cried. Her face turned a hot shade of red as her temper ignited. "Even if it's over your dead body!"

Geoffrey blinked at her in surprise. I imagined he didn't

get threatened very much. Buckley stepped forward and grabbed Cara's arm again. This time another valet grabbed her other arm and together they marched her from the premises.

Whispers began to fill the tent, and Geoffrey looked like he wanted to choke someone.

He made a curt announcement that the rest of the winners for the silent auction would be notified personally later in the day, and he strode from the tent.

"Well, that was something, wasn't it?" Andre asked.

"I'll say," I said. "I'm really glad Viv ran interference for Dotty, poor thing. She really didn't seem to get it, did she?"

"And thank goodness for that," Andre said. "Can you imagine how she would have reacted, having her delusions of thirty years shattered?"

"It would not have been pretty," I agreed.

A plume of glittery purple was working her way through the crowd. She was stopping at clusters of guests armed with waiters bearing trays of sparkling cider and wine. With just a short conversation, she smoothed over the social awkwardness like a fairy godmother waving a wand. In fifteen minutes the guests seemed to have regained their equilibrium.

"Even though I don't like Marilyn Tofts, I have to admit she's quite talented," I said.

"Hmm." Andre made a noncommittal humming noise in his throat.

I glanced at him out of the corner of my eye. "Okay, spill it. What aren't you telling me?"

"Nothing!" he protested. "You're so suspicious!"

I narrowed my gaze at him. "Fine. But I'll figure it out."

He rolled his eyes at me as if I was a pesky little sister, but I ignored him.

A bell rang signaling the start of the tea. Andre was not joining us, as he was taking pictures, so I promised to save him some cake and he moved off into the crowd.

I found Viv standing up on the patio beside a white-clothed table with teapot-shaped place cards at each seat, two of which bore our names.

"How is Dotty?" I asked, fingering the calligraphy that spelled out my name on my card.

"Right as rain," Viv said. "I walked with them to the house and Lily did a great job of distracting Dotty with a fabricated problem with the caterers. She was fine when I left and seemed to have no idea who Cara Whittles is or why she appeared here."

"Good. I feel very protective of her, since she was Mim's friend. Tina is the hostess for our table," I told Viv. I glanced at her out of the corner of my eye. "She felt we needed to be spared Liam and George. Unless, of course, you'd rather not be spared?"

Viv turned to meet my gaze. She smiled but said nothing. Oh, why wouldn't she tell me if she liked Liam or not? It was maddening, truly.

The guests were taking their seats at their tables on the patio. There was no sign of our hostess Tina. I waited a moment, but when two other ladies joined our table and sat down, I figured we could as well.

"How do you do?" one of the women, a friendly looking lady with short dark hair and a fabulous raspberry-colored trilby, addressed us.

"Very well and yourselves?" Viv asked.

"Enjoying a beautiful day in the garden," the woman answered. "I'm Linda Pankhurst, and this is my sister Jacqueline Pankhurst."

Jacqueline was wearing a seafoam-green sun hat, which matched the piping on her black dress perfectly. She gave us a warm smile.

"A pleasure," I said. "I'm Scarlett Parker and this is my cousin Vivian Tremont."

"Oh, I've heard of you," Jacqueline said. "My dear friend Sally Abbingdon raved about the hat you made for her for her son's wedding."

Viv beamed and I glanced away as they all began to talk hats and what the latest trends were in the hat world.

The rest of our tablemates began to sit and more introductions ensued. I glanced across the wide veranda and noticed that most of the other family members who were acting as table hosts were already seated. The only one I didn't see was Geoffrey.

As I made my visual sweep, George, looking quite fabulous in his caterpillar-inspired fedora, waved at me. I waved back unable to suppress my grin when he tipped his brim at me and finished it with a wicked wink.

"Is it just me or should Tina be here by now?" Viv whispered in my ear.

"She should be," I said. "And Geoffrey is missing, too."

"Do you think she found out—" Viv began but I interrupted.

"I don't know," I said.

I knew she was thinking the same thing I was: that maybe Tina had found out about him and his secretary groping in the garden.

"Why don't you act as hostess and I'll go look for her," I said.

Vivian nodded and I rose discreetly from my seat and stepped back until I could fade into the open door behind me. Once in the house, I retraced our steps from before. I knew the best person to ask about Tina's whereabouts would be Buckley, assuming he was done assisting Ms. Whittles out the door.

I didn't see Buckley in the foyer, but I saw a caterer in an apron hurrying off in what I assumed was the direction of the kitchen. Sure enough, after a long hallway and three sharp turns and down a short staircase, I was standing in the heart of the house: the kitchen.

The catering staff had overtaken the room and they were buzzing in and out with full trays as a cluster of chefs prepped each one. Buckley was overseeing the events with a critical eye and I thought the Grisbys were lucky to have such a detail-oriented man at the helm.

"Ms. Parker," Buckley said when he noticed me standing there. "How can I assist you?"

We moved off to the side of the room and out of the waiters' way.

"Actually, I was just wondering if you'd seen either

Geoffrey or Tina," I said. "The tea is about to start and neither of them were at their tables."

Buckley frowned. "I have not. I was busy escorting our visitor into a waiting police car and then had to hurry back to make sure the tea got off. I'll send some staff up to their rooms to make certain they are aware that the tea has begun. I'll have someone check the grounds as well."

"Thank you," I said. "That would be most helpful."

With a nod, I left him to go back to the tea. On my way, I got turned around. I was in a hallway that I was pretty sure I had not been in before when I saw a door that led outside. I decided to go out, thinking I'd just walk around the side of the mansion to get to the veranda, as it would be easier than getting lost in that maze of a house.

A gravel path led from the door and into the gardens. I was in a section of rosebushes that were so lovely and pungent that they took my breath away. Deep-crimson blossoms mixed with cool lavenders and vibrant yellows. I told myself I had to bring Viv back here if we got the chance, because the blooms were positively inspiring.

I heard the trickle of a fountain and found myself in a section of garden that was sculpted yew bushes. A herd of galloping horses towering above my head circled the fountain as if in a perpetual race with forelegs raised and heads thrashing; it was something to behold. I spun around, amazed at the talent it would take to prune these bushes with such fine detail.

I had all but forgotten the tea when I saw a flash of bright blue underneath the edge of the sculpted bushes. I crept forward, thinking maybe it was an exotic bird or flower. Yeah, no such luck.

As I crept through the opening in the bushes and stepped into the next section of the garden, I saw that the bright blue was the Mad Hatter's hat and facedown on the ground beside it was Geoffrey Grisby.

Chapter 8

I hurried forward and crouched on the ground beside him.

"Geoffrey, are you all right?" I asked. "Geoffrey? Mr. Grisby, can you hear me?" Did I really think he was more likely to answer to Mr. Grisby than Geoffrey?

I shook his shoulder, but he remained unresponsive. Could he be passed out drunk? I hadn't seen him drinking, but that didn't mean anything. Maybe the clinch I'd seen him in earlier had been booze induced.

Oh Lord, this was going to be mortifying for the both of us if he was pickled. Still, I couldn't leave him facedown in the dirt. Geoffrey wasn't a small man, so I had to crouch down, reach across him and haul him over onto his back. It was like trying to heave a very large sack of potatoes. I thought he would grunt or flail or make some sort of groan or moan. But no, and when he landed on his back, I understood why.

Geoffrey Grisby's vacant eyes stared up past me at the leafy canopy overhead. He was dead.

The scream that emerged from my mouth sounded as if it had been forcibly ripped from my chest. I scooted back from the body, tripping on my own skirt in my haste to get away.

I caught myself on a stone bench and braced myself while the shock and horror poured over me in waves. I couldn't catch my breath and my lungs felt tight as if they couldn't expand to let air in. I stared at Geoffrey's chest: there was no rise and fall, and he never blinked.

I needed to get help and fast. I'd only gone two steps when Andre came skidding down the steps.

"I heard a scream," he panted. "Scarlett, are you all right?"

"No," I said. I grabbed for him, craving the reassurance of a warm body next to mine. "I found Geoffrey Grisby."

I pointed and Andre let out a scream that was equally as high-pitched and terrified as mine.

"Is he—?" he asked.

"Dead? Yes, I think so." I heard footsteps coming through the garden and I yelled, "Over here."

I heard a shout and in seconds Buckley appeared with several servants in tow. He glanced at me, and I pointed to Geoffrey. Buckley took over. He knelt beside the body and did a quick examination. After a few moments, he shook his head.

Looking gray and drawn, he pulled out his phone and called for an ambulance. The conversation was short, and as he ended the call, he turned to one of his men and said,

"Go back to the house. When the ambulance comes, have them use the side entrance. I don't want to disturb Mrs. Grisby or the tea."

"It's a bit late for that, I'd say," his assistant said and nodded over Buckley's shoulder. He glanced back and saw Dotty Grisby making her way down the stairs toward us.

Buckley strode forward as if he could shield Dotty from the sight of her son. Her mind might not be all there, but there was nothing wrong with her eyesight.

"Geoffrey? Is that Geoffrey?" she asked. "Whatever is he doing down there?"

Buckley took her arm and whispered in her ear. Dotty frowned at him. Then she moved around him with a strength of purpose I wouldn't have suspected.

She knelt beside her son. She studied his face. I heard her breath catch and then she released a wrenching sob.

"Oh, my dear boy," Dotty said. "My precious boy."

With a shaky hand, she reached up and smoothed his thin hair. She laid her palm against his cheek and her face crumbled as if the force of her grief snapped her composure to the breaking point.

Andre stood beside me and I pressed my shoulder against his. He put his arm around me and we stood as silent as the statuary in the garden as we witnessed the grief of a mother, grappling with the heart-wrenching blow life had just dealt her.

We didn't move until one of the staff appeared with several medical personnel in tow. More staff were dispatched to hold the party guests at bay. Fancy hats kept popping up over the hedge, and I realized the entire party must have heard what was happening by now.

Andre and I were pressed back as the medical team set to work. It took them very little time to confirm the obvious. Geoffrey Grisby was dead.

I heard a commotion in the assembled guests. I glanced up and saw Daphne push past the servants trying to keep the area clear.

She took one look at her mother kneeling beside her brother, and she shrieked. Mayhem ensued. The rest of the family pushed forward. People were yelling and screaming. Andre and I were pushed even farther back.

Rose was cowering in a corner of the garden while George kept a protective arm around her, Daphne was shouting, demanding to know what had happened. Liam was trying to calm his mother down while Dotty was sobbing onto her son's still form with Lily kneeling beside her, holding her mother's hand.

Buckley put two fingers to his lips and let out an earsplitting whistle of such a high pitch that I was pretty sure that every dog in the city would start to bay in protest. It worked and everyone quieted down as they turned to stare at him. He took the opportunity to command the situation.

"Please get back to the house, all of you!" he ordered. No one argued. Not even Daphne.

He then knelt beside Dotty and helped her to her feet. With a gentleness that bespoke great affection, he escorted her out of the garden. When she would have turned back, he said, "No, I'll take care of him, Ma'am. I promise."

Andre and I were about to follow when Tina came trip-ping into the garden from behind us.

She took in the scene with wide eyes. "Whatever has happened?"

Then she glanced past me. "Is that—?"

"Geoffrey," I said. "I'm so sorry, Tina. He's dead."

The medics were just loading him onto a stretcher when she raced forward.

"No! No!" she cried. She pushed up against them, clutch-ing at Geoffrey. "Stop! I'm his wife. His wife!"

The medics paused and gave her some space. I glanced over to where Buckley and Dotty had been, but they were already out of sight.

"I don't understand," Tina said. "What happened?"

"I don't know," I said. I felt horribly inadequate as if there could be some reasonable explanation for finding a middle-aged man dead in a garden.

I twisted my fingers together and felt Andre's hand squeeze my shoulder.

"I'm sorry, Ma'am, we have to take him away now," the medic said.

As they took Geoffrey away, Tina curled one arm about her middle as if holding her shock and grief in tight against herself. I left Andre's side and approached her.

"I'm so sorry," I said. "Here, let us walk you back to the house."

She nodded. "What was he doing out here?"

"I don't know," I said. "When I found him, he was already gone."

"You found him?" she asked. Her steps were unsteady

as we made our way up the stairs. I reached out a hand to brace her.

"Yes," I said. "I was looking for you."

"Oh," she said. She glanced away.

"Where were you?" I asked.

"I was freshening up," she said. She didn't meet my gaze. "Excuse me, I should go to Dotty."

She pushed away from me and strode ahead. It was then that I noticed a smear of dirt on the back of her dress, the same dirt that had been on Geoffrey's jacket that was now on my dress from turning him over.

"I have to tell you, Scarlett, this is the absolute last time I am going on a photography assignment with you," Andre said as we made our way back to the house.

"You make it sound like it's my fault," I protested.

"Not your fault, just—" His voice trailed off.

"Just what?" I pressed. We walked through the remaining section of garden and across the small stretch of lawn to the house.

"I don't want to offend you," he said.

"Too late," I growled. "Tell me what you were going to say."

"Well, you're ruddy bad luck, aren't you?" he asked.

"Ah," I gasped. "That was rude."

"Sorry," he said. "But you can't deny that you've invited me out twice, and twice, we've—"

"Stumbled upon bodies?" Viv supplied as she met us at the bottom of the stairs that led to the terrace. She put her arm around me and gave me a bolstering hug. "You all right, cousin?"

"You mean other than being ruddy bad luck?" I asked, giving Andre a sour look.

"Well, you do seem to attract the stiffs," Viv said.

"Exactly," Andre said. "It's just not normal."

I sighed and glanced around the veranda. The party had taken on a macabre feel, with everyone clustered into groups whispering about Geoffrey and speculating about what could have happened.

Marilyn Tofts was in the corner by the bar. I could see her big purple hat moving as she was having an animated conversation with the caterer. I imagined she was trying to concoct a way to spin the events of the day around to make it the most fabulous dead man's tea ever. Uncharitable of me for certain, but finding a body will do that to you.

I scanned the crowd but I didn't see anyone from the family and I imagined they were holed up in one of the mansion rooms somewhere, trying to cope with what had happened.

"I don't think you comprehend me," an older woman was saying to Buckley. "I wish to have my car brought round, and I wish to leave now."

"I'm so sorry, Mrs. Pennyworth," Buckley said. "The police have asked us not to let anyone depart, as they wish to ascertain whether anyone saw what might have happened to Mr. Grisby."

"They want to question us? I won't have it." The woman looked outraged. She was a tiny little bird of a woman whose white curls peeped out from beneath the brim of her smart sunflower-yellow hat. Her dress was a drab brown, but she wore a wide patent leather belt and loafers in the same eye-poking shade of yellow as her hat. "Did you hear me? I won't have it."

"No, not questioning," Buckley said swiftly. "Merely, they wish to know if anyone saw Mr. Grisby take ill."

Mrs. Pennyworth narrowed her eyes at him. "So it was natural causes, then, that caused his—"

She seemed at a loss for words, but Buckley finished the sentence for her.

"Collapse," Buckley said. "Yes, it appears so."

I could tell by the way he glanced away from her that he really had no idea what had happened to Geoffrey but this was the official story for now.

"I don't feel well," Andre said from beside me.

I glanced at him and noted that his dark complexion had gone ashen.

"You're not going to throw up this time, are you?" I asked.

"No," he protested. "Maybe. Oh, bloody Nora! I've got my gallery opening in a few days. I can't be having a turn like this."

"Settle down," I said. "Your opening will be fine. I promise."

"What if *he* had some dreadful disease that was contagious?" Andre asked. His eyes were wide with fear.

"Oh, good grief, I'm quite sure it wasn't," I said. I could see the guests standing closest to us were leaning nearer as if to listen. "Probably, it was just a heart attack."

"But you don't know that, do you?" Andre insisted.

Viv was watching us with a worried expression. Then she stood up on her tiptoes and waved to someone behind us.

"Over here," she called. "We're over here."

I glanced over my shoulder to see who she could be greeting. I felt my insides lurch when I recognized the thick head of brown hair and the bright-green eyes of Harrison Wentworth.

Chapter 9

He shouldered his way through the crowd toward us, looking every inch the man in charge, from his perfectly tailored charcoal-gray suit to his shiny black shoes. For some reason, I found this particularly annoying.

I turned to Viv. "Did you call him?"

"Yes." She didn't add it, but I could hear the unspoken "duh" in her answer.

"But why?" I asked.

Viv gestured to Andre. "He is in no shape to drive us home. Did you want to try and take the tube?"

I glanced back at Andre, who was enthusiastically shaking Harrison's hand. "Thanks for coming out, mate."

"No trouble," Harrison said. "What's happened? Your text message was quite cryptic, Viv."

"Geoffrey Grisby was found dead in the garden," Viv said.

"What?" he asked. He glanced at the three of us and then his eyes narrowed on me. "Who found him?"

"I did," I said. I tipped my chin up in defiance. I wasn't really sure what I was being defiant about, but I didn't like the way he was looking at me as if he had suspected that I would be the one to find the body, so up my chin went and I crossed my arms over my chest for good measure.

"Oh, Ginger," he said. The sympathy in his eyes almost had me walking right into his arms for a comforting hug. I shook it off.

"I'm fine, Harry, completely fine," I said.

He raised his brows at my use of his childhood nickname.

"Well, I'm not," Andre said. He shuddered. "Gah, I am going to be sick."

"Come with me," Viv said and she grabbed his hand. "I know where the loo is."

Together they hurried through the crowd. I watched until they were inside, hoping Andre wouldn't get sick on anyone along the way.

I turned back to Harrison to find him watching me. Still, he looked like he wanted to give me a hug. It would have been nice, too nice, so I forced myself to think of something else.

"I'm surprised you didn't bring Fee with you," I said.

He frowned.

"Why would I do that?" he asked.

"Well, you two seem awfully chummy lately," I said.

He tipped his head to the side then a small smile tipped the corner of his mouth up.

"Nice of you to notice," he said.

"I did not—" I began to protest, but I was interrupted by Buckley.

"Excuse me, Ms. Parker, but the police are here and they'd like to ask you a few questions," he said.

"I'll come with you," Harrison said.

I would have refused, but given that I wasn't sure what the police wanted to ask me, I couldn't refuse the backup, especially when Harrison was looking so respectable and all.

We followed Buckley into the main house. He led us down a richly carpeted hall.

Halfway down, I turned to Harrison and asked, "Do you think it will be Detective Inspector Franks this time?"

"No, he's in the Kensington Borough. We're a bit north, in the Barnet Borough, so it will likely be someone else."

"Oh," I said. I figured the odds were slim, but I had grown fond of inspectors Franks and Simms when they'd investigated the murder of one of our clients.

Buckley rapped his knuckles on a thick white door. A murmur from inside bade us to enter.

Buckley pushed open the door and stepped aside to let Harrison and me pass into a small parlor. The room had east-facing windows and was done in pale yellows. It overlooked the garden, and I felt my insides clench when I recognized the bushes sculpted into running horses. Had I just been admiring them without a care when Geoffrey Grisby had been struck by a heart attack or some other life-threatening condition with no one there to help him?

A uniformed constable stood talking to another man in a blue suit coat and tie. They looked up when we entered, and I felt Harrison take my elbow to guide me toward them. What, did he think I was going to run?

"Detective Inspector Finchley," Buckley greeted the plainclothes man, "this is Scarlett Parker and Harrison Wentworth."

I saw Finchley's eyebrows rise just a fraction at the mention of Harrison's name. Interesting.

"Thank you, Wolcott," Finchley said to the constable, dismissing him.

The constable nodded to us and departed from the room. I got the feeling he was on assignment.

"Ms. Parker. Mr. Wentworth." Finchley extended his hand and we shook.

"Inspector," Harrison returned, and I muttered the same when it was my turn.

"I wasn't aware that you were attending the tea, Mr. Wentworth," Finchley said.

"I wasn't," Harrison said. "I was called to come and collect Ms. Parker and her cousin Ms. Tremont. The person whom they came with is not in a state to drive just yet."

"And who would that be?" Finchley asked.

The Inspector had some impressive jowls, I noticed. They wobbled when he talked and gave a droopy look to his face. It was a face that didn't look as if it laughed very much. I thought that was unfortunate, but then again, in his line of work, I didn't suppose there was much to yuck it up about.

"His name is Andre Eisel," I said. "He's a photographer and has a studio just down the street from our hat shop. He's a bit sensitive."

Finchley's gaze moved from Harrison to me. His

deep-brown eyes looked sympathetic and he said, "You were the one to find the body, Ms. Parker?"

"Yes," I said.

"Could you tell me exactly what happened?" he asked.

"Of course," I said. I started with the tea beginning and our hostess not being present. I said that after I talked to Buckley, I decided to go around the outside of the house so as not to get lost, and that's when I found Geoffrey. I described exactly how I saw the hat first right up until I realized he was dead and called for help.

Finchley nodded slowly and his jowls wagged at me. "Did you see anyone else in the garden when you were walking through it?"

"No," I said. "It was empty."

Again, he nodded. He seemed to be turning over my words in his mind. I could hear the carriage clock on the mantel ticking, and I began to get nervous as if there was something I had missed.

"Did you know that Geoffrey Grisby wasn't at his table when you went to look for his wife?" Finchley asked.

"Yes, I did mention it to Buckley," I said. "We assumed after the scene with Cara Whittles that they were freshening up."

He seemed to mull that over for a minute. He didn't ask me about Cara Whittles, so I assumed he'd already been brought up to speed.

"Is there anything else that you saw that could be important?" he asked. "Any behavior that struck you as odd or out of character by any of the family members or guests, other than Ms. Whittles, of course?"

"You mean other than seeing Geoffrey Grisby in a passionate clinch with his secretary?" I asked.

Finchley's jowls flapped, and I felt Harrison stiffen beside me.

"You're quite certain?" he asked.

"Oh yeah," I said. I wandered over to the window that overlooked the terrace where the guests were still gathered. "See that woman there? In the orange? That's her. I came upon them in the garden earlier when both Mrs. Grisby, Tina that is, and I went to look for him to start the auction."

Finchley and Harrison both followed me to the window. They each glanced over my shoulders out the window. The woman I pointed to was sobbing into a handkerchief. I noticed that no one was standing near her and I wondered if it was her copious weeping or the status of her relationship with Geoffrey Grisby that caused her to be shunned.

"You're quite sure it was a passionate clinch?" Finchley asked.

"Positive," I said.

"Is there anything else that you can think of that might be important?" he asked.

I reviewed the events of the day. No, interrupting a passionate embrace and then finding a body pretty much capped out the tea for me.

"Nothing comes to mind," I said.

"Is Scarlett free to go?" Harrison asked.

"Yes," Finchley said. Then he fished a card out of his jacket pocket and handed it to me. It was white with an embossed Metropolitan Police Service emblem of a shield with a knight's helmet over it with a lion on each side. His name and number were at the bottom of the card. "If you think of anything else, please contact me at the number listed."

"Absolutely," I said.

We watched as he left the room. I wondered what Harrison was thinking about all of this. Not surprisingly, it didn't take him long to weigh in with an opinion.

"How is it you happened to stumble upon Geoffrey and his secretary?" he asked.

"I'm lucky like that," I said.

I could feel his gaze on the side of my face, but I refused to engage.

"'Lucky' is not the word I would choose," he said.

Now I did turn to face him. "What's that supposed to mean?"

"Why do you suppose you're always in the wrong place at the wrong time?" he asked.

I did not like the direction this was going. I began to walk to the door.

"We should gather Viv and Andre," I said. "What are we going to do about his car?"

"I'll drive it," he said.

"What about your car?" I asked.

"I had a colleague drop me off," he said as he fell into step beside me.

"Oh," I said. "That was thinking."

"It's been known to happen."

The dryness of his tone made me smile.

"That's better," he said.

"What is?" I asked. His gaze was focused on my face.

"Your smile," he said. He reached up as if he was going to touch my face but then he didn't. "You looked rather rattled when I got here."

"A dead body will do that to a girl," I said.

"Are you two ready?" Viv appeared in the door with Andre in tow. He still looked pasty and shaky.

"Yes," I said. "Let's get Andre home."

Viv and Andre led the way while Harrison and I fell into step behind them.

"Just so you know, I did notice," Harrison leaned close and whispered in my ear.

"Notice what?" I asked. My first thought was that he meant my dress, my hat or my hair, but he ruthlessly squashed my vanity like a bug under a rock.

"That you didn't answer my question," he said. "Why are you always in the wrong place at the wrong time? It positively mystifies."

I said nothing, knowing I really couldn't argue the point.

Chapter 10

We were a subdued crew at the shop over the next few days. Fee was fretting over the Butler-Coates wedding. The bride hadn't liked any of the hats she'd come up with and Fee had refused Viv's offer to help. She wanted to do it alone. As she banged around in the back room grumbling to herself, I decided to hide out in the front of the shop while Viv worked on her own projects beside Fee.

With summer's arrival, our sun hats were fairly flying off the shelves. Viv had fashioned a number of hats in an ecru sinamay and then finished them with denim hatbands and trim along the brim. They had a delicate yet sporty look about them, and I noted that they seemed to be most popular with the mothers of small sticky-jam-fingered children.

I was just restocking the window display when I saw Tina Grisby hurrying down Portobello Road toward the shop.

When she saw me in the window, she blinked and then waved. I waved back.

The bells on the door chimed when she entered and I climbed out of the window to greet her.

"Tina, how are you?" I asked. I wanted to pepper her with questions, but it seemed rude, so instead, I asked, "Can I get you a cup of tea?"

"Thank you, no," she said. "I can't stay long."

"Of course. I'm sure you're needed at home," I said.

"Oh no, we're not staying at the house," she said. "We've all moved into suites at the Savoy. No one could bear to stay after . . ."

I nodded. I noticed she was wearing a conservative navy-blue dress with matching pumps. She was a widow now. It hit me like a slap upside the head. No matter what I thought of Geoffrey Grisby personally, she was his wife and had to be struggling with his loss.

"Honestly, Scarlett, I came to ask you a favor," she said.

"Of course," I agreed. One would think I would have learned to wait until the specifics were stated before I agreed, but no, I had yet to apply caution to my helpfulness.

She twisted her fingers together and then looked me square in the eye and said, "I'd appreciate it if you didn't tell anyone about the conversation you overheard between me and Geoffrey."

"You mean about you getting pregnant?" I asked.

"Yes."

I took a deep breath. I couldn't imagine that I would have a need to tell anyone about that conversation, but then I remembered Detective Inspector Finchley. Would that conversation be of interest to him? I had a feeling it might.

As if she could tell where my thoughts were going, Tina stepped forward and clutched my hands in hers. Her fingers were cold, and I felt my skin shrink as if recoiling from her touch.

"Please," she said. "I'm begging you not to tell anyone."

"Tina, what happened to Geoffrey?" I asked. Suddenly, nothing about this seemed normal.

She dropped my hands. "I don't know, I swear. But if there was— If someone— I just can't risk it."

"Risk what?" I asked.

The bells on the door jangled again and I glanced over to see three ladies enter the shop. I glanced around but both Viv and Fee were in back, working.

"I'll be right with you," I called to the ladies.

They smiled at me and began to peruse the shelves. I noticed they were looking at the sun hats, so I figured they were looking to buy off the rack, which was a lucky break.

"I'd better let you get back—" Tina began, but I grabbed her elbow and guided her to the far corner.

"Oh no, you don't," I said. "What's going on? Why are you worried about someone asking questions? What aren't you telling me?"

Tina glanced over her shoulder at the other ladies to see if they were listening. They were giggling as they tried on hats and made ridiculous duck lips in the mirror. What was it with that duck-face thing? *I want to marry a girl who looks like a duck*, said no man ever.

"They can't hear you," I said. "Now tell me what is going on."

"I don't know," she said. She fretted her lip between her teeth. "I just don't want anyone to think I had something to do with Geoffrey's death."

"Why would anyone think that?" I asked. I tried to keep my voice from sounding speculative, but I couldn't help but remember the streak of dirt on her dress and how she was missing until after Geoffrey's body had been found.

"Because Geoffrey was poisoned," she said. "They did a preliminary autopsy and found that—oh God—his insides were essentially corroded, which is indicative of being poisoned."

I dropped her elbow. I felt my jaw go slack. Here I had just thought that he'd had a heart attack and died. Yes, it had been odd in a man so young but not completely out of the realm of possibility.

"How? Why? Who would do such a thing?" I asked.

Tina's eyes were darting all over the shop. She looked as if she was afraid of being seen here, and I knew that she was hiding something from me.

"Tina, what's going on?" I asked. "What do you know that you're not telling me?"

"Nothing," she said. "I swear. I don't know who would have done that to him, but things are complicated, and I'm afraid—"

"Excuse me," a voice called from across the shop. I glanced over to see the three women who had come in, standing at the register. They each had a hat in hand.

"Don't move," I said to Tina. Before I could get away,

her cold fingers clamped on to my arm. "Please don't say anything to anyone about Geoffrey and me," she hissed. "It could put someone in danger."

I stared at her for a second. Was she telling me that it would put me in danger if I blabbed? Was she threatening me?

I studied her face. There was no menace there, just desperation. No, I couldn't imagine that she meant to do me harm. Still, she looked frantic.

"Don't go anywhere," I said. "I have more questions."

With that I left her by the window and approached the ladies who were waiting for assistance. I felt as if my smile was forced, and I shook my head, trying to dig deeper to offer up a sincere greeting.

"I see you ladies were quite successful," I said.

"Honestly, I had to restrain myself," the one in the middle said. "They are all so lovely, and blue is my favorite color."

"Did you want them boxed or were you planning to wear them out of the shop?" I asked.

"We'll wear them, please," The oldest of the three said. She had a head of tight curls. "We're off for a stroll in Hyde Park and the sun is quite ferocious today."

The other two nodded. I began to ring up the sale when I heard the bells on the door jangle. I glanced up just in time to see the door shut behind Tina as she hurried down the sidewalk away from the shop.

Damn. I still had so many questions. I debated calling Fee out to finish the sale while I raced out the door after Tina, but it seemed bad form. I consoled myself with the fact that I knew where she lived and if I had to trot on over to Bishops Avenue to talk to her, then I would, assuming she wasn't still at the Savoy. I could always go there; in fact, that might be even better because it was a public place.

Geoffrey Grisby poisoned. It boggled. As I handed the third customer her credit card back and watched as they left the shop, I couldn't help but think who would have the most to gain from Geoffrey's death. There was no doubt about it, it was Liam, as he was the next in line to inherit the family fortune.

I tried to picture the jovial young man as a coldhearted killer, but it just didn't work. Now, his mother, Daphne, on the other hand, she seemed to be up to playing the part without much difficulty.

Why was Tina worried about me telling everyone how Geoffrey had been treating her? That he had been pressuring her to have a baby? Surely, since she had nothing to gain by his death, she couldn't be a suspect. Could she? Again, I thought of the dirt mark on her dress. Could she have seen Geoffrey with his secretary and killed him in a jealous rage?

I supposed anything was possible, but poison did not strike me as a crime of passion. No, it seemed more the sort of thing someone with an axe to grind would use to get rid of their enemy.

"Oy, Ginger, you in there?" a man's voice said in my ear, and I jumped with a yelp.

I snapped my head to the right to find Harrison standing there. He looked amused.

I put my hand over my rioting heart and scowled at him. "You scared me!"

"Sorry, but you were practically in a trance," he said.

"You didn't hear me come in, and when I said hello, three times, you didn't answer. I thought you were in a stupor or something."

"I was thinking," I snapped.

"I hope you didn't strain yourself," he said.

I glowered.

Harrison rocked back on his heels with a smirk. He was wearing a black suit over a black shirt, which was open at the throat. He looked annoyingly handsome, like he belonged at an art show.

The art show! Ack! I turned and ran into the back room. Viv and Fee were both seated at the big wooden table with a couple of open bags of Hula Hoops, sort of like a potato chip but in a ring shape, and half-empty glasses of pop.

"You guys are back here snacking?" I asked, although the answer was obvious.

"Well, we were going to call you in, but you were helping customers," Viv said. She looked slightly shamefaced when she added, "And then we forgot."

"Uh-huh," I said. I stuck my hand in the bag of cheese-and-onion-flavored potato rings. They fit perfectly onto the ends of my fingers, and I munched on them to stave off the hunger I felt coming on strong.

"Don't tell me you all lost track of time," Harrison said as he walked into the room behind me.

Viv glanced at the clock. "Ah! Is that the time? Andre's gallery opening! We have to hurry."

Fee hopped off her seat and lifted a garment bag from where it was hanging on one of the supply closet doors.

"All right if I change upstairs?" she asked.

"Absolutely," Viv said. "Use the guest bedroom."

Fee hurried out of the room, brushing by Harrison as she went. They smiled at each other.

"Come on, Scarlett," Viv said. "We can clean up the mess later."

"I'll get it sorted," Harrison offered.

I was sipping out of Viv's glass, which she took out of my hands. Apparently, I wasn't moving fast enough for her, as she grabbed my arm and dragged me toward the door.

"Keep an eye on the shop, Harry!" I cried as we left the room. I saw him frown. I knew he hated that nickname, so naturally I used it as often as possible.

"Will do, Ginger!" he called back.

Unlike him, I liked my nickname, especially when he said it. I was relieved that I had my back to him, so he couldn't see my face get warm.

As we hurried up the stairs, Viv glanced at me.

"Are you blushing?" she asked.

"Certainly not," I said.

"Then why are your cheeks so pink?" she persisted.

"I'm allergic to potato rings," I lied.

"Is that a euphemism for being allergic to Harrison?" she asked.

Her bright-blue eyes might as well have been laser beams. We crossed through the flat and paused by her door. I forced myself to meet her gaze with a bland look of my own. I refused to acknowledge her words on the grounds that I might incriminate myself.

"We'd better hurry," I said. "We don't want Andre to think we stood him up."

I slipped through the door that led up the stairs to my room and the guest bedroom before Viv could say another word.

I closed my door and hurried over to my closet. I did not like Harrison that way I assured myself. Yes, he was handsome and charming when he wanted to be, but he was also insufferably bossy.

After my last relationship had caused me global humiliation—no, not exaggerating—I had promised myself that I would take a year off from dating men. As my mother had pointed out to me, the longest I had ever gone without a boyfriend was two weeks. She thought perhaps a relationship sabbatical would be good for me.

I was quite sure that if I was responding to Harrison at all, it was merely because I had not had a boyfriend in a few months, a personal best, and was therefore much more susceptible to any male presence. See? Perfectly reasonable.

Earlier, I had picked out the dress I was going to wear to the art opening. It was my classic little black dress: very flattering but also very unassuming. Suddenly, however, I felt the need for something with a little more zip zap. I shuffled through my closet until I found my Tadashi Shoji party dress. A formfitting aqua textured lace with sheer tulle trim, this was not a dress to be ignored. I slipped it on and then added a pair of beige open-toed pumps.

I put my red hair up in a twist, freshened up my makeup and I was ready. This was exactly what I needed to take my mind off of any inappropriate thoughts about Harrison. After all, the art show was sure to have loads of men there.

I could flirt with abandon and get it out of my system, thus stopping myself from being an idiot over Harry.

When I stepped out into the hallway, I bumped into Fee coming out of the guest bedroom. We stared at one another for a moment, neither one of us speaking as we took in the absolutely horrific sight before us.

We were wearing the same dress!

Chapter 11

Fee bit her lip as she gazed at me. "It looks better on you."

"No, it doesn't," I sighed. I wished I were lying, but no. Fee was all youthful curves and long legs. She looked amazing.

"We could go as twins, yeah?" Fee offered with a shy smile.

I grimaced. "That'd make me the ugly sister. I don't think my ego could take it."

"It would not," Fee said with a laugh. "You look gorgeous. Honestly, I don't fancy being seen with you in the same dress because I would be the hideous one."

"No worries," I said. "I'll go change."

"Are you sure?" Fee asked. "I'd offer to, but I don't have any other dresses here."

"Absolutely, not a problem," I said. "You go ahead. I'll be right down."

Fee nodded and headed down the stairs. I sighed and went back into my room. It appeared it was going to be the demure little black dress after all.

Viv insisted that we all wear hats to Andre's art show, as she never missed an opportunity to advertise the shop. Since I was wearing black, I decided to jazz things up and wear a black pillbox hat with a nest of fluffy white feathers in the front that had long black eyelash feathers bursting out of it. It was very Audrey Hepburn and made me feel a bit less dowdy.

Fee found a hat to match *our* dress. It was an aqua fascinator in the shape of a bow that had a pouf of matching netting that draped just over her forehead. Viv was wearing a chemise in shimmering pewter. She added black elbow-length gloves and wore a black cloche with a pewter hatband. She let her long blonde curls hang loose down her back.

Walking to Andre's gallery, which was just down Portobello Road from Mim's Whims, I felt like I was the ugly duckling in a flock of swans. I tried to shake it off, but as Fee and Harrison walked ahead of Viv and me with their heads pressed together as they talked, I found myself getting more and more grumpy.

"I think we need to spread out and work the room," Viv said as we walked.

"Huh," I replied not really listening. Fee had just laughed and brushed her shoulder up against Harrison's. I couldn't imagine what he might have said that could have been that funny.

"Andre said a reporter from the Times will be there to take pictures and do a write-up for the Arts section," Viv said. "I think we should try to get into those photos."

"Sure," I said.

"You know, if you were to rip off your dress and twirl it over your head, that would really get their attention," Viv said.

"Sounds good," I said.

"Scarlett! You are not listening to a word I say!" she accused.

"What?" I asked. "Don't be ridiculous. Of course I'm not going to rip my dress off in public. I've had more than my share of notoriety, thank you very much."

Viv pursed her lips as she considered me. I blinked.

She glanced ahead at Fee and Harrison. "Those two seem awfully chummy."

"Really?" I asked. Harrison stood at the door to Andre's gallery, holding it open for us. "I hadn't noticed."

"Uh-huh," Viv said. She patted Harrison's cheek as she walked past him into the gallery.

I did not. In fact, I didn't acknowledge him at all but strode into the gallery with my head held high.

"Scarlett, there's my girl!" a voice cried.

I glanced across the room to see Nick Carroll, Andre's life partner, striding toward me with his hands outstretched. He grabbed my upper arms and we did the air-kiss thing on both cheeks.

"Well, aren't you a vision," Nick said.

"Thank you," I said and I gave a practiced twirl. I looked him over. "Nick, you look positively debonair."

He really did. His blond hair was thinning, but he had obviously plumped it up with some well-used product. He wore a pinstripe navy suit over a light-blue dress shirt, which was open at the throat.

"Shall we strut and preen and show off?" he asked.

"Yes, definitely," I said and put my hand on his arm.

Andre and Nick had been working on the gallery for months. This was the grand opening, and it was packed to bursting with people trying to see and be seen.

A waiter paused beside us and Nick snagged us each a glass of champagne. We worked our way toward the back of the room, where we could see Andre talking animatedly to a group of people.

"He's really in his element, isn't he?" Nick asked.

Andre was dressed in black trousers and a white loose-fitting dress shirt with a rich plum-colored vest over it. His dark skin and close-cropped hair accentuated his fine-boned good looks. He looked like a rock star and had the requisite solar system of women orbiting around him to prove it.

"Those girls are doomed to disappointment," I said to Nick.

He grinned. "Oh no, most of them know he's my partner. They just want him to take pictures of them, sort of like they want me to fix their teeth. They are users, one and all."

"Which is fine, since they fill out the party, don't they?" I asked.

"Indeed they do," he said.

Another waiter stopped by and we helped ourselves to the cherry tomatoes stuffed with pesto.

"There are some salt-and-pepper cheese puffs circling about," Nick said. "Keep an eye out."

"Yes, sir," I said.

I scanned the room, looking for Viv. She was easy to spot. She was standing in front of one of Andre's cityscapes, talking to two older gentlemen and their wives. I could tell she was chatting about the shop, as she touched the brim of her hat with a gloved hand.

"Beg pardon, Mr. Carroll," a waiter joined us. "We have a small situation in the kitchen."

"What sort of situation?" Nick asked around the tomato in his mouth.

"A fire," the waiter said.

"Gah!" Nick waved to me as he shot off across the room toward the back of the building.

"It was just a small one," the waiter said, following him. "We got it out."

I watched them go, wondering if this was cause to evacuate. I glanced up. I didn't see a sprinkler system. Then again, that would be bad for the photographs.

I dropped my small plastic plate and napkin into a trash can. I supposed it was time to do my duty and work the room, except I didn't really feel up to being my usual charming self. I scanned the crowd, looking for a flash of aqua. Given how tall Fee was in her platform heels, it didn't take me long to spot her. To my surprise, there was no sign of Harrison hanging on her every word.

I turned around, checking to see where he might be. Not that I cared, I told myself. I was just trying to keep track of the people I had come with, which was only polite.

"Looking for someone?" a voice asked from behind me.

I turned to find Harrison standing there. My breath caught in surprise, but I refused to show it. Instead I gave him a closed-lip smile and said, "Just assessing the situation."

"And what have you determined?" he asked.

"That Andre's gallery is destined to be a success," I said.

"To Andre," Harrison said and lifted his glass.

"To Andre," I repeated. We clinked glasses and I took a sip of the crisp, fruity champagne.

"Have you had the tiny tomatoes?" I asked. "They're very good."

"No, I missed those," he said.

He glanced over my head in the direction where I'd seen Fee. Now, that was just rude. I frowned at him.

"What?" he asked when he met my gaze.

"If you're so bored with me, you can go elsewhere," I said.

"I'm not bored," he said.

"Yeah, that's why you're looking right around me at someone who is entirely too young for you," I snapped.

He was in the middle of a sip when I spoke, and I must have caught him off guard, because he choked on his beverage and began to cough to clear his throat. His eyes were watering, and I could tell he really needed to have a good hacking fit to clear the airway.

"Come on," I said. I took his glass and put it down with mine on a nearby table, then I led him by the arm out the front door to the street, where he could let loose with a coughing jag.

It was quieter out here. The dull roar of the crowd was replaced by the occasional rumble of a car going past. Until Harrison burst into a coughing fit that was so violent, it hushed the birds chirping in the nearby trees. I thumped his back, possibly with more force than was strictly necessary, but hey, I was trying to help.

When his cough diminished to a small wheeze, I ceased whacking him.

"Better now?" I asked.

"Yeah, thanks," he said. His voice was gruff and a tear leaked out of the corner of his right eye.

"Excellent," I said. I made to go back into the gallery, but Harrison stopped me by catching my hand in his and tugging me back.

"Not so fast, Ginger," he said. His green eyes narrowed. "What exactly did you mean I was looking around you at someone entirely too young for me?"

"Nothing," I said. I tried to pull my fingers out of his grasp but he tightened his hold.

"I don't believe you," he said.

I gave him my best affronted look. I even put my free hand over my chest in a protestation of shocked innocence.

"No, still don't believe you," he said.

"Well, that's just—" I began, but he interrupted.

109

"Spill it," he said. "Who do you think I was looking at?"

"Fee," I said.

"Oh, well, I was looking for her."

"Aha!" I poked him in the chest with my finger. "I knew it."

Chapter 12

"Knew what?" he asked. He rubbed the spot where I'd jabbed him.

"She's too young for you," I said. "You could be her father."

Harrison's eyes widened in surprise, and he said, "Perhaps if I'd spawned her when I was eight."

I crossed my arms over my chest. "That's a huge age difference."

"You are mental," he said. "I can't believe you think . . . ugh . . . I refuse to participate in this conversation any further."

He strode past me, back into the gallery. Viv was just coming outside, and he brushed past her without even checking his stride.

"What's got Harrison's knickers in a knot?" Viv asked.

"He's just being oversensitive because I said that Fee is too young for him," I said.

"Is there a reason you felt the need to point that out?" she asked.

She was holding a glass of champagne in her gloved hand, and she took a sip while she waited for my answer.

I glanced at the gallery behind us, but I couldn't see either Fee or Harrison through the windows. I did see Viv's and my reflections. In our party dresses and hats, we looked like we belonged on the cover of a vintage *Vogue*. I turned away.

"I just thought the obvious might be escaping him," I said. I reached out and took Viv's glass out of her hand and helped myself to a fortifying sip.

"Scarlett, jealousy does not become you," Viv said.

"What?" I gasped. "I am not jealous!"

One of Viv's delicate eyebrows rose higher than the other as she considered me.

"Really? Then why meddle with whatever might be happening between Fee and Harrison?" she asked.

"He's eight years older than her!" I protested.

"Correct me if I'm wrong," Viv said, "but wasn't the blighter who broke your heart *ten* years older than you?"

"Exactly, my point," I said. It wasn't, but that didn't mean I couldn't cling to it like a life raft in the North Sea.

"Harrison isn't like that," Viv said. "He's a good man and just because he is a few years older doesn't mean he's a lying, cheating git."

"I know, but Fee is so young and innocent," I said. "She really needs to be dating people her own age."

Viv studied me for a moment. I didn't like the look in her eye.

"What?" I asked.

"Jealous," she said in a singsong voice.

"No, I'm not," I said. Why are family members so good at twanging your last nerve like a banjo string?

"You can't escape your nature," she said.

"Now, what's that supposed to mean?" I asked.

"Do you remember when we were teenagers and that silly musician boy liked you?" she asked.

I sighed. I did not like the direction this conversation was headed.

"No, I don't," I said. I drained her glass and handed it back to her.

"He was a swarthy, dark-haired fellow named Chad or Todd or something like that," Viv said. "He was completely uninteresting to you until Chrissy Hupper took a shine to him."

"I have no recollection of this," I said. Big, fat lie. I still remembered Chrissy. Still hated her, too.

She was one of those girls who didn't have any girl-friends. I always consider that an indicator of whether a woman can be trusted. If a woman has no female friends, there is usually a reason why. In Chrissy's case, it was because she loathed any competition in the wide-open field of men.

She tagged around with all of the boys in the neighbor-hood, preening under their attention. She didn't like it if any other girls cut into her turf, so needless to say she was less than thrilled when Viv and I appeared on the scene.

Chrissy spent a lot of time making fun of my American accent and making me feel like an idiot because I didn't know all of the local slang and television references that the neighborhood kids shared. She was particularly irritated by me because the silly musician boy liked me so much.

"You were oblivious to Chad/Todd until he showed a glimmer of interest in Chrissy, after weeks of you rejecting him, of course, and then you full-on stalked the boy just to take him away from her," Viv said. "Because you were jealous."

"No, I wasn't. Besides, that was completely different," I said. "I did flirt with the musician boy, which I admit was not nice of me, mostly because I couldn't stand Chrissy, but it was also to protect him. I wouldn't let a guppy date her, never mind an actual boy. I don't feel that way at all about Fee. I adore her."

"And yet you showed no interest in Harrison until he showed interest elsewhere," Viv said. "Then you got jealous."

"I am not jealous," I protested. "This whole conversation is ridiculous. I don't care who Harrison or Fee date; I just don't think they're right together."

"Which is none of your business," Viv said.

"Fine," I said. "I'll butt out. Can we go back inside now?"

Viv looked unconvinced but then shrugged as if resigned to whatever happened.

I opened the door, determined not to look for Fee or Harrison. Instead, I made a beeline over to Andre to give him my congratulations.

Thankfully, he had a moment between being interviewed and fawned over and opened his arms wide when he saw me.

"Scarlett, you look amazing," he said as he hugged me. "I should grab my camera."

"And this is why I love you," I said, hugging him back. "You know just what to say to a girl when she's feeling dowdy."

"You? Dowdy?" he asked. "Never."

I gave him a doubtful look.

"You don't believe me?" he asked. "Come here. I have something to show you."

He led me to a corner of the gallery I had yet to visit. A series of three huge prints were on the wall. They were done in black and white with just one object in the photo in color.

"Oh my God," I murmured. "That's me and Viv!"

The photos were the ones he had taken of us at the Wonderland tea when I'd been telling Viv about seeing Geoffrey and his secretary.

The first photo was a profile shot of me with my hand almost up to my mouth. It was easy to see I was about to tell a secret. The second shot was of Viv and me, huddled together with me whispering in her ear. And the third was of Viv looking surprised at what she'd just heard. In the first one, only my lips had color, rum raisin, in fact—my favorite lipstick. In the second, the feathers on Viv's hat were the only burst of color. And in the third, it was Viv's big blue eyes that were the spot of color.

"When did you put these up?" I asked. "They weren't here when we helped set up the other night."

"They weren't ready yet," he said. "In fact, I hung them this afternoon, and they were the first prints to sell."

"Oh, Andre, they are magnificent," I said. "You made us beautiful."

"You already are, love," he said.

I was feeling a bit too emotional to talk, so I put my hand on his cheek and whispered, "Thank you."

"No, thank you," he said. "I'm sorry I said you were ruddy bad luck. You're not, you know."

"You're forgiven." I stepped back and glanced around the room. "Andre, this is fantastic. You are the toast of the town."

He put a hand on the back of his neck and tilted his head to the side as if studying the room through the lens of his camera.

"It is brilliant, isn't it?" He looked equal parts relieved and awed.

"Andre, pet, you've got a buyer for your series of boats on the Thames," Nick said as he joined us. "They want to talk to you about light in dark or shadow or some such artsy stuff."

"Keep an eye on my girl," Andre said.

"I do hope he is referring to me," Nick said to me with a wink.

Andre grinned and kissed first Nick's cheek and then mine before he moved in the direction of the art buyers.

"How is the fiery situation?" I asked Nick.

"Under control," he said. "Honestly, caterers these days. A little oil fire and they all act like we're in a bad disaster movie."

"Scarlett Parker, is that you?"

The voice came from behind me. I didn't recognize it. I gave Nick a wide-eyed look and he glanced over my shoulder. Given the paparazzi's fascination with me a few months before, I was always leery when approached by persons unknown. Nick shrugged, which I took to mean he had no idea who it was but that it didn't look like a media type.

I turned slowly, bracing myself for a camera or a mic to be shoved into my face. There was none of that. Instead, I found Marilyn Tofts standing behind me, sipping champagne and nibbling on a cheese puff.

"I thought it was you," she said. "Nice hat."

"Marilyn, how good to see you," I said. I can recover and lie pretty quickly like that. Given that the last time I'd seen her was at a dead man's tea, I was surprised she was even willing to be seen talking to me.

"Likewise," she said. From the cool expression on her face, I could tell she was being as insincere as I was.

"Nick Carroll, I'd like to introduce Marilyn Tofts." I grabbed Nick's hand before he could disappear into the crowd.

He gave me a put out look and then he glanced at Marilyn as if recognizing the name. "Marilyn Tofts? The event planner?" he asked.

"Yes, that's me," she said. She tossed her long honey hair back over her shoulder and gave him a bright smile. "You've heard of me?"

"Heard of you?" Nick asked. "You were the talk of the Berringers' dinner party last week."

"Was it the Wonderland tea they were talking about?" I inquired.

Marilyn gave me a sour look.

"No, this was before that unfortunate incident," Nick said.

"It *was* unfortunate, wasn't it?" Marilyn gave a delicate sniff. "All of my hard work and for what? The host up and dies in the middle of the tea. There was simply no saving it."

"You tried?" I asked.

"But of course; that's what I do," Marilyn said and sipped her champagne. "The family was extremely difficult. I could not get any of them to come out of hiding and take control of the situation."

"But the head of the family had just been discovered dead," I protested. "Surely, the guests understood the extraordinary circumstances."

Marilyn Tofts rolled her eyes. "It was a pathetic display. That family is a disaster, I tell you. If you ask me, it serves them right. Letting me believe the queen would be there when obviously they are not of that social caliber. *Humpf.*"

I glared at her. She was just as shallow as I had supposed.

"Everyone has challenges," Nick said. He patted Marilyn's hand sympathetically. "It makes you stronger."

She gave him a grateful smile. I glanced between them. He looked positively giddy to meet her. I had to give it to her: she did make an impression.

In her usual vintage-starlet style, Marilyn was wearing a Maggy London satin sheath dress in jewel green. It had a wide portrait neckline and a cascade of fabric on one hip that gave her an amazing silhouette. She'd finished the look with a pair of black platform heels, which caused me a severe pang of shoe envy.

"And you're so brilliantly talented that the tea will be no more than an insignificant memory as you blaze a trail through the upper crust's social network," Nick said.

"Oh, go on," Marilyn said. There was a pause and she raised a perfectly sculpted eyebrow at Nick. "No, seriously, go on."

Nick grinned and suddenly I felt like the third seat on a bicycle built for two.

"I heard that you arranged to have the lead singer of Oasis just pop in at the Dashavoys' wedding and sing a bit to the bride, is that true?" Nick gushed.

"It is," Marilyn preened.

"That's brilliant!" Nick cried.

"I know!" Marilyn cried in return. "This is how amazing I am . . ."

I backed away. Neither of them noticed and no one tried to stop me. I decided I liked Marilyn Tofts even less now than I did when I first met her, and that had been in the negatives already.

I worked my way through the crowd and decided to console myself with a tray of goat cheese–stuffed dates that I found unattended. I was working through my fourth when Fee joined me, looking smashing in *our* dress.

"Scarlett, what are you doing here playing the part of the wallflower?" she asked.

"Muh muh," I mumbled through a mouthful of date.

Fee blew an errant blue curl out of her eye and studied me with a look of concern.

"Something's wrong, yeah?" she asked.

I wanted to stomp my foot and howl, yes, that this was the worst party ever because she had my dress and Harrison was too old for her and Nick was suddenly besotted with a true mean girl. Thankfully, a smidgeon of maturity kicked in and instead, I gave her a small smile and said, "Just a tiny headache, no big deal."

Fee didn't look like she believed me. Smart girl. But she didn't say anything.

"Well, my lovelies," Viv said as she joined us. "Have we done enough promotion for the shop?"

"I thought we were here to support Andre," Fee said.

"Of course we are," Viv said. "But mostly, we're walking advertisements for Mim's Whims. You did work the shop into every conversation, didn't you?"

Fee looked stricken, and I felt sorry for her.

"Go easy on her," I said. "She's a rookie."

Viv gave me a look as if to say she was surprised I was standing up for Fee, which was ridiculous. I didn't have a problem with Fee. If anyone, my issue was with Harrison for looking at a girl who was too young for him.

"Are you ladies calling it a night?"

Speak of the devil. Harrison appeared on the other side of Fee.

"We are," Fee said. "And you?"

"I've eaten all of the tiny food I can cram in," he said. "I'm ready to go."

"Excellent," Viv said. She waved at Andre over the heads of the crowd until he waved back. I waved, too, and nodded when he gestured that he'd call me later.

As we cleared the door, Viv slipped her hand through Fee's arm and said, "So, I was thinking that since I am finished creating the hats for the Wonderland tea and I've caught up to all of the special orders, you might like an assist on the hats for the Butler-Coates wedding."

"Do you mean it?" Fee gasped. Viv nodded and Fee clapped a hand to her forehead. "Oh, thank you. I know I said I wanted to do it myself, but that bridezilla is about to drive me right out of my mind."

She glanced over her shoulder at us—okay, mostly at Harrison—and asked, "Did you hear? Viv is going to save me!"

He grinned at her and I smiled. I knew Fee had been struggling with the big event. The Butler-Coates wedding had a high-maintenance bride with seven bridesmaids in it, so it was a doozy.

"Maybe we can start all over, because goodness knows, I am getting nowhere," Fee said. She looked so relieved, I couldn't help but be happy for her.

Viv laughed and hugged Fee close to her side. They continued walking and I heard Viv say, "Tell me some of your latest ideas."

Fee took a deep breath and out poured a flood of hat talk. I glanced at Harrison. He was watching them with a small smile on his lips as if he was charmed by the sight of them, which I found very irritating.

I picked up the pace of my walk so that I was right on Viv and Fee's heels, not that they noticed, since they were discussing the different types of fabric they could use for the bride's veil. Harrison kept pace with me, but when I would have slammed into Fee's back because she stopped short for a woman walking her dog, he caught me by the elbow and kept me from crashing.

Viv and Fee kept walking, but the little black-and-white dog danced right in front of my feet, blocking my path.

"Hey there, little fella," I said. I knelt down and patted his soft head. He wagged and panted. Harrison knelt down beside me and scratched the dog's back. The dog pranced on his feet and licked Harrison's wrist before trotting off with his owner, who smiled at us.

When I straightened up, I saw that Viv and Fee were half a block ahead of us. For a moment I wondered if Viv had planned this whole thing, but that seemed over-the-top even for Viv.

The streetlamps glowed bright white, while the shops that remained open beat back the night's darkness from their windows with warm squares of yellow light.

"Listen, Scarlett," Harrison said before I could continue walking. "About before—"

"No." I held up my hand. "It's none of my business."

"But you need to know—" he began, but again I interrupted.

"No, I really don't need the particulars of your whatever," I said. "If college girls are what you're into, it's none of my affair."

"College girls are what I'm into?" he repeated, sounding confounded.

Two older gentlemen walking around us stopped, and one of them nudged Harrison with his elbow. "Nothing wrong with that, Batch; enjoy your youth while you can."

Harrison gave him a dark look and he and his friend hurried off. I surmised from the wobble in their walks that they'd been indulging in a pint or three of Fuller's ale.

I'm partial to Fuller's London Pride myself. It's a nice pale ale that goes amazingly well with a pasty or a plate of roast beef and Yorkshire pudding. Of course, they don't generally serve it as cold as I was used to in the States, but I've found that I liked it better that way.

"What does 'Batch' mean?" I asked.

"It's short for 'bachelor,'" he said.

"Huh." I resumed walking, but again Harrison stopped me with a hand on my elbow.

"So why does it bother you?" he asked.

"What?" I blinked at him. When all else fails, I've discovered playing dumb is a fabulous diversionary tactic.

"Me and Fee."

My eyes widened. He admitted it! My expression must have given my thoughts away, because he looked at me and shook his head.

"Not that there is a me and Fee," he clarified, "but why does the idea bother you so much?"

The man was like a dog with a bone, and I was beginning to feel like the marrow. Honestly, how was I going to get out of this one?

Chapter 13

His green eyes narrowed as he waited.

"I already told you," I said. "Fee's too young for you."

"Oh, codswallop!" Harrison said. "Eight years is not too young, but that's not the point. The point is I don't believe you. What's really bothering you?"

I stared at him, refusing to answer. He shoved his hands into his pants pockets and rocked back and forth on his heels as if he had all the time in the world to wait for my answer. When he started to whistle, I glowered.

"You really think you're all that, don't you?" I asked. I decided to go for the offensive strike.

"Hey, now, what do you mean by that?" he asked.

I turned and began walking. When he would have grabbed my elbow again, I dodged.

"You refuse to believe that I am just looking out for a

friend," I said. "Because your male vanity insists that it must be something else."

"No, it doesn't," he protested as he matched his stride to mine.

"Then why don't you believe me?" I asked.

We were nearing Mim's Whims when Harrison slowed his pace. There was no sign of Viv or Fee, so I assumed they must have gone inside. The shades were drawn over the windows, but the overhead security light illuminated the walkway in front of the shop.

"I'll tell you why," he said. He stopped in front of the door.

"This should be good," I said. I crossed my arms over my chest and tapped my toe on the sidewalk.

"You have no problem throwing Viv at that adolescent Liam Grisby, and their age difference is about the same as Fee's and mine," he said. "So, Ginger, why the double standard?"

I felt my insides sink like a deflated cake after a loud bang. He had me. Why did I think it was okay for Viv and Liam to hook up but not Harry and Fee?

"That's different," I protested.

"Really?" he asked. "How?"

"Because you're an older male and Viv is an older female and the relationship dynamics are completely different."

He crossed his arms over his chest, mimicking my stance.

"I have another theory," he said. "Care to hear it?"

"Not really, no," I said.

"Excellent, here it is," he said, completely ignoring me. "You're jealous. That's why you're so interested in whether Fee and I have something going."

"I am not," I argued.

He leaned close and grinned at me. "Yes, you are."

I wasn't sure what annoyed me more, the fact that he looked so smug or that he was right, a fact I was not even willing to admit to myself just yet.

"I will have you know, Harry, that I couldn't be less interested in you if you were three feet tall, bald, and had hair sprouting out your ears."

He grinned at me. "Right."

With one word, he mocked. I desperately wanted to kick him but even more I wanted to win the argument if for no other reason than to preserve my dignity.

"And even if I had taken complete leave of my senses and was jealous, which I'm not, it wouldn't matter because I have taken a vow of celibacy for at least one year."

"What?" he asked. He looked shocked and appalled.

Ah, now I had his attention. I reached around him and grabbed the handle to the door, relieved to find it unlocked.

"You heard me," I said. "Good night."

I stepped inside and shut the door without inviting him in.

Viv was putting away the hats she and Fee had worn. I lifted the pretty pillbox off of my head and handed it to her.

"Everything all right?" Viv asked.

"Peachy," I said.

She raised her eyebrows, but I didn't elaborate.

"Where's Harrison?" she asked.

"He had to go," I said. Which was not a complete lie in the sense that he really needed to get away from me.

"Oh, I was hoping he'd come and cook something for us," Viv said.

"I can cook," I offered.

"And by that, you mean you can place an order for take-away?" Viv asked.

"Exactly," I said. I do like to play to my strengths.

Fee came down the stairs with her dress returned to its garment bag, which was hanging over her arm. She was back in her capri pants and flats, looking very Cinderella-back-from-the-ball.

"I have to run," she said. "My brothers will wonder where I am."

"You really need to bring them round sometime," Viv said. "They might trust you more if they met us."

"Or they'd start bossing you about, too, yeah?" Fee said.

Viv and I exchanged a look. That would not go over well.

"See you tomorrow," Fee said.

She sailed out the front door and I wondered if Harrison was out there waiting for her. Not my business, I told myself. Still, as I locked the door behind her, I shifted the blinds to peer out the glass portion of the door.

The street was quiet and Fee was striding off on her own, chatting on her cell phone as she went. I wondered if she was calling her brothers to assure them that she was fine. Then I wondered what her brothers would think about her and Harrison. Not that I would tell them about the pair, I'm not that meddlesome; still, they were awfully protective. I bet they'd think Harrison was too old, too.

"Trouble over there, Scarlett?" Viv asked.

I dropped the blind and turned around. "No, not a bit. So, what's your fancy for dinner? We could walk over to

Notting Hill Gate and get takeaway soup and sandwiches from Le Pain Quotidien."

"Sounds perfect," Viv said. "I could use a tasty tartine, and if we walk, it won't stick to my arse."

I laughed. Viv never was one to candy-coat things.

We locked up and stepped out into the cool June night. Soup and a sandwich would surely put things right, and if not, there was always treacle tart with cream.

With Fee and Viv preoccupied with the Butler-Coates wedding, I was left to man the shop, which was not a bad thing since of the three of us, I had the best people skills. Thank goodness or I'd really have nothing to contribute to our enterprise.

It was midafternoon and business had tapered off enough that I decided to sit in one of our squashy blue chairs and put my feet up. Yes, the minute I put my feet up I should have known something bad would happen. You can almost always bank on that sort of thing in retail.

I did not see the bad thing coming as Detective Inspector Finchley arriving with his own entourage of crime-scene investigators. I was so engrossed in the latest issue of the *Daily Mirror*—don't judge; a customer left it behind—that I didn't even hear them enter the shop until the detective was standing right beside me.

"Good afternoon, Ms. Parker," he said.

"Ah!" I yelped. My feet came down, my paper flew up and my heart about smashed through my rib cage. I put a hand over my chest and tried to catch my breath.

"Sorry, I didn't mean to startle you," he said. His jowls wobbled, and I suspected he was trying not to laugh at me.

"No harm done," I lied. I was pretty sure a few days had been shaved off of my life, but yeah, no biggie. I stood and faced him. "I take it this isn't a social call, or are you all looking for new hats?"

One of the female techs behind him stifled a laugh, and I decided that I liked her.

"Actually, this is quite serious, I'm afraid," Finchley said. His brows met in the middle in a severe frown, eradicating any of the humor that had flitted briefly across his face like a cloud over the sun.

"Oh, I'm sorry," I said. "What can I do to help?"

"The forensic pathologist has discovered that Geoffrey Grisby's death was not from natural causes," Finchley said. His face was grim.

I said nothing. I suppose I should have told him that Tina had already told me he'd been poisoned, but I wanted to wait and see where this was going before I volunteered any information.

"Are you saying he was murdered?" I asked, because I like to be specific like that. I raised my eyebrows to indicate my surprise.

Finchley pressed his lips together as if he was trying to determine how much to say. Finally, he gave me an abrupt nod.

"But how?" I asked. "There was no blood or sign of a wound or anything to indicate a struggle."

"Looked at him that closely, did you?" Finchley asked me.

"I was the one to find him," I said. "I did turn him over."

"Indeed," Finchley said. For one word, it sure packed a punch.

"Hey!" I protested. "I don't know what you're thinking, but I have absolutely no reason—"

"Didn't you flee the States after battering your lover with his anniversary cake?"

I felt my heart, which had finally resumed its normal rhythm, stop and fall down into my stomach. My face felt hot with shame. My voice was very quiet when I spoke.

"I don't really see what one has to do with the other."

"Neither do I," he said. "But I promise you, if there is a connection to be made, I will make it."

It didn't feel like a threat so much as a promise. Okay, that was intimidating.

"And I can assure you, there is no connection," I said. "We were commissioned by the Grisby family to design the hats for the Wonderland tea. That is all."

"Then why does Mrs. Grisby refer to your cousin as her old friend Ginny when your cousin's name is clearly Vivian?" he asked.

I glanced over his shoulder at the crime-scene techs who had come with him. The woman was checking out our hats. The man was absorbed by his cell phone. So no backup there.

"Surely, you noticed that Mrs. Grisby is not operating at full mental capacity," I said.

"She does seem a bit addled," he conceded.

"My cousin felt it was kinder to let Dotty think of her as her old friend instead of insisting that she wasn't. We're very nice like that." I gave him a pointed look, which he ignored.

"Is your cousin here right now?" he asked.

"Yes, she's in back, working on some hats," I said.

"You make them here?" he asked.

"Yes," I said. "Why?"

"We'll need to see your work area," he said.

"All right, follow me," I said. I led them through the shop to the workroom, where Viv and Fee had music playing. Fatboy Slim's "Praise You," to be precise.

Fee was singing along while Viv was bobbing her head. Finchley seemed to take the room in at a glance—an unhappy glance.

"Viv," I called to my cousin, but she couldn't hear me over the music.

I hurried across the room to the computer, which was live streaming the XFM radio station. With a click of the mouse the music switched off and both Viv and Fee glanced up with What-the—? looks on their faces.

"Viv, this is Detective Inspector Finchley," I said. "He's here to ask you some questions."

Viv tossed her long blonde curls over her shoulder and stared at him. "Whatever about?"

"Poison," he said.

Chapter 14

"Poison?" Viv, Fee and I all asked together.

Finchley took a moment to study all three of us. He handed me a sheaf of legal-looking papers. Sadly, I'd been on the receiving end of these before, and I knew it was a warrant allowing them to search the shop.

"All right, team, you know what to look for," he said.

The man put his phone away and the woman looked up from where she was examining the ruffled tulle on the edge of a fascinator.

"Excuse me, Detective Inspector Finchley," Viv said. "But why would I have poison in my shop? And why are you here, anyway?"

"Geoffrey Grisby was poisoned and traces were found on the hat you made for him," Finchley said.

"But I have no reason to have killed Mr. Grisby," Viv said.

"Possibly," he said. "But what of your employees?"

"I had no reason to murder him," Fee said. "I wasn't even at the tea."

"Why not?" Finchley asked.

"Because I was here working," Fee said. Her brown eyes were wide, and she looked worried.

"Can anyone verify that?" Finchley asked.

Fee looked alarmed. "I'm sure I had customers who could."

"That'll do," Finchley said.

"Well, I had no reason to murder him either," I chimed in. "And whatever I did in the States is not relevant and you know it."

Finchley studied me from under a pair of bushy eyebrows. "How do I know someone in the family didn't hire you to do it for them?"

"Oh, please," Viv said. Her exasperation was showing. "Do you really think we run a hat shop with a little murder business on the side? Honestly."

Finchley shoved his hands in his pockets and scowled. "Scoff if you want, but you are connected to the murder whether you like it or not. Besides, hatters are known for being mad, aren't they? Why couldn't it be you?"

"I am getting bloody tired of people telling me I'm mad!" Viv snapped.

"I didn't say you were," Finchley corrected. "I said hatters are known for it, but since you brought it up, who else has called you mad and why?"

I glanced at Viv. This was not good. The last person I knew who had called hatters mad was Geoffrey Grisby.

"It is a social stigma," Viv said, not answering his question. "And if you had done your research before coming here, you would know that the origin of the term 'mad hatter' comes from the hat-making industry in the 1800s. A mercury solution was used during the process of turning fur into felt."

"Mercury?" Finchley asked. "But that's poisonous."

"We know that now," Viv said. "They didn't then, and it caused the hatters to have symptoms such as trembling, loosening of teeth, memory loss, depression, *irritability*"— she dragged that word out for impact—"loss of coordination, slurred speech and anxiety. It was called Mad Hatter Syndrome."

Finchley stared at Viv and I could tell she'd made an impression upon him. I just couldn't tell if it was good or bad. Finally, he nodded at her and said, "Fascinating."

Amazingly, Viv seemed mollified by this.

"Excuse me."

I was leaning against the cupboard when the forensic woman with Finchley gestured that she needed to get in there. I moved. The forensic man did the same to Viv and Fee as he swabbed the table and then carefully put the swabs into a plastic kit that he put in his bag.

"Oh, this is ridiculous. How are we supposed to work like this?" Viv asked, and she strode to the front of the shop.

"Go check on her, would you?" I asked Fee. She hurried after Viv and I turned to Inspector Finchley. "What sort of poison was it?"

He looked like he wasn't going to say. I crossed my arms over my chest and tipped my chin up. He considered me for a moment. I don't know if it was the sheer stubbornness of my stance or the fact that he was beginning to believe that we had nothing to do with it, but he gave me a brisk nod.

"Formaldehyde," he said. "Mr. Grisby died of acute exposure to formaldehyde."

I frowned. I don't know why, but I had expected it to be arsenic or cyanide or even a bad mushroom. Formaldehyde threw me for a loop.

"But we don't use anything like that here," I said.

"Then you should be in the clear shortly," Finchley said. "If you'll excuse me. This shouldn't take very long. Am I correct in assuming you live above the shop?"

"Yes," I said.

"Excellent. I'll let you know when we're ready to go up there."

He did not leave it open to discussion. I left the room, feeling somewhat like I'd just been run over by a semi.

I found Viv and Fee sitting in the shop, which was quiet. Viv had picked up the copy of the *Mirror*—see, it's like a train wreck: you just can't look away—and was flipping through it and muttering to herself.

"I don't know about you, but I'm having flashbacks of the last time the police wanted to search the place," Fee said to me.

"A little bit," I agreed.

The bells on the door chimed and in walked Andre and Nick. They were looking very dapper in jackets over dress pants with crisp shirts, open at the collar, underneath.

"You two are looking disgustingly respectable," I said. "What gives?"

"Off to the bank," Nick said. "We're going to go for a loan to refurbish the studio a bit."

"The opening went well, did it?" Viv asked.

"Better than I could have imagined," Andre said. He looked amazed at his own good fortune and I couldn't help but be happy for him.

"Well, you might want to clear out of here so that our bad luck doesn't rub off on you," I said.

"You could never be unlucky," Nick protested.

"Oh, I don't know," I said. I jerked a thumb at the door behind me that led to the workroom. "Inspector Finchley is here looking for traces of formaldehyde."

"Formaldehyde?" Viv slapped the tabloid onto the table. "But that stuff smells disgusting. I would never let that in my shop."

Fee wrinkled her nose. "I do think we would have noticed, yeah?"

I sighed. "They're saying that's what Geoffrey died from and there were trace amounts on the hat you made for him. Thus, they're looking here."

"That's ridiculous," Andre said. "Have you called Harrison? He'll get it sorted."

"I don't think—" I began but Viv interrupted.

"Already done," she said. "He's on his way over."

"What?" I cried. I glanced at a standing mirror nearby. Why had I chosen to wear my most unflattering top today? I wondered if I had time to change. Then I mentally smacked myself. What did I care if Harrison saw me in a blousy peach shirt that made me look ten pounds heavier than I was? I didn't.

I glanced away from the mirror and saw Nick smiling at me. I scowled.

"So, how did your chat go with Marilyn Tofts?" I asked. "The two of you seemed awfully chummy."

"I know," Nick preened. "I can really turn on the charm when I want some dish."

"You mean she's not your new BFF?" I asked.

"Oh, ick, no. Andre invited her just for promotion," he said with a dismissive wave of his hand.

"You invited her?" I asked Andre.

He shrugged, which I took as a yes.

"So that's what you weren't telling me that day at the tea. There I was going on about how I loathed her and you had already invited her to the opening," I said.

"Guilty," Andre said and hung his head.

"She's a horrible woman," Nick said. "But she is seriously connected, and you know how I love the gossip. Hey, is that a copy of the *Mirror*? Can I have it?"

He snatched up the magazine Viv had smacked down on the table.

"Time, Nick—we have to go," Andre said, checking his cell phone. "Wish us luck."

The three of us waved as they left the shop. The door had barely closed behind them when Finchley reappeared from the workroom with his minions.

"We're ready to examine your living quarters," he said.

Viv looked like she was going to growl, so I cut her off before she could cause any more suspicion to rain down upon us.

"I'll take you up," I said. "Viv, why don't you get back to work. Fee, would you mind watching the shop?"

I turned away before they could balk. Sometimes, I think sharks have it right: stay in constant motion and nothing bad can catch you.

The bells on the door rang again, and I glanced over my shoulder to see Harrison stride into the shop. So much for my shark theory.

Harrison shook hands with Finchley in quite the courteous, nothing-suspicious-here manner. Finchley indicated that I had the paperwork, so I handed it to Harrison before leading the way upstairs.

"Go ahead with Ms. Parker," Finchley instructed. "I'll follow shortly."

"Hi, Fee, how are you?"

I heard Harrison greet Fee but I refused to look to see if they were giving each other goofy grins. I pulled open the door that led upstairs and turned to see if the two detectives were following me. Now, I can't help it if I happened to glance behind them and saw Harrison watching me.

We held each other's gaze for just a moment before he gave me a small smile and turned back to Detective Inspector Finchley. Now what was I supposed to make of that?

I led the way up the stairs. I toured the two detectives

around our apartment, where they continued their snooping. You can call it whatever you like, but I'm going with "snooping," especially when I caught the male portion of the twosome sniffing all of my hair products.

"Scarlett!" a voice called to me from the living room. I gave the male a look until he put down my very expensive conditioner.

"Coming!" I called back. I hurried down the stairs.

I moved across the flat, feeling weird about leaving the two detectives in our rooms, but saw no alternative. When I got to the sitting room, Viv was there, looking agitated.

"What is it, Viv?" I asked.

"I think you should tell Finchley about Tina," she said in a hushed tone.

I glanced at her. "What do you mean?"

"You should tell him how they were, how mean Grisby was and how you were afraid for her," Viv said.

"I already told him about running into Geoffrey and his secretary, and I found the body," I said. "He's going to think I'm some sort of crazy stalker."

"Oh, here you are," Harrison said as he stepped through the door from downstairs with Finchley on his heels.

Viv gave me a meaningful look, but I shook her off like a pitcher rejecting a catcher's signal. Maybe it was because Tina had just been here pleading her case, or maybe it was because I didn't want to look like I was trying to steer the investigation away from us, but I thought that I would wait

139

for another opportunity to mention the baby dilemma Tina and Geoffrey had been having.

"Your detectives are finishing their search upstairs," I said.

"Thank you, Ms. Parker; sorry for the intrusion," he said. He moved past us to join the others.

When he was out of earshot, Viv hissed, "Why didn't you say anything?"

"Not now," I said and tipped my head in Harrison's direction.

"Not now what?" he asked.

"Nothing," I said.

"This is definitely not nothing," Viv argued.

"It might be nothing," I said. "When Tina was here the other day—"

That was as far as I got before Viv interrupted.

"Tina Grisby was here? The other day? In our shop?" she cried. "And you're only mentioning it now?"

"Oh, good grief, don't have a cow," I snapped. "It was no big deal."

"Look, Scarlett, in case you haven't noticed, our premises are being searched because the police think we've poisoned someone. I can assure you, it is a big deal."

"No, it isn't!" I argued. I turned so Viv and I were face-to-face. We didn't fight much, but when we did, it went from a lit match to volcanic fairly quickly. "We've been searched before. Oh, wait, that's right, you weren't here for that because you were off chasing down feathers in Africa."

"Oh, pick a new instrument already," Viv cried. "Because

you've been playing the pity harp ever since I got back and it's getting old."

"Ah!" I gasped.

"Girls," Harrison said as he tried to wedge himself in between us. "Let's all just calm down."

"We are calm!" Viv and I both yelled.

"Is there a problem here?" Finchley asked from the doorway.

I was surprised he didn't go up in smoke, so hot were the glowers we directed at him. Viv opened her mouth to say something, but I spoke before she could.

"Just business issues," I said. "You know, boring tax stuff."

His jowls wobbled as he jerked his head to study each of us in turn. I didn't care what Viv said. There was something in the way Tina looked the day she stopped by, something desperate, that made me not want to say anything to the police. At least, not yet anyway.

To Viv's credit, she gave him just as bland a stare as I did. The inspector and his team left shortly thereafter.

Fee had made a pot of tea to calm all of our nerves and we convened in the workroom over tea and biscuits and a nice block of cheese I'd picked up at the local Waitrose market over on Bayswater Road.

No one spoke while the tea steeped. I wasn't sure why, but it seemed we were all gathering our thoughts. I'm sure Viv was reeling at having the police going through our things, but Fee, Harrison and I had been through it before, so it was a bit less unsettling this time.

Viv took the cozy off of the teapot and began to pour. This must have signaled that it was time to discuss the situation. Not surprisingly, Harrison spoke first.

"So, who wants to tell me what that was all about?" Harrison asked.

Chapter 15

"Whatever do you mean?" I asked as I blew on my cup of tea. "It seemed perfectly understandable to me. Someone poisoned Geoffrey Grisby. Traces of the poison were found on his hat, so the police had to do a thorough search of our shop to make sure we aren't the point of origin."

Viv was staring at me. It went without saying that she felt I should mention the whole Tina-Geoffrey situation, but I refused. I didn't want Harrison's opinion on the matter; in fact, I didn't really want him here at all. He confused things.

Harrison frowned. "Fee, help me out. What are these two hiding about Tina Grisby?"

Fee looked from me to Viv and back. Whatever she saw there must have convinced her to keep her trap shut.

"No idea," she said.

Harrison lifted an eyebrow at her and then sipped his tea.

"I really don't see any cause for concern," I said. "Finchley isn't going to find any poison in our shop, so there's nothing to worry about. We'll be in the clear as soon as they run the tests."

"I still say you should have told him what you overheard between Geoffrey and Tina when they were here looking at hats," Viv said. "It might have gotten us out of the hot seat a lot faster."

"Maybe, but he still would have searched the shop for poison," I said. "So what's the difference?"

"The difference is that Tina is the most likely person to have murdered Geoffrey," Viv said. "She's his wife and he was cheating on her with his secretary while putting incredible pressure upon her to get pregnant."

Harrison and Fee both looked at me for confirmation. I sighed.

"Well, I guess you don't have to badger us for the information anymore," I said to them. "Consider yourselves in the loop."

"Thanks," Harrison said. He looked puzzled.

"What?" I asked.

"Why don't you want to tell the police about this?" he asked.

"Because I like Tina and I don't think she did it," I said. "I mean, it's not like I'm keeping a big secret. He was nasty to her, just awful, actually, and I'm sure others will divulge that, and they were trying to have a baby, which seemed very stressful for them."

"Denial," Viv said. "You're obviously in a state of denial.

The fact that she asked you not to tell anyone about the altercation makes it suspicious."

"No, I'm not. It just doesn't make sense given the circumstance of the Grisby estate," I argued. "Without Geoffrey, Tina gets nothing. I would think a more likely candidate would be Daphne or her sons, as they stand to inherit it all with Geoffrey dead."

"You can't mean that," Viv said. "Liam would never harm his uncle."

"How could you possibly know that?" I asked. "You barely know him. He could be a cold-blooded killer beneath all of his charm and good looks."

"He's not," Viv said. She picked up a crisp and nibbled on it.

"Talk about denial," I said. "So, you do like him?"

Yes, I was fishing for information. It was too good of an opportunity to pass up.

"Not relevant," Viv said.

"Oh, I don't know," Harrison said. He looked at me when he said, "Isn't he younger by several years than you, Viv?"

"What does age have to do with it?" she asked. "If I like a man, I don't care if he's younger or older. I only care that we are compatible."

"Uh-huh." Harrison grunted. I noted he was looking at me and not Viv. Whatever.

"Moving right along," I said. I didn't like the triumphant gleam in Harrison's eyes. We were so not circling back to his theory that I was jealous. "Tina looked frightened the day she came in and she asked me specifically not to mention what had happened between her and Geoffrey."

"But don't you see?" Viv asked. "That's because she whacked him."

"No, I don't see that," I said. "It makes no sense. Why would you kill off your meal ticket?"

Viv pursed her lips. She always hated losing an argument.

"Didn't you say that Geoffrey Grisby was germ-phobic?" Harrison asked. "How could he not have noticed the smell of formaldehyde? It's not like smelling roses, after all, now, is it?"

"He has a point," Fee said. "You can't ignore a stench like that."

I thought back to the day of the party when Geoffrey had walked passed me in the garden. Did I smell anything then? Not that I remembered.

There was just no way to know what could have happened. I wondered how the Grisby family was handling the tragedy. I wished there was a reason to pop in on them and find out.

"You know," I said. "Given that Dotty thinks you're her old friend Ginny, maybe we should pop in and see how she's doing."

"Scarlett, did you not see their mansion?" Viv asked. "These are not the sort of people you pop in on. They'd set the dogs after you."

"Agreed, no popping," Harrison said. "You need to steer clear of the whole situation."

Viv and I exchanged a look. I was absolutely not down

with Harrison telling me what to do. Viv, however, gave him a small smile and a hair toss.

"You're right," she said.

I would have opened my mouth to argue, but I felt her step on my toes in what had to be a signal for me to keep my yap shut.

Harrison looked at me and I mimicked Viv's hair toss and smile and said, "Quite right."

Harrison narrowed his green eyes at us, but we maintained full eye contact.

"Excellent," he said. "I'm glad you're both showing such good sense."

He drained his cup of tea in one big swallow and rinsed the cup out in the sink.

"Nothing but," Viv said. "We are merely diligent milliners with our heads twisted on all proper—ouch!"

Yes, I pinched her just above the elbow. The way she was babbling, Harrison was no doubt going to know we were flat-out lying.

"All right, Viv?" he asked.

She rubbed her arm where I'd pinched her and gave me a dark look. "Yes, fine. It must have been a pest of sorts."

"I'll ring you later," Harrison said as he made his way to the door.

"Sounds good," Viv said with a wave.

Fee and I waved, too, as Harrison disappeared through the door.

"So, when did you want to pop over to the Grisbys'?" Viv asked me.

I grinned. That was the cousin I knew and adored.

"Aha! I knew it!" Harrison jumped back into the doorway, causing me to start and spill tea all down my front. I wasn't the only one.

"Oy, you about gave me a bloody heart attack!" Fee snapped as she brushed at the front of her blouse.

"Sorry, but I knew these two were up to their usual shenanigans," he said.

"For your information," Viv said. "I knew you were listening at the door, and I was just tricking you."

"You did not!" he argued.

"Yes, I did," she said. "Here, stand here and look in that window," she said, indicating where she was standing and pointing to the window to her left.

She then hurried through the door and stood just past it. She held her thumbs to her ears and waved her hands while she stuck out her tongue. Though we couldn't see her in the doorway, her reflection in the window was perfectly clear.

I busted up laughing while Harrison looked chagrinned.

"Hey, how many fingers am I holding up?" she cried.

Mercifully, she shot us a peace sign and not the other equally well-known hand gesture.

"Two, you daft milliner," Harrison said.

Viv danced back into the room laughing. She hugged Harrison hard and ruffled his hair.

"You're just so easy to tease," she said.

He huffed out a breath before he hugged her back.

"Now I'm leaving for real," he said.

"Like we're going to believe that," Viv said.

"You will, because Scarlett will walk me out," Harrison said. "Won't you?"

"Uh, sure," I said. I glanced at Fee to see if she looked disappointed that he hadn't asked her. She was smiling at us, so I took that as a no.

Harrison led the way through the shop and paused before the front door.

He stood with his hand on the door handle, yet he didn't push it open. Instead he studied me. Uh-oh.

"Were you waiting for an invitation to leave?" I asked. "Because I can assist with that."

"Charming," he said. "Actually, I am trying to choose my words carefully so that there is no mistaking what I'm about to say."

"Well, don't hurt yourself," I said. What? Too antagonistic? I can't help it; Harrison just brings it out in me.

"You and Viv are not to set one toe on the Grisby estate," he said. "And by one toe, I mean anything that might be attached to said toe, as in no other part of your body should find itself on the Grisby estate either. How am I doing for clarity?"

"Pretty clear," I said. "You are aware that you're not the boss of us, aren't you?"

He blew out a breath. "Perhaps but consider this: if I quit doing your books for you, who are you going to get to replace me?"

"A passive little pencil pusher who minds his own business?" I suggested.

"Right," he said. "Because you two won't take the Mickey out of the poor bloke in the first week."

"Are you calling us scary?" I asked. I was pretty sure I should be offended.

"With the amount of dead bodies springing up round you two, yeah, I reckon I'd say you're scary," he said.

He had a point, not that I was about to acknowledge it.

"I'll have your word, Scarlett," he said. "No going any-where near the Grisbys, especially if you believe Liam might have had something to do with his uncle's death. Surely, you don't want Viv to get involved with a man like that."

"I really don't think Liam had anything to do with his uncle's death," I said.

"Someone did," Harrison said. "And if they've murdered once, they're really not going to be too concerned about doing it again."

That gave me a shiver. Harrison noticed and reached out a hand to rub my arm. His fingers were warm on my cool skin, his touch firm but gentle.

"I'm not trying to frighten you, but . . . wait, yes, I am," he said as he removed his hand.

This made me smile and I said, "Mission accomplished."

"Good," he said. "This is serious stuff. Whoever offed Grisby planned it out."

"How do you know?" I asked.

"Because shooting, stabbing, or clubbing someone might be a crime of passion, but poison requires some thought and preparation."

"I suppose you're right," I said. "Couldn't it be someone he was in business with? Does it have to be a family member?"

"Anything is possible, but with the upheaval in the family, it seems as if they'd have the most motive."

"I suppose," I said. I really hated to think of Tina or Liam as suspects.

"Which means they're really not going to appreciate anyone getting in their way. You have to stay out of this, Ginger. I don't want to see you or Viv get hurt."

"We won't," I said.

He gave me a beady-eyed stare. I stared back.

"So just out of curiosity, am I right that you are trying to ascertain whether Viv likes Liam or not?"

"What the what?" I blinked. "Careful there, you could give a girl whiplash with that abrupt subject change."

"Sorry, but I'm wondering why you're poking around in Viv's personal life?" he said. "She's very private, you know."

"Oh, I've noticed," I said. "I'm worried about her. I'd like to see her date a nice guy."

"Well, one with a possible murder charge on his head should probably be scratched off of your list," he said.

"I suppose," I agreed.

"I'm sure Viv is quite capable of finding a decent chap on her own," he said.

"Really?" I asked. "This is Viv we're talking about. She's not known for making the best choices."

"Just because you dated a particularly rank git, you shouldn't assume all women do."

"What can I say? I'm a bitter woman, Harry," I said. I was only partly kidding. I patted his shoulder. "Don't worry about me. I'm sure it's nothing a few years of therapy can't fix."

"You don't need therapy," he said. "You need to date a higher caliber of man."

"Hmm," I grunted. "Since I'm not dating anyone for a very long time, I'll take your recommendation under advisement."

He looked like he wanted to say something. He even opened his mouth to speak but then closed it and shook his head.

"Fine, but I'll have your promise to stay away from the Grisbys."

I frowned.

"You thought I'd forgotten about that, didn't you?" he asked.

"No—yes," I admitted.

"Your word, Scarlett," he said.

"But I don't want to," I said. "I want to see Tina again, and I want to know that she's okay. I'm worried about her."

"But you hardly know her," he protested.

"I know, but I like her and I feel for her situation," I said. "I get the impression she doesn't have a lot of people she can turn to, and I can't turn my back on her."

"Ginger, you are quite possibly one of the nicest people I've ever met," he said. Well, didn't that make me feel special? I smiled at him right up until he added, "And one of the most misguided."

"What's that supposed to mean?" I asked.

"Just that you're not the best judge of character, now, are you?"

"Meaning?"

"Your last relationship . . ." His voice trailed off.

"I was conned by a professional cad. You can't judge me by that," I said. "Besides, I also befriended Andre and Nick, and they've turned out all right."

"Everyone gets lucky sometimes," he said.

I rolled my eyes. "If I promise that I won't go near the Grisbys, will you quit nagging?"

"Hold up your hands," he said. I frowned at him and he said, "No crossed fingers or other loopholes."

I held up my hands.

"Now give me your word," he said.

"I give you my word that Viv and I will not go anywhere near the Grisby estate."

Harrison studied me for a moment and then he seemed satisfied.

"All right, then," he said. "I'll ring you later."

I waved at him through the door before he turned and headed down the street. I noticed several of the ladies he passed turned their heads to watch him go by. There was no denying the fact that Harrison was a very handsome man, if you were into that sort of thing, which, I reminded myself, I wasn't.

As I made my way to the back room, I noticed that Ferd, the carved bird on top of Mim's wardrobe, was watching me with its unblinking stare. I could swear it was smirking.

"No one asked you," I said and mimicked Viv by sticking my tongue out at it as I went by.

"So, did Harrison put you in thumbscrews and make you swear not to go to the Grisby mansion?" Viv asked as I returned to the back room.

"How'd you know?" I asked.

"He's fairly single-minded like that," she said.

"So, did you promise?" Fee asked. She was standing by the sink, rinsing her cup.

"Yes, I did," I said.

Viv looked surprised. "I didn't really think you'd cave in like that."

"You sound disappointed," I said.

"No, it's not that. All right, yes, actually it is," she said. "Scarlett, don't tell me that the recent events in your life have made you lose your fire."

"Me, lose my fire?" I asked. I glanced at both of them. I lifted a hank of hair off of my shoulder. "You're joking, right?"

Viv smiled. "Your fire is more than your hair color and you know it."

"Indeed," I said. "It is also my hot temper, my stubbornness and my tenacity, which is why we'll be taking tea at the Savoy later today. I hear it's where all the best families trying to get away from a murder scene hang out."

"No!" Viv cried. "Oh, you are a clever one."

"What?" Fee asked. "I'm not following."

"The Grisby family is holed up at the Savoy," I said. "Hiding from the press and I imagine getting away from the grisly scene at home."

"But you promised Harrison . . ." Fee's voice trailed off.

"That we wouldn't go to the Grisby estate," I said. "I said nothing about their hideout."

Fee shook her head. "Harrison is going to be so unhappy about this."

"Pish posh," Viv said. "We're keeping our word. Now, you have to promise not to tell him."

"I'm sure I won't have to," Fee said. "These things always have a way of coming out, but of course, I do promise."

"Good girl," Viv said. "Now what should we wear to tea at the Savoy?"

Chapter 16

The Savoy sits on the banks of the Thames River. Because Viv is a whiz at the Underground, I let her figure out the tube stop for us to get from Notting Hill Gate on the Central Line to the Embankment Underground Station on Villiers Street, which meant starting on the Central Line and switching to the Bakerloo Line. It was only three minutes from there to the Savoy, and the day was clear and sunny, so it was a pleasant walk.

Viv had insisted, of course, that we wear hats. I chose a demure navy cap with a small cluster of pale-yellow flowers on the right side, which matched my pale-yellow dress and navy sandals. Viv, being Viv, went with a bright-red cap that had black piping along the edge and three long ostrich plumes in matching red. She wore a flirty red dress and black sandals to pull the look together.

Standing next to her, I felt like I was about to check into the local nunnery and be issued my habit and wimple. It was simply not fair that we came from the same gene pool and she had panache while I had plainness.

"I haven't had a proper tea, as in one I haven't had to make myself, in ages," Viv said as we left the station behind and made our way to the Savoy. I could see the London Eye across the river in the distance, but we were walking away from it as we headed toward the hotel.

"We should have made this a priority before now," I said. "Do you remember when Mim would take us to tea at Claridge's in Mayfair?"

"Yes," Viv grinned. "We'd all dress up and have a ladies' afternoon and then she'd take us shopping at Selfridges."

"I miss her," I sighed.

Viv put her arm around me and gave me a solid squeeze. "Me, too, pet. Me, too."

We were quiet as we walked. When the Savoy came into view, I rehearsed what we'd planned. "So, while we're having tea, we keep an eye out for any of the Grisbys," I said. "If we get lucky and run into one of them, we'll take it from there and see what we can find out."

"And if we don't"—Viv paused to pat the hat box that dangled from her arm—"then we simply tell the hotel concierge that we have a delivery for Dotty Grisby."

"You did put a hat in there, didn't you?" I asked.

"Yes, it's a lovely black number with a fine veil trimmed in black lace, perfect for a grieving mother," she said.

"This makes me feel a bit like a ghoul," I said.

"The police are investigating our shop for poison," Viv

said. "We're not being ghouls; we are merely protecting our business by trying to discover what our shop has to do with Geoffrey's poisoning."

"Then we seem like cold, calculating businesspeople," I said.

"Might I remind you that this was your idea," Viv said.

"That doesn't mean it's not cold," I said.

The doorman held the door for us as we entered the glamorous Savoy. The lobby caught my attention as we stepped into a room with dark paneled walls and a black-and-white floor polished to a high gloss. Sparkly chandeliers hung overhead and I suddenly felt as if I'd walked into a world more suited to Zelda and F. Scott Fitzgerald than Vivian Tremont and Scarlett Parker.

"Come on," Viv said. "Tea is in the Thames Foyer."

I began to follow her but was distracted by the window of a chocolatier across the lobby.

"Hang on," I said.

I moved closer and watched the man in the white chef's coat working with what looked like bars of caramel that he was dipping into a vat of chocolate.

"Scarlett, come on," Viv said as she took me by the hand and dragged me past a beautiful bouquet of orchids in the center of the vestibule, across the black-and-white floor and down the steps to the tea room.

A gazebo was set up under a large stained-glass dome in the ceiling, and a piano player sat inside of it, playing softly. I glanced around to see that it was quite crowded but the conversation was muted, probably by the plush furniture that was well spaced out.

Looking at the tables, I wondered if I wanted afternoon tea, which was sweet, or high tea, which was savory. Decisions, decisions, but I was pretty sure my MoonPie-loving sweet tooth was going to win this battle and afternoon tea it would be. Is it bad that I sort of hoped we had to wait around enjoying tea for a while before spotting a Grisby?

The hostess approved of our hats and Viv took the opportunity to press her business card on her. When the woman realized it was Viv, who is pretty famous for her hats, she looked delighted.

I couldn't swear to it, but I was pretty sure our seats got upgraded to plusher ones, two wing chairs with a low table between us. Honestly, they were so comfy I think I could have taken a nap—you know, if we weren't on a mission.

Our waitress came right over and introduced herself. "Good afternoon, ladies. I'm Chris and I'll be your waitress today."

"Are you from the States?" I asked. She looked at me in surprise and I was certain my American accent had struck her as much as hers had hit me. It almost made me homesick to hear someone taking a nice bite out of their "R"s.

"Canada, actually. I'm from Halifax, Nova Scotia, to be exact," she said. "And you?"

"Florida," I said. "Just a bit south of there."

We smiled at each other and then her eyes narrowed. "You look awfully familiar," she said. "Have you been to the Savoy before?"

"Not in ages," I said. I realized that she had probably seen me on the Internet video that would not die. You know, the one of me lobbing cake at my rat-bastard boyfriend. I decided

JENN McKINLAY

to nip it in the bud. "But I get that all the time. People think I'm their neighbor, cousin, sister's best friend—"

"Husband's girlfriend," Viv added with a sly look.

"Cute," I said. "Really adorable."

I gave Viv my best quelling glance and she adjusted her hat with one hand and gave me an innocent smile.

Chris, our new buddy, seemed to think Viv was just teasing me and laughed. She then handed us menus and went over the amazing selection of tea that the Savoy offered. I decided on a rose tea and Viv and I agreed on the afternoon tea, which my sweet tooth appreciated very much.

Chris left with our order and Viv and I settled into our comfy chairs, looking very much like two ladies of leisure. At least I hoped we did. It was a hard pose to maintain, as I was keeping an eye on the door in case a Grisby happened to enter the room.

"So, if we should see one of the family, what do we say?" Viv asked. I noticed she was turning her head to scan the room just as I was.

"We're here to meet a customer to deliver her hat," I said.

"But I thought the hat was for Dotty," Viv said.

"Only if we don't see a Grisby, and then we use it to go up and visit her," I said.

"But what if it is a Grisby that we're not interested in?" Viv asked.

"Such as?"

"Rose or Lily," she said. "Neither of them strikes me as the murdering kind."

"No, Rose is too timid and Lily seems above it all," I

said. "But there is a fortune at stake here, so we really shouldn't rule anyone out."

"But which of them would be familiar with the toxic properties of formaldehyde?" Viv asked.

"That could be anyone," I said. "The information is out there."

"I suppose," Viv said. "Although to murder one's own brother seems downright evil."

"A lot of money and a really big house can harden a heart, I suppose," I said. "You know, when you were missing, Harrison actually suggested that I had something to do with it because we were business partners and I was the one with the most to gain from your death."

"He didn't!" she cried.

"Did," I confirmed. Of course, I neglected to add that I had accused him of being involved in Viv's disappearance first. No need to muddy the waters.

"Well, no wonder you're not eager to date him," she said. "Not if he could believe you to be a murderer. Of course, now it's easy to see he's quite besotted with you."

"On the contrary," I said. "I don't think it's me that he's interested in at all. I'm afraid I'm a bit long in the tooth for him."

"What does that expression mean?" Viv asked. "Do your teeth really get longer when you age? I don't think that will be a very attractive look on me."

"I don't know what it means," I admitted. "I just remember Mim used to say it and I think in regard to Harrison, it's true."

"You sound jealous again," Viv said.

"I'm not jealous," I protested.

"Really?" a voice asked from behind me. "And here I had hoped you were stalking me out of fear that some other girl might capture my interest—not that any girl stands a chance beside you, but still it would have been quite flattering to be stalked."

"George!" I cried as I stood up and turned around.

"Hi, Scarlett." He leaned forward and we kissed each other's cheek. Viv stood up and they exchanged the same greeting.

"How are you?" I asked. I gestured for him to sit down and he took the empty chair next to mine.

"I've been better," he said. His tone was rueful. "I can't say I was ever close to my uncle, but it was awful to discover he was poisoned like that. The family is a wreck."

"I'm so sorry," Viv said. "I imagine it was a horrible shock. How is Dotty taking it?"

"Grandmother seems . . . well, after the initial shock passed, I'm not sure she really understands what has happened, which I suppose is a blessing," he said.

Our waitress, Chris, returned and brought a menu for George. He said he didn't want to intrude, but Viv and I insisted, so he ordered afternoon tea as well.

"How is the rest of the family holding up?" I asked. I was hoping to get some information about Tina.

George frowned.

"I'm sorry," I said. "If you don't want to talk about it, I completely understand. I didn't mean to pry."

Sometimes I worry that my American ways are a bit too in-your-face for my British relatives and friends. I think I'm supposed to talk more about the weather and less about personal matters, but I'm not very good at checking my concern for others, even if it appears rude.

"No, it's quite all right," he said. "I'm just not sure how to reply. Everyone is reacting about how you'd imagine. Liam is probably the most distraught. I don't think he's ever wanted the responsibility of the Grisby fortune, and now that it might be thrust upon him, he's up a gum tree."

Viv glanced at me in an I-told-you-so sort of way that I chose to ignore. From my youth, I knew "up a gum tree" meant in great difficulty, kind of like "up a creek" in the States. So Liam wasn't happy about this turn of events. That didn't mean he wouldn't rally, especially when they handed him the keys to the castle, as it were.

Our tea arrived and I fell immediately in love with the smell of the rose tea and was not disappointed in the taste either. Our sweet cakes followed and I almost forgot our purpose as I set to eating my petit fours.

"So, what brings you two to tea at the Savoy?" George asked.

I opened my mouth to speak but Viv got there first and instead of sticking to our story about meeting a client, she actually told him the truth—so much for our covert operation!

"We're here to see if anyone in your family poisoned Geoffrey," Viv said.

She caught George on an inhale and he spluttered into his teacup. Several heads turned in our direction as he tried to clear his lungs out with several wracking coughs.

His eyes were watering when he choked out, "Beg pardon?"

I decided to take control of the conversation and attempt to do damage control.

"Detective Inspector Finchley stopped by the shop," I said. "Poison was found on Geoffrey's hat. They seemed to think we had something to do with it."

"Which we did not," Viv added.

"So we thought we'd stop by and visit you and see if you knew anything," I said.

"Me?" he asked. He gave me a hopeful look. "I'm flattered."

" 'You' meaning 'your family,' " Viv corrected him.

"Plus we brought a hat." I gestured to the hatbox at Viv's feet. George nodded as if this made perfect sense, which it did not.

"Oh, so it isn't me." He looked a bit crestfallen but quickly rallied. "Well, tea with two pretty ladies is still an afternoon well spent."

I patted his knee encouragingly.

"So, any idea on who might have wanted your uncle dead?" I asked.

"Aside from my mum and her sisters?" he asked. "None."

I stared at him. "You don't really think—"

"That my mum and her sisters murdered their brother?" he asked. "No, but given that they were about to sue him for their percentage of the estate, it really doesn't look good."

Chapter 17

"They were going to sue your uncle?" I asked. I hadn't heard about a lawsuit in all of the hullabaloo.

"Pretty lousy timing, right," he confirmed. "It looks terrible."

"That might be something you want to keep to yourself," Viv said.

"It's already public knowledge, like the poisoning," he said. "Not much point in pretending it wasn't happening."

"I take it Detective Inspector Finchley has been visiting you as well?" I asked.

"Frequently," George said. He looked irritated. "I know how it looks, but not one of them is capable of murder and certainly not over money. I mean, if they were planning to murder him to get the family fortune, why would they sue him?"

"What about the estate?" I asked. "It's a beautiful piece of property."

"Now it's the scene of a murder," George said. "Sort of taints the whole thing, which is why we're all at the Savoy. Well, that and the damn reporters. Speaking of which, how did you know we were here? Even the press hasn't figured it out yet."

"T—" Viv began, but I cut her off.

"Total luck," I said.

George stared at me for a moment and I knew he was trying to decide whether to believe me or not. Viv rolled her eyes as if she couldn't believe that I was covering for Tina. I was not about to tell George that she had come to the shop, however, because there would be uncomfortable questions as to why she had stopped by, and I was not prepared to divulge her secrets.

If he doubted me, he didn't question it but instead changed the subject. We discussed an art show that was currently at the Hayward Gallery. To my surprise, George knew quite a lot about art and artists, and he admitted that growing up with Lily for an aunt had been very educational. He had spent the past few years studying art in Florence, Italy. He was studying to be a curator and planned to go into museum work when he graduated.

"Would you like to come up and see everyone?" he asked as we finished tea. "I know my grandmother would be pleased to see you both, especially you, Viv."

Now that the opportunity had presented itself, I felt sort of bad that we had maneuvered George into it. Viv, obviously, did not.

"We'd love to," she said.

"Brilliant," he said. "Of course, I'm sure my brother will be delighted to see you as well."

Viv ignored his knowing look, and I tucked my lips in to keep from smiling. We followed George to the elevator, which took us up to one of the top floors.

The doors opened onto a black-and-white foyer with dark wood paneling, much like the lobby below. George led us to a door at the far end.

A uniformed doorman stood beside the heavy wooden door. With a nod at George, he pushed it open. We stepped into a small foyer that led into a large main room, which boasted a lovely view of the city and the Thames River. The room held lots of large soft-looking furniture on one side and a grand piano on the other.

A woman was sitting at the piano, playing a classical piece quite softly. It was Rose, and I marveled that she played piano much like she spoke, so as not to be noticed.

"Stop it!" a voice shouted. "Stop coddling her!"

George stopped in his tracks and Viv bumped into his back. Unprepared to stop, I slammed into hers and we stood like a three-car pileup on the motorway.

"Ouch!" Viv yelped.

I stepped back and George stepped forward. The piano playing stumbled to a halt and the people in the drawing room all turned as one to look at us.

It was easy to see who had done the yelling. Daphne stood in the middle of the room with her arms held out wide and her face an unpleasant shade of red.

I glanced to see who her adversary could be—obviously

not Rose, who'd been at the piano, which left only Lily or Liam. Liam was texting on his phone and Lily was flipping through a magazine. Of the two, my money was on Lily.

"Oh, look, company," Lily said. "Your temper tantrum will have to hold, sister."

"George," Daphne spoke through clenched teeth. "This really isn't a good time."

"I thought seeing Viv might perk Gram up," he said. "Since she thinks she's an old friend and all."

Lily tossed the magazine onto the table and tipped her head. "I think you might be right. I'll go get her."

"I don't think—" Daphne began to protest, but Lily cut her off.

"I don't really care what you think," she said. "Vivian, Scarlett, it's good to see you. I'll be right back."

Liam shoved his phone in his pocket strode across the room to greet us. It was impossible not to notice how his eyes lit up at the sight of Viv. He greeted her with a kiss on the cheek and then turned and exchanged the same greeting with me. I noted he didn't linger near me like he did with Viv, however.

"Brother, how did you stumble upon two of the city's finest ladies when you only stepped out for a smoke?" Liam asked. "You have the devil's own luck."

George grinned. "I like to think my animal magnetism drew them to me."

"Like a pair of oxpecker birds to a hippopotamus," Daphne snapped. It was clear the insult was directed at Viv and me. I wasn't too happy to be compared to a scavenger bird that eats the bugs off of a hippo's butt.

"Does that make me the hippo?" George asked his brother in mock alarm. Then he turned to me. "You'd tell me if I was getting hippy, wouldn't you?"

"And damage that fragile ego?" I asked, trying not to laugh at his mock look of horror. "No, I don't think I would."

Whatever George had been about to say was interrupted by the appearance of Dotty and Lily.

Dotty looked strained. Her face was pale, and her wrinkles seemed more deeply etched into her sagging skin than they had a few days before. Her grief was evident, and it changed the tone in the room as effectively as a shroud being drawn over a body.

"Oh, Ginny," she said as she stepped forward. "So good of you to come."

Viv stepped forward and took Dotty's hands in hers. "I am so sorry for your loss, dear."

"Loss?" Dotty repeated. She turned to Lily and said, "Did I lose something?"

I frowned and turned to look at Liam and George. Liam shrugged and George twirled a finger by his temple, which I took to mean that Dotty wasn't processing her son's death in the expected way.

"They're talking about Geoffrey, Mum," Lily said. Her voice sounded encouraging as if she was willing her mother to put it together on her own.

"Oh, Geoffrey—he's away on business, you know," Dotty said. "Such a hard worker, just like his father. I quite worry about him."

I heard a scoffing sound coming from Daphne, and this

time Liam glared at his mother. She appeared to want to argue but instead she gave us a patronizing look.

"You really need to be resting, Mother," she said. "I'm sure your friends can come back another time when it is more convenient."

Well, didn't I feel like the stray dog who'd snuck into the house and peed on the carpet.

"It is always the right time to visit with friends," Dotty said, giving Daphne a reproving glance. She led us over to the squashy furniture by the window and gestured for us to sit down.

Viv took a seat on the couch beside Dotty while I commandeered an armchair nearby. Lily sat on the other side of Dotty while George took the wing chair next to mine and Liam stood leaning against the wall that offered him the best view of Viv.

Dotty glanced over at the piano where Rose sat with her hands held in her lap as if she was afraid to move.

"Go ahead, dear: play something pretty," Dotty said.

Rose's fingers faltered a bit but then she found her rhythm and a soft melody filled the suite. It was a lovely tune with a heartbreakingly sad melody carrying the weight of the piece.

"I never thought I'd be here," Dotty said.

"No, I expect you didn't," Viv said.

I thought it was very diplomatic of Viv to agree, since we really had no idea what Dotty was talking about. Did she mean she never pictured herself at the Savoy? Because, clearly, she was not grasping the fact that her son was dead.

In fact, she seemed to have transferred the way she dealt with her husband's abandonment right onto her son's murder, which just showed how incapable of dealing with reality she truly was.

"Ginny, do you remember when we were young, before I married into the Grisby family and you had just arrived in Notting Hill? Oh, the times we had."

Viv and I perked up. Were we about to get some dish on Mim?

"Yes," Viv said. "That would have been the late sixties and early seventies, wouldn't it?"

"Oh, the parties," Dotty gushed. "I remember the time we were all at All Saint's church hall and you jumped up on the stage and began to dance. Oh, you had all the men following you around that night. I was sure one of them was going to propose to you."

"Right," Viv said. She glanced at me and I could tell she was thinking the same thing I was—that Dotty was proving to be quite a source of information about our grandmother.

"You didn't go for him, though," Dotty said as if confused by Mim's choice. "Good call, since he died of an overdose a few years later. Musicians."

I felt my eyebrows lift as I gazed at Viv. Mim had been hooking up with musicians? No way! And, while I'm sure there were a lot of musicians who overdosed back in the sixties in Notting Hill, the most famous one was Jimi Hendrix in 1970. Mim and Hendrix? It boggled. Viv looked as intrigued as I did, but like me, I suspected she didn't know what to say to get more information out of Dotty, who, quite frankly, was not the most reliable source of information to begin with.

Still, the time line fit. Mim was widowed by the time the hippie counterculture had swarmed the Notting Hill area. She would have been right at the epicenter of the movement.

She and my grandfather had met and married in their small village in Yorkshire and moved to London for his career as a barrister. Shortly after my aunt Grace was born, my grandfather was killed in a car accident. My mother remembers her father a little, but not clearly, since she was only three when he died. Instead of moving back to her village, Mim had found a cheap shop to buy in Notting Hill, which was a bit of a hippie ghetto back in the day, and had started up her millinery business much to the disapproval of her own family.

She would have been a widow in her twenties. And given that Mim, like Viv, had quite the artist's temperament, it was easy to picture her as part of the scene.

"No, I never loved anyone as much as my Emerson," Viv said. She glanced at me. Mim had always said this about our grandfather. Whenever we asked why she didn't marry again, she said she never met another man with her Emerson's spark.

"I chose Geoffrey," Dotty said. She said it with an air of puzzlement as if she wasn't quite sure now why she had chosen to marry him.

"And now he's going to have a hospital wing named after him," Viv said. She glanced at Lily and Liam to see if this was all right. Liam gave her a small nod.

"Quite right," Dotty said. "He sacrificed so much for our family, always away on business, you know."

Another gagging sound was emitted from Daphne, who was pacing around the piano. She met my gaze and pointedly looked at her watch.

If Dotty heard her, she didn't show it. Instead, she had a far-off look in her eye. "Dear Geoffrey, such a devoted father, and what an excellent role model for his son."

Daphne opened her mouth to speak, and I had no doubt it would be a caustic comment about her father, but Lily cut her off.

"He would be proud, just as we all are," she said.

"Quite right," Dotty said and she patted Lily's hand affectionately.

"Stop it! Just stop," Daphne snapped. "Why must we participate in this sham? Mother, Geoffrey, your son, our brother, is dead—not away on business, dead."

Rose's fingers faltered on the piano while everyone in the room froze to see how Dotty would react.

"Daphne, how can you say such a thing?" Dotty pressed her hand to her throat. "I know you're unhappy about the terms of your father's will, but to declare your brother dead is just vile. I am not amused, young lady."

"Oh, for God's sake, Mother," Daphne cried. She was so angry she was shaking. She began to pace. "I get that you have altered reality for the past thirty years, but you can't alter this. Geoffrey is dead."

Dotty rose to her feet. She looked even more pale and pinched than when she'd entered the room, but her eyes blazed with heat as she glared at her daughter.

"You are being beastly!" she declared. "In front of guests, no less. I am appalled. Ginny, Scarlett, I am so sorry. Lily, please take me back to my room."

Viv and I rose with Lily. I glanced at Daphne to see her raise her chin in defiance while Rose hissed at her to behave herself. She shrugged her off.

George glanced around the room in bemusement as if he wasn't quite sure how he could be related to these people. I didn't blame him a bit on that one.

"Really, sister, I think you need to go to your room as well and calm down," Lily said.

"She's right. You're going too far," Liam hissed between his teeth. "George, let's get her out of here."

Daphne glared daggers at her son. "Why? Because I spoke the truth? Here's a little more for you. Not only is our dear brother dead, Mother, but it quite possibly could be someone in our family who murdered him."

The room was silent. No one was making eye contact. I couldn't tell if it was guilt, shame or embarrassment blanketing the room, but either way I'm not very good at awkward pauses and generally feel compelled to fill them with mindless chatter.

I suppose it's the pleaser in me, but I can't help but try to get everyone to a happy place, and if happy can't be achieved, then I settle for a diversion.

"But I assumed the most likely person would be Cara Whittles," I said. "I mean, she had motive and opportunity."

Viv looked at me with both eyebrows raised as if she couldn't believe I was going there. But given that Daphne had just accused someone in her own family of killing their brother, I really didn't think what I had to say was that bad.

"Who is Cara Whittles?" Dotty asked.

Ah, and this is where I open my mouth and enjoy a nice shoe-leather sandwich. What exactly was I supposed to say here? *Why, darling, Cara Whittles was your husband's lover of thirty years, who was left nothing, crashed your tea party and threatened your son's life—you remember, the party where your son was murdered.* Yeah, not even the threat of electric shock could make me say that sentence.

"I don't understand what's happening," Dotty said. She sniffed as if she was about to cry, causing both Viv and Lily to give me dirty looks.

"Geoffrey is a charming, hardworking boy. He's away on business and he'll be back when he's done. You'll see."

There was a heartbreaking plaintive note in her voice that made my throat close up. I couldn't shake the feeling that Dotty clung to her belief that her son was away on business because the reality of his death was too much to bear. It seemed criminal to take the escape away from her.

"Of course, you're right, Mum," Lily said. She put an arm around Dotty's shoulders. "Daphne is just being dramatic. You know how she gets."

Daphne looked like she would argue, but I honestly thought Lily would punch her in the mouth if she said another word. Daphne tossed her hair and stomped across the room to stand by the piano.

Rose hadn't moved. I suspected she was doing what she

always did when voices got heated and tempers flared. She sat perfectly still and quiet as if she could blend into the wood of the piano and remain unseen and unengaged. These were some crazy family dynamics at work.

Lily led Dotty from the room. Viv nodded at me and we began to move to the door, making awkward good-byes as we went. We were almost there when the door to the suite opened and Tina came in. She looked pale and shaky and when she took in Viv's and my appearance, she looked wary and startled.

I didn't want her to think I had betrayed her confidence, so I snatched the hatbox from Viv's hands and handed it to Tina.

"Here," I said. "This is for you."

I could feel George's eyes on me, but I figured I'd explain, okay, yes, I'd make something up later. For now, I just wanted Tina to know that her secret was still safe with me and that I hadn't come here to blab her secrets.

"Oh, how thoughtful," she said. Her eyes met mine and I saw an imploring look in them. I gave her a tiny nod to let her know we were okay.

"It's just a little something from the shop," Viv said. She glanced over her shoulder at where Dotty had gone. "You know, in case you might need a black hat for some reason."

Daphne made another derisive sound and Liam frowned at her. "Not now, Mum."

"What do you mean, not now?" Daphne said. "Is there a better time for me to show my contempt?"

Tina flinched and Liam took his mother's elbow in an attempt to lead her away while George stepped up and stood beside Tina. This show of support was obviously too much for Daphne.

"What's the ruckus now?" Lily asked as she returned to the room. "Daphne, you really need to get a hold of yourself. Mum isn't well and blasting her with reality is not helping. Oh, hello, Tina. Are you all right? You look peaky."

"No, she's not all right," Daphne said. She turned her angry gaze on Tina. "You're finally figuring it out, aren't you? You're his widow, not his heir, you know. Once his funeral is over, you'll need to leave the estate, since you won't be getting a pence from it."

"Surely, she is provided for," Lily said. She sounded aghast at the thought that Tina would be tossed to the curb.

"No, I've already spoken to the solicitor. Geoffrey had no will," Daphne said. "He never got around to it, so as things stand, the entire fortune will go to Liam."

Liam turned a ghostly shade of white and then a hot shade of red. He glowered at his mother.

"This is neither the time nor the place to have this discussion," he said. He cast a glance at the door to Dotty's room.

Tina had paled as well, as if the reality of her situation was becoming clear to her. She leaned heavily on Liam.

"Are you all right?" he asked.

Tina shook her head. "No, I'm afraid I'm not."

"Help her to a seat," Lily said.

George stepped forward and both he and Liam guided

her into the padded chair I had vacated. She sat down on shaky knees.

"What is it, dear?" Lily asked. Worry lines creased her brow with concern as she gazed at her sister-in-law.

When Tina spoke, her voice was faint but unmistakable.

"I'm pregnant."

Chapter 18

"Liar! You're lying!" Daphne shouted.

"Sister, control yourself!" Lily said. She looked appalled by Daphne's behavior.

"Control myself?" Daphne roared. She spun around, staring at everyone as if daring them to challenge her. "I'm not the one who is lying, trying to get my hands on our fortune."

Tina looked miserable, but her gaze was steady when she met Daphne's accusing glance. "I'm not lying. You can call my doctor if you want."

"That won't be necessary," Liam said. "We believe you, and both you and your child will be cared for, just as Geoffrey would have wanted."

He put his hand on her shoulder. I glanced at Viv to see if she was getting this. I thought this spoke very well of Liam and wondered if she was thinking the same.

Rose left the piano and went to sit in the chair beside Tina. She didn't say anything but patted her sister-in-law's hands where they were clasped in her lap in an obvious show of support.

I glanced at Daphne, who looked like she was frothing at the mouth. I have to admit I was a little bit afraid of her.

"Well, we can see you have some personal business to mind, so we'll just carry on back to our shop," Viv said.

"But it's just getting interesting," George whispered in my ear.

I glanced at him and saw the mischief sparkle in his eyes. I refused to smile and encourage him and tried to give him my best censoring glance, but he didn't appear hampered at all by it. Clearly, I needed to work on that.

Viv was out the door and I scooted right after her, calling a general good-bye over my shoulder. I saw Lily kneel beside Tina and put a comforting arm about her shoulders. This made me feel better. I didn't want Tina to feel abandoned, but between Liam, Rose, Lily and George, she looked to be in good hands. Hopefully, they would all run interference and shut Daphne down.

"Well, if that wasn't the equivalent of dropping a bomb, I don't know what is," Viv said as soon as the elevator doors closed behind us.

"Poor Tina," I said. "Here Geoffrey was giving her such a hard time about getting pregnant, and now she is and he's dead."

"I suppose they'll keep her in the family until they know whether she's having a boy or a girl," Viv said.

"Well, I think if Liam has anything to do with it, he'll

make sure she's provided for," I said. "He seemed very solicitous of her, didn't he?"

"Yes, yes, he did," Viv said. She glanced away from me and I couldn't tell what she was thinking. Very irritating.

The elevator doors opened and we crossed through the opulent lobby to outside. The streets were crowded with people and the sound of car engines as they growled their way through the traffic.

I could hear smatterings of different languages as I followed behind Viv. It was too crowded to walk side by side. It reminded me a bit of market day on Portobello Road, crowded and noisy as people worked their way to their various destinations.

We hurried down the entrance to the Underground. Viv scanned her Oyster card and I followed behind her in the turnstile. The white brick tunnel led us down several flights of stairs until we got to our platform. In minutes the train arrived and we hopped on board.

We only had a few stops and then we switched trains and were soon jostling our way back to Notting Hill Gate on the Cental Line. The Underground train stopped and we both lurched forward. There had been no seats available, so we were standing.

The automated female voice of the Underground announced the next stop, which was ours, and we took our positions by the door. We hadn't talked much and I wondered if Viv was thinking about the Grisby family as much as I was or if she was designing hats in her head. She did that a lot.

When the doors opened, we rode the two escalators up

and then climbed the stairs to Notting Hill Gate. It was a bit of a walk back to our shop, but the day was sunny and warm with a cool breeze. I matched my steps to Viv's as we cut through Pembridge Mews. I knew Harrison lived somewhere along this stretch of row houses, but I refused to look for him.

"Who do you think killed Geoffrey?" I asked, more to distract myself than for a real answer.

Viv stopped and turned to look at me.

"What?" I asked. "Come on, you must have someone in mind."

"Actually, I was thinking it was probably a freak accident," she said.

"Formaldehyde in his hat, an accident?" I asked. "How do you figure?"

"Well, if I knew that, I'd be a detective, now, wouldn't I?" she asked.

"He was murdered," I said, ignoring her question.

"Now, why do you say that?" she asked. "It could have been an accident."

"The police don't seem to think so," I said. "Don't you find it suspicious that his father's mistress threatened him and hours later he's dead? Or how about Daphne? She's practically psychotic about the whole inheritance situation."

We turned off Pembridge Road to Portobello Road. The sidewalk was narrow and our shoulders brushed as we walked. Viv's high heels made her a bit taller than me, and I remembered that when we were girls I was always trying to be as tall as she was. I was an inch taller than her when we finally topped out, but she always wore high heels, which kept her even or taller. Today she was a smidge taller. I felt a flicker of the old competitiveness about height, which was ridiculous, but cousins, like siblings, I suppose, always have a teeny bit of competitiveness amongst them.

"Inspector Finchley is just being thorough," Viv said. "I bet they discover that a cleaning lady accidentally doused his hat in some chemical that had formaldehyde in it and that's what has caused the whole hullabaloo. Perhaps it was just a severe allergic reaction."

"You're not serious," I said.

"Of course I am," she said. "Listen, I grant that his sisters certainly have motive, but I don't believe that they did him in, not even Daphne, who is the most vocal about her bitterness toward the terms of the estate. In fact, it is her very loud complaining that makes me think she is innocent. If she had done him in, she'd be playing the grieving sister, not the bitter daughter."

The road sloped down and we continued on our way, passing Andre's studio shop and several others until we reached Mim's Whims. The door was unlocked and Fee was behind the counter, helping a stout-looking woman with a wide-brimmed bucket hat in a startling shade of fuchsia.

"Well, if you follow that logic," I said, "then the person who is grieving the most, Tina, would be the likely suspect because she seems so wrenched by the loss of her husband."

"Yes, her lying, cheating and possibly abusive husband," Viv said. "A real tragedy for her, I'm sure."

With a chipper hello to Fee she kept walking toward the back room, but I stood in the center of the shop, feeling stunned.

Could Viv be right? Was it an accident? And if it wasn't, could Tina be guilty? I hated to even think it, but I couldn't deny that since she was pregnant her motive was hard to beat.

Chapter 19

"Do you really believe that the old bird has no idea what's going on? That she's not even aware that her son is dead?" Nick asked. "I mean that's just mental."

Nick, Andre, Fee, Viv and I were sacked out in the front of the shop, eating our way through several cartons of Thai food and a couple of bottles of wine. We had drawn all of the blinds down over the windows and locked the door. Viv and I had spent the past fifteen minutes while we divided up the takeaway order, telling them all about our afternoon adventure.

It was a noisy conversation with Nick and Andre bellowing in outrage at Daphne's horrid behavior. They were so loud, in fact, that we didn't hear the front door open until a voice called out.

"What's this? Are you having a party and didn't invite

me?" Harrison stood in the doorway, holding a bakery box in his hands.

Fee shot up from her seat and crossed the room toward him. She kissed his cheek and peeked inside the box. "Oh, cupcakes!"

He grinned at her as she took the box and brought it back to the table. Viv stood and kissed Harrison's cheek while Andre grabbed a chair from nearby and brought it over for Harrison to sit in, shoving it right next to mine. Nick shook Harrison's hand and wagged the wine bottle at him. Harrison gave him an enthusiastic nod while he dropped into the seat beside me.

"So, what's the occasion?" Harrison asked.

Before Viv or I could derail him, Andre said, "The girls were just telling us about their adventures with the Grisby family."

"What?" Harrison bellowed. He turned and glowered at me.

I refused to engage but merely poked my pad Thai with my plastic fork. Nick had brought the food all the way from the Thai restaurant housed in the pub The Churchill Arms on Kensington Church Street, and I wasn't about to let it get cold.

"Harrison, it's not what you think," Viv said.

"Not what I think?" he repeated. "Please tell me what I think."

Nick handed him a wineglass and Harrison gulped it down in one long swallow.

Nick and Andre exchanged a look, which clearly said they were delighted to have front-row seats for this show.

"We didn't go to the Grisby estate," Viv said. "We were merely having afternoon tea at the Savoy when we ran into George—you know, Daphne's son."

"Uh-huh."

Harrison was still glaring at me. I could feel the heat of his gaze on the side of my face. I kept moving my noodles around my plate like they were racing each other to the finish line, which was my mouth.

"And what do you have to say for yourself, Scarlett?" he asked.

I shoved a forkful of the spicy noodles into my pie hole and indicated that I couldn't talk with my mouth full. He glowered.

"Of all the irresponsible, juvenile, reckless, wrongheaded—" He began a tirade that I desperately wanted to interrupt, but I couldn't unless I risked spitting noodles all over the both of us.

I chewed vigorously, washing down my mouthful with a slug of wine. Harrison was still going strong.

"—ridiculous, foolish, idiotic . . ." He paused to hold his wineglass out for a refill, and I jumped in.

"It was not," I protested. "We simply had tea. I promised you we wouldn't go near the estate, and we didn't, but now that I think on it, you had no right to ask me to make such a promise."

"I have every right," he protested. He tossed back his second glass before continuing. "I am your business manager. It is my job to look after you just like it was my uncle's job to look after Mim."

"You are to look after our accounts," I snapped. "Not us.

187

I am a grown woman and I will go where I want when I want and I bloody well don't need your permission."

"Oh, you're tapping into your inner Brit there," Viv said. She was smiling at me in approval. "She's right, Harrison, you really do treat us like we don't have a brain between us."

Harrison looked at Nick and Andre. "Help me out, mates: tell them they need to stay away from this mess."

"I would," Nick said. "But I'm the teensiest bit afraid of her."

"Me?" I asked. "Really?"

"I saw what you did to that cake," he said.

"Oh, right," I said. I had shown Nick and Andre the video that had gone viral of me throwing fistfuls of cake at my unbeknownst-to-me married boyfriend. I flexed my right arm and looked at Harrison. "You should be afraid, too."

He glanced at the cupcake box on the table. "Take your best shot."

"Don't you dare," Fee said. She covered the box with her upper body. "These are from Buttercup Cake Shop around the corner, and they have my favorite rose-flavored one."

"Fine," I said. "Still, you're not the boss of me, Harry."

"Harrison," he corrected with a grimace. "And actually, I am the boss of you. Tell her, Viv."

"Tell me what?" I asked Viv.

She was studying the inside of the cupcake box as if all of her future happiness resided on picking the right cupcake. It was clearly a ploy to avoid me, although I did appreciate the seriousness of the decision at hand.

"Viv," I said. "Explain."

"It's nothing," she said. Both Andre and Nick were

hovering over the box. Fee had already grabbed a gorgeous pink cupcake that made me drool just a bit at the sight of it.

"Halfsies?" Nick negotiated with Andre as they both went for a vanilla cupcake with what looked like a thick carpet of vanilla shavings on top.

"Hey!" Viv protested. "I wanted that one."

"Oh, for Pete's sake," I cried. "Would you all quit it with the cupcakes and explain what Harrison is talking about?"

Viv turned to me, her blue eyes wide. "Are you yelling?"

"No!" I cried. I lowered my voice. "Maybe—just please explain what he means."

Harrison had reached around me and selected a chocolate cupcake also with a thick layer of chocolate shavings on top. It was all I could do not to snatch it out of his hands if for no other reason than to wipe the smug look off of his face. Plus, I really love chocolate.

"When Harrison's uncle turned over his duty as business manager, some changes were made to the original contract," Viv said.

"Why wasn't I told?" I asked.

"You were, actually," Viv said. "The changes were sent by certified letter and you signed off on it. I believe you were caught up in your personal life at the time."

I felt a warm flush heat my face. This was Viv's nice way of saying I had been blowing off her and the business for my boyfriend, currently known as the rat bastard. Aren't bad life decisions great? Every time you think you've moved on, they come back to bite you in the unsuspecting butt.

"What were the changes?" I asked.

"Only that . . ." Viv shoved a bite of pistachio cupcake in her mouth and talked through it, making her answer unintelligible.

"Beg pardon?" I asked.

"I have final approval over any and all business decisions," Harrison said. His cupcake was already gone and he wiped his fingers on his napkin.

"Meaning what exactly?" I asked.

"You can't sell the business or refinance or move or, well, basically, anything unless I approve it."

I frowned. "And why did this come about?"

Viv and Harrison exchanged a glance. Viv looked a bit guilty and Harrison disapproving. I really didn't need more to go on than that. It was pretty clear that the arrangement had been made to save Viv from her impulsive self.

"All right," I said. "I can see where it could be a system of checks and balances."

"Quite right," Nick chimed in. "Always smart to have a second opinion."

I gave him a look and he resumed chomping on his cupcake.

"But I don't see how you think it gives you the right to tell us what we can and can't do when it comes to visiting clients," I said to Harrison.

" 'Clients' is the key word," he said. "Tina isn't your friend. She's a client. The reason you're in this mess is because you were working for the Grisby family, making this a business association, therefore giving me the right to tell you to stop—for the good of the business, of course."

While he spoke, I could feel my temper getting hot. I

don't like being told what to do. In fact, usually, when I am told what to do I do the opposite out of sheer contrariness. What can I say? I'm flawed like that.

"Fine," I said. "You want us to stop having anything to do with the Grisbys and as 'the boss' you feel you have the right to demand that. Yes?"

"That sounds a bit harsh," Harrison said. His brows lowered in a frown over his bright-green eyes and his mouth twisted to one side in an unhappy pucker.

"Yes or no?" I asked as I rose to stand. I dumped my dinner plate in a nearby trash can.

"Well, then yes, I do think I have the right as your manager to insist," he said.

"All right," I said. I brushed my hands together over the trash, getting rid of any crumbs. "Then I quit."

I heard a collective gasp. Viv and Andre both called my name, but I had already turned on my heel and bolted for the stairs that led up to our apartment. On the scale of dramatic exits, this was a solid seven. I slammed the door behind me, discouraging anyone from following.

I didn't stop until I reached my bedroom upstairs, where I slammed the door again, hoping that they heard it all the way downstairs.

Miffed, piqued, perturbed—all were dramatic understatements to how I was feeling. My palms positively itched with wanting to slap someone, but of course, I would never.

The nerve of Harrison Wentworth to think he's the boss of me. I grabbed my laptop off of my desk and moved to my bed, where I could open up the pertinent files while lying down. Now that I knew the situation, I would not rest until

I had read through the previously ignored paperwork and corrected anything that declared Harrison in charge.

I woke up to a soft knocking on my door. It took a minute for it to penetrate my sleep fog and when it did I found myself fully clothed and snuggling my laptop like it was a teddy bear.

"Scarlett, are you all right?"

It was Viv's voice. I thought about ignoring her, but I knew she'd just come in.

"What do you want?" I asked.

The door pushed open and Viv walked in cautiously as if she expected me to lob a pillow at her head.

"Still wobbly?" she asked.

"If by that do you mean am I still mad, yes," I said.

Viv sighed and sat down on the end of the bed. "Listen, I'm sorry this was such a shock for you, but truly, I sent the paperwork and you did sign it."

"I'm not mad at you," I said. "I'm mad at myself for not paying attention and at Harrison for being so heavy-handed."

"Well, it's not entirely his fault. His uncle had the job before him and he actually recommended the arrangement."

"But why?" I asked. "I don't understand."

Viv glanced around my room. "We really need to make some time to freshen up this room. This pink thing you've got going is making my eyes water."

I had painted the room a retina-searing pink when I was twelve. It was pretty awful, but I got the feeling Viv was stalling.

"Viv, what aren't you telling me?" I asked.

"It was Swarovski crystals," she said. "There was a huge deal on them and I couldn't pass them up, so I went and bought all that he had."

"Who had?" I asked.

"A dealer here at the Portobello Saturday market," she said.

I closed my eyes. I had a feeling I knew exactly what had happened. "Were we completely wiped out?"

"Very nearly," she said. "I would have told you, but you were otherwise occupied."

"How did we manage to survive?" I asked.

"Harrison used his own resources to save the business," she said.

"So he owns the major share of the business," I said.

"Yes," she said.

"When were you planning on telling me?" I asked.

She pressed her lips together.

"Never?" I asked.

"Well, I've been paying him back every month, and in a few years . . ." Her voice trailed off.

"A few years!" I cried. I flopped back onto the bed and put my hand over my eyes. "Oh my God, Harrison really is the boss of me."

"Well, technically, since you quit, he really isn't," she said.

"That was just me doing my drama thing," I protested. "I'm not quitting."

"That's what Andre said," Viv said. She sighed. "Well, that's a relief. So you'll stay?"

"Yes," I said. I said it grumpily so she wouldn't think she was completely off the hook. She grinned at me.

"You know, I really think Harrison is so bossy because he has a thing for you," she said. "I think he really likes you, Scarlett."

"Yes, I could really feel his concern when he was telling me off," I said.

"Do you really think if he didn't care about you that he'd give a rip if you got yourself into danger?" she asked.

"Well, since he's my boss, he might be concerned about me from an employer-employee standpoint," I said.

"Oh, what a lot of tosh," she said. "You know he likes you and I think you like him, too."

"We are definitely not going there," I said. "I am man free and planning to stay that way for a very long time."

Viv shook her head and said, "About him and Fee . . . I have some information—"

"No, thank you, no," I said. I held up my hand to ward her off. "I'm not interested. It's not my business."

"But—"

"No!"

"If you'd just lis—"

"Viv, no," I said. "Seriously, I'm good. Now, how long did you all talk about me after I stormed out?"

"About fifteen minutes," she said. "Andre was mad at Harrison, who looked contrite, but Nick said that Harrison was showing good sense, which set Andre and Nick into a spat."

"Oh no," I said.

"No, no, they seemed to be enjoying it," she said. "And

194

then Fee had to run because of her brothers, so Nick and Andre walked her out. Harrison thought about coming up here to talk to you, but I discouraged it."

"Wise choice," I said.

"Yeah, well, he'll be round to see you tomorrow," she said.

"What?" I cried.

"Well, you did quit," she said. "He wants to talk to you about it."

"Nuts!" I glanced at the clock. It was midnight. I had no idea when I'd fallen asleep or for how long I'd been out. Apparently, legal paperwork gives me the yawns. "What are you still doing up?"

"Elvis movie," she said. "You know how I get."

Yes, I did. Viv loved Elvis, and if an old movie of his came on, everything stopped while she watched.

"And you didn't wake me?" I asked. Yes, I love him, too.

"I was afraid you'd still be mad," she said.

"Was it a good one?" I asked.

"*Blue Hawaii*," she said.

"Aw, man," I complained. She laughed just as I'd hoped and then reached out to hug me. I squeezed her back.

"So we're okay?" she asked. She studied my face closely but there was no need.

"Yes, we're fine," I said. "But tomorrow, I want all of the gory details."

"Over eggs and sausages," she agreed. "It'll go down easier that way."

She slipped out of my room with a wave and I rose to put my laptop back on my desk.

So, Harrison wanted to talk, did he? Fine, we would have a nice chat tomorrow about how he was going to give me the business back and there would be no more telling me what to do.

Determined, I marched across the hall to brush my teeth, feeling quite sure that I could manage this situation with Harrison as effectively as I had juggled mishmashed reservations in the hotel business. How hard could it be? Right?

Chapter 20

"Scarlett, where are you going?" Viv asked as I jogged through the kitchen, pausing only for a piece of toast and a cup of coffee.

"Meeting," I said.

"Where and with whom?" she asked.

"Tina Grisby," I said. "I just got a text from her."

"Oh no, you can't!" she wailed. "Harrison—"

"Can't say anything about it," I said. "I no longer work here, remember?"

"But—" she protested.

"No, I'm off. Tina will be waiting," I said.

"Oh, this is not going to end well," Viv said.

I was sure she was referring to Harrison's reaction to my absence, but I refused to acknowledge it.

"It'll be fine," I said. "I'll be back before we open. You'll see."

I didn't give her a chance to offer up any more protests but dashed down to the shop and out the door.

Yes, a very large part of my decision was to avoid having to see Harrison. I was really unhappy that no one had told me he owned controlling interest in the shop. I felt betrayed by the omission, but then I felt guilty because if I had been available instead of being self-absorbed, Viv could have turned to me. What a mess.

Portobello Road was quiet this early in the day. Most of the shops hadn't opened as yet. Tina and I had agreed to meet up at the Caffe Nero near Notting Hill Gate.

I couldn't help but wonder what she wanted to talk to me about. Her text had sounded, well, desperate. I thought about the Grisby family and in her situation, I wondered who in that family I would turn to if I discovered I was pregnant, offsetting the entire chain of succession. No one leapt to mind, although Lily seemed trustworthy, as did Liam and George.

I was so deep in thought as I turned onto the road in front of the coffee shop that I didn't notice the huffing and puffing behind me until it grew so loud it was impossible to ignore. I whipped my head around and assumed a fighter stance, anticipating an attack. What I saw made me double up with laughter.

Nick and Andre were jogging in matching running suits of neon green and orange with white reflector stripes down the sides. While Andre was hardly even sweating, Nick looked like he'd just finished a 10K. His face was red, his thin hair was soaked with sweat and his orange jogging suit looked wilted.

"For the love of oxygen," he wheezed. "Can we please stop?"

Andre gave him a bland look and jogged in place. Nick wiped his brow off with the towel around his neck and gave me a pleading look.

"Save me, Scarlett, please," he said.

"No, I don't think I will," I said. I feigned looking irritated at him. "I heard that while Andre defended me, you took Harrison's side. I don't know if I'm speaking to you yet."

"Oh, love, don't be like that," Nick wheezed. "I was only looking out for you. There's a murderer out there. And Harrison is right. You have to be careful."

"No one likes to be bossed about," Andre said.

"Oh, don't you start," Nick grumped.

"Scarlett!" a woman's voice called and I turned to see Tina waving to me from in front of the café. I waved back and she hurried over to join us.

"Tina, these are my friends Andre and Nick," I said. "They were just on their way to finish their jog."

Nick gave me a pouty face, but I ignored him.

"Hi, Tina," Nick said. He was still a little breathy but he managed to shake her hand without sweating all over her. "You look familiar. Do you live in the area?"

"Oh no," she said. "I just pop into Mim's Whims now and again."

She looked uncomfortable and despite the overcast day,

she wore oversized sunglasses that she pushed up on her nose as if hoping to hide behind them.

"Come on, Nick, let's leave the ladies to their coffee," Andre said. "We have another lap to do."

"I think I have a blister," Nick whined.

Andre gave him a look and turned back to us and said, "A pleasure to meet you, Tina. Call me later, Scarlett."

"Will do," I said with a wave as he began to jog away.

Nick began to limp-run after him, "I'm in agony, I tell you. What if the blister pops? It could get infected."

Andre didn't slow down and Nick was forced to hurry to catch up.

I glanced at Tina and said, "My neighbors on Portobello. Andre took the pictures at the Wonderland tea."

"I thought he looked familiar," she said. "I don't suppose he recognized me."

"If he did, he'd be too polite to mention it," I said. "Andre's good like that."

I saw Tina's shoulders sink with relief. "The media has been ferocious."

"Oh, I know all about that," I said. It had been a few months since my own days of infamy, but the term "hounded by the press" would forever have new meaning for me.

"That's one of the reasons I wanted to talk to you," Tina said.

We entered the shop and ordered our coffee at the counter. They gave us a number and we sat at a small table in the corner. Although the shop was busy, our coffee was delivered within minutes of our arrival.

I stirred in some brown sugar—not the type you used for

baking but the kind we call raw in the States—into my latte and waited for Tina to talk.

She had ordered a decaf and stirred it for a moment as if trying to gather her thoughts. I studied her face while I waited. She looked pale and tired with dark circles under her eyes and anxiety pinching her mouth into a thin line. Her long brown hair was dull and shoved into a clip onto the back of her head. When she put her spoon down, I noticed her hand was shaking.

"I don't know how to say it," she said. "So I guess I'll just lob it out there. I think someone tried to kill me last night."

"What?" I cried. "Tina, you have to call Detective Inspector Finchley. He needs to know this."

"But what if I'm wrong?" she asked. "What if I just dreamt it?"

"What if you didn't?" I countered. "Tell me what happened exactly."

"Well, there was a big row after you and Viv left," she said. "I packed my things and decided I'd rather be home at Grisby Hall with Geoffrey's ghost than stay another night in the hotel with the lot of them."

"Does he have a ghost?" I asked. This would be a game changer.

Tina frowned. "It was just an expression. I mean, I don't know. When I left the hotel, Dotty, Lily and Rose came with me, while Daphne and her sons opted to stay at the Savoy."

"So what makes you think someone is trying to kill you?"

"I woke up to someone, a presence, in my room," she said. "When I cried out, no one answered but I heard something drop and then the door banged open.

"When I turned the light on, I found one of my pillows on the floor and the door to my room was wide-open. I think whoever it was may have planned to suffocate me but gave up the idea when I woke up. I called Buckley but he had retired for the night and didn't see anyone in the house on his way to me. Together we woke the others."

"Could it have been any of them?" I asked.

"They all looked genuinely groggy with sleep," Tina said. "I'm not sure what to do. I've decided that I'll stay for Geoffrey's funeral, but as soon as it's over, I'm leaving the country. That's what I wanted to talk to you about."

"Me?" I asked.

"Can you help me get settled in the States?" she asked. "I just need a safe place to go until I get on my feet." She put a protective hand on her belly. "For my son's sake."

"You know it's a boy already?" I asked. This seemed early to me.

"It has to be a boy," she said. "That was all Geoffrey wanted. It just has to be."

I wasn't sure what kind of crazy pregnancy hormones were rocketing through her system, so I didn't press the point, but I was worried about her—very worried.

"My parents are settled in New Haven, Connecticut," I said. "I know that they'd be happy to help you find a nice safe place to live, maybe a nice old farmhouse in the country or a cottage on the shore."

"That sounds perfect," she said.

"In the meantime, you really should talk to Inspector Finchley. He'd want to know if you feel unsafe in your own home. Maybe he could post a man to keep watch," I said.

"But the family," she said. "They're everywhere. He can't keep them out of their own home, now, can he? And what if it's not the family at all? It could be anyone."

"Like Cara Whittles?" I asked.

"Perhaps she's gotten to a member of the house staff," Tina said. "It could have been one of them." The maniacal gleam in her eye freaked me out a bit, but I reasoned she was pregnant and obviously hadn't slept.

"Maybe you should consider staying at a different hotel. Just so you can get a good night's sleep. Everything is always better when you've gotten some rest."

"Maybe," she said.

But I could tell by her tone that she was just saying it to make me happy.

We finished our coffee and she hurried off into the Underground, leaving me to feel perplexed and worried. Had someone tried to kill her? If so, then it had to be someone who didn't want her baby to inherit the entire fortune. But who?

Chapter 21

When I arrived back at the shop, Harrison was waiting for me. Not a total surprise. Still, I had nothing to say to him. I didn't technically work for him and I wasn't about to stand there and listen to a lecture.

He was leaning against the front counter, where Fee was working, obviously waiting for someone. Me.

"Hi, Fee," I said as I walked past them. I was halfway to the door that led to the stairs when he yelled, "Oy. We're really not talking, are we?"

"You can talk," I said with a shrug. "But that doesn't mean I have to listen."

I opened the door and jogged up the stairs to the apartment above. The toast I'd had earlier wasn't enough to keep a sparrow alive, so I headed for the kitchen and grabbed a banana out of the fruit bowl and a yogurt from the refrigerator.

I was just slicing the banana into the yogurt when Harrison walked into our small kitchen from the living room and took a seat at the counter.

"Viv said you went to see Tina Grisby," he said.

"She did?" I couldn't believe she had ratted me out. Not cool.

"She was worried about you and she figured it was either tell me or call the police, so she opted to tell me," he said.

I glanced from my yogurt cup to him. His dark-brown hair flopped over his forehead. He was casual today in jeans and a form-fitting Henley. Had he always been that well muscled? My inner girly girl wanted to bat her eyelashes at him and get him to lift heavy things for me, but the new independent happily single me was refusing to allow any such nonsense.

"What exactly did she think you would be able to do if I was in danger?" I asked.

"I think she thought I would call the police if it seemed warranted," he said.

"Did you?" I asked.

"Well, if you hadn't come back to the shop in a timely fashion, I might have," he said.

We were both silent as I ate my yogurt. I wanted to ask him why he cared, but then that would sound needy, wouldn't it? I scraped the plastic cup as I finished, more for something to do than because I needed those last remnants of yogurt.

"Ginger, we need to reach a truce," he said.

I put my spoon in the sink and rinsed out my yogurt cup.

"You make it sound like we're fighting," I said.

"Well, you did quit and storm out of the room last night," he said. "I'd say if not a full-fledged fight, we're definitely in a tiff."

"I have a right to be irritated," I said. "I can't believe you and Viv didn't tell me about the business situation."

He sighed. "I left it to Viv, but I think she was worried you'd be upset."

"You think?"

"So, what did Tina have to say?" he asked.

"Abrupt subject change," I observed.

"It seemed pointless to pursue the business talk," he said.

"Why would I tell you about Tina?" I asked. I placed my hands on the counter and leaned forward. He was sitting across on one of the stools. We were definitely at a standoff.

"Perhaps I can help," he said.

"Why would you do that when you are always telling me to stay away from the Grisbys?" I asked.

"Because maybe solving Geoffrey's murder is the only way you will stay away," he said. His exasperation with the situation was more than evident.

"Tina thinks someone tried to kill her last night," I said.

"What?" he asked. "She needs to report it to the police."

"I know," I said. "But she's afraid that they can't protect her, so she's planning to stay for Geoffrey's funeral and then wants me to help her find a safe place in the States to live with her baby."

"Can you do that?" he asked.

"My parents will help," I said.

"Ginger, who do you think killed Geoffrey Grisby?" he asked.

"I don't know," I said. "Viv thinks it was an accident."

"Could it have been?"

I gave him a long look. He nodded and I knew he didn't believe it was an accident either.

"It has to be someone who has access to formaldehyde," I said. "But that could be anyone."

"How do you figure?" he asked.

"Geoffrey Grisby Senior died a month ago," I said. "They were all at his funeral. Someone could have gotten the chemical there."

"Really?" he asked. He leaned back on his stool. "Think about it. Don't you think the funeral home would notice if someone helped themselves to their embalming fluid?"

"Maybe," I said. "Maybe not."

"And there is still the dilemma of how they poisoned Geoffrey with it," he said. "I mean, that stuff has a serious stench."

I drummed my fingers on the countertop. "All right, tabling that dilemma for now, there is also the question of who in the family is the most likely to have poisoned him."

"If Tina is pregnant with a boy, I say it's her," Harrison said.

"Oh, good grief, not you, too," Viv cried as she entered the kitchen. "You're supposed to be talking to her about the business, not playing *Inspector Lewis*."

"I tried," Harrison protested. "But she's stuck in neutral and the only way to move forward is to resolve the Grisby situation."

I frowned at him. "Did you just compare me to a car?"

"An adorable little sports car," he amended.

"Huh." I let it go. "For the record, I'm Hathaway and you're Lewis."

"That makes me your boss," he said.

"Apparently," I said. "But I'm also younger and cuter."

Viv glanced between us. "Do I see a truce in the making?"

"Yes, you do," I said. "So long as we're agreed that we're going to help Tina."

Harrison rolled his eyes. Viv frowned.

"You really don't think Geoffrey's death was an accident?" she asked.

"No," I said. "Tina doesn't either. She thinks someone tried to kill her last night and I believe she's in danger."

Viv's eyes went wide. "Who do you think it is?"

"No idea but it stands to reason that it's someone who will gain if Tina's baby is never born," I said. I watched her face closely when I added, "The same person who killed Geoffrey."

She frowned and tugged at her lower lip. "Liam."

Harrison and I exchanged a look. Did she know something?

"What makes you say that?" Harrison asked.

Viv glanced away from us.

"Viv, what do you know?" I asked.

"Nothing," she protested.

Harrison and I both stared at her. Hard.

"Fine," she said. "Maybe he was acting strange at the Wonderland tea."

Harrison sat up straight. "Strange how?"

"I heard him having an argument with his brother, George," she said. "About Cara Whittles."

"Their grandfather's mistress?" I asked.

"Liam wanted to have her arrested for trespassing, but George wouldn't hear of it," Viv said.

"When did you hear this argument?" Harrison asked.

"Just before Scarlett screamed her head off whilst finding Geoffrey's body."

A shudder rippled down my back. It sounded so harsh when she said it like that.

"Why do you suppose George didn't want to call the police?" I asked.

"I don't know, but Liam intimated that George had some affection for Cara," Viv said. "Liam sounded very, well, jealous about it."

"And you didn't mention this?" I asked.

"It sort of slipped my mind after the body was found," she said.

"Didn't George tell us he studied art in Italy for a few years?" I asked. Viv nodded. "So that would have put him in close proximity to his grandfather and Cara. Still, it doesn't make any sense. Liam is the one who will inherit it all; even if George was fond of Cara and wanted to protect her, there'd be no purpose in him harming Geoffrey because he'd still get nothing. Besides, didn't Lily say that Tom Mercer, George and Liam's father, was rich? They don't need the money."

"Yes, the Mercers are extremely wealthy," Viv said. "Which is why it makes no sense for Liam or George to be involved in this. There is no gain for them."

"Maybe it's more than affection between George and Cara or Liam and Cara," Harrison said.

"Oh, ew," I said.

They both looked at me.

"She's old enough to be their mother," I said.

"Ageist," Viv accused.

"I am not," I argued. "A certain amount of years is all right between an older woman and a younger man, but if she's old enough to have birthed the boy, well, that's just . . . ew."

No one spoke for a moment. I wondered if I had been too adamant and had offended them. I was about to retract my words when Harrison spoke.

"So, funeral home?" he asked.

"Excuse me?"

"Do you want to go visit the funeral home where Geoffrey Grisby Senior was embalmed?" he asked. "Maybe the funeral director remembers something hinky."

"Brilliant," Viv said. "What should I wear?"

"You are not going," I said. She pouted. "You have to help Fee with the Butler-Coates wedding before she has a nervous breakdown."

"Brides ruin all of my fun," Viv said with a scowl.

"There's a message in there somewhere," Harrison said. He turned to me. "Shall we?"

"You know where to go?" I asked.

"Geoffrey Junior's funeral was listed in the paper and the article mentioned that it was to be in the same parlor as his father," Harrison said.

"Oh," I said. "If you give me the name, I can check it out."

Harrison nodded and then said, "No."

I frowned at him. I was pretty sure he was mocking me.

"What kind of boss would I be to send you off on your own into a potentially dangerous situation?" he asked.

I pushed away from the counter. "You're not my boss. I quit. Remember?"

"Oh, I forgot to mention that if you want the information about where the funeral home is, you have to take your job back," he said.

"Power play," Viv said behind her hand to me.

I crossed my arms over my chest. "I don't need you. You told me you read it in the paper. I'm confident I can find it on my own."

"Ah, but I didn't say what paper or what day I read it. Let's see. Was it the *Times*, the *Evening Standard*, the *Daily Mail*, the *Irish Independent* . . . shall I go on?"

I heaved a sigh. It would be hours of work to go through them all, and yes, I could try to find it online, but really, what was the point? I was pretty sure I wasn't going to be able to shake Harrison loose. And truth be told, I thought I'd have better luck getting information if he was with me. Like it or not, he gave me an air of legitimacy I clearly lacked on my own, being American and all.

"Okay, fine," I snapped. I didn't have to be happy about it, now, did I? "I'll take my job back. Now let's go."

"Yay!" Viv cheered behind us.

I turned and gave her a dark look and she promptly lost her smile and tried to look serious, but I could see it was an effort.

I led the way downstairs with Harrison right on my heels.

When we arrived in the shop, Fee was still behind the counter. She glanced up and smiled at us, and I couldn't help but glance between her and Harrison. They looked happy to see each other, but I didn't get a romantic vibe off of them. Now, what did that mean? Were they over each other already?

"Call if you find anything out," Viv said as we left. "And be careful."

"I promise," I called and led the way out of the shop.

Had I known what was going to happen, I would have put a bit more sincerity in my vow.

Chapter 22

We nabbed two seats on the tube just as they were vacated. I glanced at the map on the wall above the seats to see how many stops and train switches we would have to make to get to Highgate. The funeral home was just around the corner from the Underground stop.

Despite his casual attire, Harrison had a watchfulness about him that reminded me of a guard dog. He seemed to be taking in every passenger who arrived onto or departed from our train car. I wondered what he was looking for and then thought maybe he knew something I didn't.

I thought about asking him on the train, but I didn't want to yell at him and be overheard. I waited until we'd reached our last stop and had climbed the steps up to the surface street.

"You seem awfully on edge," I said.

"Do I?" he asked.

He began to walk down the sidewalk, leaving me no choice but to follow.

"Care to share? I prodded.

"Not really," he said.

Well, wasn't that maddening. Clearly, he was underestimating my curiosity.

"What were you looking for on the train?" I asked.

He slowed and turned to look at me. Then he sighed. "You're not going to give up, are you?"

"No," I said.

"All right, I was trying to determine if we were being followed," he said.

"Who would follow us?" I asked. "And why?"

"Anyone who saw you having coffee with Tina Grisby this morning," he said. "You know, the same person who tried to kill her last night."

My heart did a little shiver in my chest. I hadn't really thought about it like that.

"Come on, I don't fancy loitering on this errand and making targets of ourselves," he said. He turned down a narrow side street and I hurried after him.

Assuming someone had tried to kill Tina last night and assuming that they had followed her this morning and seen me, then maybe Harrison's caution was warranted. But it seemed like an awful lot of assumptions to me, so I shrugged it off as Harrison stopped in front of a small stone building with dark windows.

Two large wooden doors led inside, and he pulled one

and gestured for me to lead. As you would expect, there was a hush about the place, which was accentuated by its thick burgundy carpet and heavy gold drapes.

A receptionist sat at a small desk off to the side of the front room and she greeted us with a small smile, the sort that was offered in times of sadness, as if she didn't want to offend us with too boisterous of a greeting.

She was somewhere in her fifties, I guessed, wearing a tailored blouse and navy slacks. Her gray hair was styled in a becoming cut. She looked like the kind of woman who knew how to fold a fitted bedsheet without breaking down and swearing at it. I liked her.

"Welcome to Buskers and Sons," she said. "I'm Marjorie. How may I help you?"

Harrison and I exchanged a glance. We hadn't really thought this out. How were we going to explain our presence to this nice lady?

"Oh, uh, I'm Steve Waterstone and this is my wife, Sally. We're newlyweds and we've just begun drawing up our wills." Harrison lied so smoothly even I almost believed him. "We aren't sure what to instruct the other to do upon our deaths. We were looking to talk to someone about the different options."

As if to cement the story, he threw his arm around my shoulders and hugged me to his side. I gave Marjorie a small smile of my own.

She clapped her hands together and said, "Well, isn't that wonderful. Not enough young people take into account their ever after. You would not believe some of the tragic stories we hear."

"I expect not," Harrison said. He really seemed to be embracing his role.

"Let me just call Mr. Busker," Marjorie said. "He's between appointments and I'm certain he'll be happy to talk to you."

She hurried back around her desk and picked up her phone. While she spoke softly into the receiver, I shrugged Harrison's arm off of my shoulders.

"Now, don't bury your feelings, love—let me know how you really feel," he whispered in my ear.

I rolled my eyes and made quotation marks in the air with my fingers when I said, "You'll have to 'urn' my trust first."

"Very punny," he said, but he wrinkled his nose as if he smelled something bad.

"Why do I never get credit for my wordplay?" I asked. "That was a good one."

"Sorry, that one belongs six feet under." He laughed at his own joke. I did not.

"Mr. and Mrs. Waterstone, if you'll follow me," Marjorie said. She gestured to a door behind her desk. Harrison motioned for me to go first so I followed Marjorie through the door, hoping we weren't making a grave mistake. See? Another good one.

Mr. Busker's office was as pristine as Marjorie's front desk. I suppose some people find compulsive neatness reassuring. Me? Not so much. Then again, given that we were in a funeral home, it wouldn't do to find bodies stacked up against the wall like old newspapers, now, would it?

I don't know what I expected out of a funeral home

director. I have not made the acquaintance of that many, but Mr. Busker wasn't it. Instead of a skinny, pale man who rubbed his boney fingers together as if sizing you up for a casket, this guy was round and robust with a deep voice that seemed incapable of a whisper.

"Welcome, Mr. and Mrs. Waterstone," he called as Marjorie ushered us into his office. He shook our hands and gestured for us to take the two seats across from his desk. His office was plush but less opulent than the main room, with a forest-green carpet and brown leather furniture.

"Thank you for seeing us," Harrison said.

"I understand you want to discuss the options of what to do after you've passed on," he said.

"That's right," I said. More to insert myself into the conversation than anything else.

"The traditional methods are burial or cremation," Mr. Busker said. He leaned his elbows on the desk and then placed his hands together at the fingertips in a thoughtful pose. "But things are changing as the world becomes more environmentally minded."

"Such as?" Harrison asked. He raised one eyebrow higher than the other and I thought he looked every bit the skeptical husband.

"Well, there's resomation, a process where they use a solution to liquefy the body before pulverizing the bones—a lot like cremation, but instead of burning the body, it's melted."

"Oh," I said. My voice came out fainter than I intended and Harrison patted my hand.

"There's also cryonics, mummification, plastination or

freeze-drying," Mr. Busker said. "Some of those are still in the experimental stage, but by the time you two are looking at your ever after, they could be viable."

A part of me desperately wanted to ask about the freeze-drying, but I figured we'd better stay on task.

"Let's go with the more traditional methods," I said. "For example, if we were to go with being buried, then our bodies would be preserved?"

"Yes," Mr. Busker nodded. "We do offer embalming to keep the body from immediately putrefying, allowing the family and friends a last memory picture of the deceased to help with the grieving."

I did not see how looking at a stiff version of me would help anyone say good-bye to me. In fact, I preferred that they remember me as I was, but I didn't say as much.

"How does embalming work?" Harrison asked.

"It's a chemical process where the body is prepared with a solution of formaldehyde, glutaraldehyde, ethanol, humectants and other solvents," he said. He rattled it off as if he was asked this question a lot.

"Do you do the process here?" I asked.

"Yes, we have a mortuary, where our embalmer works on the bodies," he said.

"So you have all of those chemicals here?" Harrison asked.

"Yes, all of the chemicals and equipment to embalm a body are here." His face lost its engaging look and his eyes turned speculative as he studied Harrison.

"And if we choose cremation, would that happen here as

well?" I asked. I hoped to distract him from thinking we were ghouls.

Mr. Busker's face relaxed and he said, "No, we would facilitate that for you by going through a crematorium. There are many within the city of London, as about seventy percent of people now use cremation as their preferred method."

"Really, seventy percent?" I asked.

"Would we be able to tour the mortuary?" Harrison asked.

Mr. Busker frowned. There was no keeping him from thinking Harrison was a creep now.

"I really don't see . . ." Mr. Busker began, but I interrupted.

"My husband is deathly afraid of needles. He faints every time he sees one. It's just so adorable," I said. I patted Harrison's hand as if I was reassuring the big lunk.

"Well, you would already be dead," Mr. Busker said. "So you would have nothing to fear."

"Yes, but I'd still like to see where my darling wife will be embalmed," Harrison said. He patted my hand in return a little harder than necessary. "You know, where her cold, stiff body will lie in order to be prepped."

"I suppose that would be all right," Mr. Busker said. He rose from his seat and gestured for us to follow him back into the main room. Marjorie was on the phone at her desk, and as we passed by, he said, "Just giving a tour."

Marjorie nodded and continued her call.

Harrison fell in beside me as we followed Mr. Busker through a doorway that led down a short hallway and out into a garage. The garage had several gleaming hearses parked, ready to shuttle the deceased to their final resting place.

"It occurs to me that you and I are spending a lot of time in funeral homes together," Harrison whispered. His breath tickled my ear and I moved slightly away and tried to ignore him. "They're becoming our place, don't you think?"

I gave him a dark look. "No, I don't."

I turned to glance at him and he looked amused, which I found highly irritating. What was it with this man's ability to get under my skin? Just because we had been to a wake together a few months ago and now we were touring a funeral home did not make it "our" place.

Mr. Busker opened a door on the other end of the garage and peeked his head inside. After a moment, he pushed the door open and gestured for us to follow.

We entered a room that resembled a doctor's office, sort of, with a tile floor, a large steel sink, and an autoclave in the corner. Much to my relief there was no body on either of the two medical tables that were placed in front of a wall of cabinets.

The room had the acrid smell of disinfectant about it and I wrinkled my nose against the assault.

Mr. Busker knocked on a door at the far end of the room and when it opened a man in a lab coat stepped through. A draft of cold air came with him, and just over his shoulder, I could see a wall of steel cabinets. I didn't need to be told that's where the bodies were kept. A shudder wracked my body before I could stop it, and I felt the warm press of Harrison's hand against my back, steadying me.

"This is Mr. Peakes, our embalmer," Mr. Busker said. "Mr. Peakes, this is Mr. and Mrs. Waterstone. They were interested in seeing our operation."

Mr. Peakes was a large man with a shaved head and a skull earring in one ear. His hand was large and it felt as if it swallowed mine whole when we shook hands.

"How do you do?" Mr. Peakes asked.

"Better than most of the people you see, I imagine," Harrison said.

To my surprise, Mr. Peakes busted out a laugh. "That's the truth, isn't it?"

Mr. Busker cleared his throat and said, "This is where the deceased are prepped for their final viewing. Mr. Peakes is a true artist. He takes great care to make sure our clients look quite peaceful."

"What's all that?" Harrison asked. He pointed at a rolling cart loaded with big bottles of chemicals.

"Those are the solutions I use to preserve the bodies and also some colorants to give the deceased more of a lifelike look—a blush of life, if you will," Mr. Peakes said.

"Oh, so it's not all makeup?" I asked.

"No, I pump formaldehyde under ten pounds of pressure right through the heart with a trocar," Mr. Peakes said. He held up a very long, very big needle.

I felt Harrison lurch beside me and when I glanced at him, his face was very pasty. Oh, wow, he really was looking queasy.

"Oh, dear, Mr. Busker, I think my husband needs some air," I said. I pushed Harrison in Mr. Busker's direction and I looked at Mr. Peakes and said, "Needles."

"Ah," Mr. Peakes said with a nod.

Harrison looked reluctant to leave, so I gave him another shove.

"I'll be right along," I said. I waited until the door closed behind them. Mr. Peakes had put his large needle back on his workstation.

"Do many people tour this area?" I asked.

"No, I expect most don't want to know what happens after they're gone."

"I believe you took care of a friend of mine, recently," I said. "An older gentleman named Geoffrey Grisby."

Mr. Peakes frowned. "That was several months ago. I heard we're getting the son, too, as soon as he's released from the forensic pathologist."

"Did you hear that Geoffrey Grisby was poisoned with formaldehyde?" I asked.

Mr. Peakes stared at me. "What are you getting at?"

"Nothing," I said. My voice came out in a high squeak. "It's just an unusual sort of poison, don't you think?"

I was suddenly aware that I was alone in a room with a very large man and a lot of medical equipment that could easily render a girl dead.

"Why are you here?" he asked. He took a step forward and I took one back. His face looked as dark as a thundercloud and I found my tongue was stuck to the roof of my mouth, which had gone suddenly dry. I swallowed, trying to create some saliva. It made an audible gulp sound.

"No reason, really, I was just looking around and it occurred to me that someone could have come in here and taken some of your chemicals and poisoned Geoffrey Grisby, the son," I said. My words came out in a rush.

"That's what I told the police!" Mr. Peakes slammed his hand on one of the steel tables. The crash made me jump and the table rattled ominously. A glance at his meaty fist made my whole body clench, fearing I might be next.

Chapter 23

"The police?" I asked, hoping to redirect this anger.

"Yeah, an Inspector Finchley was here sniffing around, asking me if I saw anyone in here—I hadn't—or if I'd had contact with anyone from the family, insinuating that I might have something to do with the murder. Right, because I don't see enough dead bodies.

"Now the Buskers want me to keep my chemicals under lock and key, as if it's my fault someone came in and helped themselves to a half-pint. You know, it only takes thirty milliliters ingested to kill a person. Bloody pain in the arse, I say," he growled.

The door slammed open and Harrison stood there. "All right, Sca . . . uh . . . Sally?" he asked.

"Fine, just fine," I said. I hurried to the door. "Well, I

don't want to keep you from your work, Mr. Peakes; have a nice day."

He grumbled something after me, but I grabbed Harrison's hand and yanked him back through the garage past Mr. Busker, who was waiting at the door to the funeral home.

"So sorry to cut the tour short, Mr. Busker. Bye, Marjorie, you've all been very kind," I cried over my shoulder as I dragged Harrison through the lobby and out onto the street.

My last glimpse of the funeral home was of Mr. Busker and Marjorie exchanging bewildered looks.

"Scarlett, what's going on?" Harrison demanded.

"Not yet," I said. "Keep moving."

A small public garden nestled in between two residential streets beckoned up ahead. I dragged Harrison across the street and through the wrought iron fence. There was an older couple, admiring the roses on the far side of the small enclosure, so I pushed Harrison down onto a stone bench and sat beside him.

We were both huffing and puffing—okay, mostly it was just me. As the older couple shuffled past us, we smiled and nodded.

As soon as they left, Harrison turned to me. "Are you all right? What happened back there? He didn't touch you, did he?"

"Yes," I said. "It's complicated and no."

Harrison shook his head. "Again and with more detail please."

I took a deep breath and told him what Peakes had told

me about the police already being there and how he was going to have to lock up his chemicals and how he had no idea who might have wandered into his embalming room and siphoned off his formaldehyde and how he didn't seem to like the idea that they were looking at him. Also, that it only took thirty milliliters to kill a person.

"How much is thirty milliliters, anyway?" I asked.

"About an ounce," he said. "He is a bit of a scary bloke."

"Frankenstein the embalmer," I agreed. We were quiet for a moment and then I said, "So, fear of needles, eh?"

"I was merely acting to give you the opportunity to question him on your own," he said.

"Really," I said. I opened my purse and began to search inside. "Because I grabbed one of his needles for evidence."

Harrison's face drained of color.

"Ha! Gotcha!"

"That was cruel," he said as his shoulders slumped down from around his ears.

"But very funny," I said. "Come on, we'd best get back to the shop or Viv will send the police to look for us."

I led the way out of the walled garden. As I pushed open the gate, I turned to glance back at Harrison. Maybe I wasn't ready to tell him, but the truth was that I was glad he was with me. I would have been nervous to go to a funeral home by myself, and the cover of husband and wife had certainly made our visit seem less odd, at least initially.

Harrison met my gaze and gave me a small smile. I liked the way his hair fell over his forehead and the sparkle in his green eyes when he looked at me.

He opened his mouth to say something but was distracted by something behind me.

"Scarlett! Look out!" he cried.

I turned to see what was behind me—lion, tiger, mugger—but Harrison grabbed my arm and yanked me down, covering my body with his. I heard a sickening thump and then Harrison slumped on top of me with all of his weight pressing down on my back.

"Oy! What are you doing there?" a voice yelled.

I heard footsteps pounding down the sidewalk away from us.

"Help!" I cried from underneath Harrison. I was trying to brace his unconscious form with my body, but he was too heavy and I was in an awkward position.

"Hang on, Miss, I've got him," a man's voice said.

Abruptly, Harrison was lifted off of me and I popped up to see a stocky man in construction attire holding Harrison. Together we gently lowered him to the ground.

"He took a right bashin' on the noggin," the man said. He was fumbling in his pocket for his phone. Two women and a bicyclist joined us.

I knelt beside Harrison while the man called an ambulance. I felt under Harrison's jaw for a pulse. It was strong and steady. I could hear the people around me talking about an attacker in a hooded sweatshirt and how Harrison had protected me by covering me with his body.

"Why'd you do it, Harry?" I whispered. His face remained slack, his eyes shut, having seen something I could only guess at, because with my back to the attacker I hadn't seen a thing.

In moments a bright-green ambulance roared up and out jumped a paramedic in a dark-green suit. Following the ambulance came a small blue metro police car.

The construction worker who'd called explained what happened to the officer while I stood and watched the medics work on Harrison. I felt as if all of my insides had shriveled.

"Ginger?" A groggy voice called my name and I pressed forward to see Harrison regaining consciousness. "What happened?"

"We got jumped," I said. "I didn't see who did it."

"Blimey, what did they hit me with—a cricket bat?" he asked.

"I don't know," I said. "I didn't see that either."

"Pretty close, yeah?" the construction worker said as he leaned over Harrison. "The guy was wearing a dark hooded jacket and carrying a heavy satchel. He must have had bricks in it, because he hit you and you went down. Nice save on the lady, though."

"Thanks," Harrison said. He closed his right eye and squinted at the man.

"Trying to make sure there's just one of him?" the paramedic asked.

"That obvious?" Harrison asked.

"Yeah, we're going to take you in for a proper look-see," he said.

"Can I ride with you?" I asked. "I don't want to leave him."

"Sure," the paramedic said. "The more the merrier."

The police officer asked both Harrison and me what we'd

seen. I was useless, having seen nothing, but Harrison confirmed what the construction guy had said about the man in the dark hooded jacket and the heavy bag that he wielded like a club.

The officer took our names and addresses and asked us to be in touch if we remembered anything. He planned to file a report on the chance that this was a mugger who would likely strike again. Harrison and I exchanged a look. This was no mugger.

"We're taking you to the A&E at the Royal Free Hospital over on Pond Street," the medic said. "It's not far."

I knew that "A&E" meant "accident and emergency," the British version of the emergency room in hospitals in the States. I wondered if they were truly worried about Harrison or if they were erring on the side of caution because he'd suffered a head injury.

It didn't take long to get to the hospital, and Harrison was whisked inside.

"I'll be right in," I told Harrison as they off-loaded him from the ambulance. "I'm going to call Viv."

He nodded, and I could tell by the way he winced that the motion caused him significant pain. The next hour was a blur. Viv was worried, but I reassured her that Harrison was conscious and that no, I wasn't the one who had hit him. Yes, she actually asked.

When I joined Harrison in the A&E, a doctor was checking his pupils and feeling the lump on his head.

I stood to the side while he asked Harrison questions. He seemed satisfied that Harrison was okay but then warned him not to be alone for twenty-four hours and to have someone wake him up every two hours to check for signs of a concussion.

A surge of guilt hit me hard right in the chest. Harrison was now holding an ice pack to the lump on his head because he had protected me. And he wouldn't have had to protect me if we hadn't been attacked and I was pretty sure we wouldn't have been attacked if we hadn't gone to the funeral home and asked questions about Geoffrey Grisby. In other words, this whole mess was my fault and I felt horribly guilty. A sob burbled up in my throat and came out like a half cough, half hiccup, and it hurt.

"You all right, Scarlett?" Harrison asked. He had a handful of papers in one hand and his ice pack in the other.

"I'm fine." I sniffed and then wailed, "But you could have been killed!"

Harrison's eyebrows shot up and the doctor gave him an alarmed look before ducking out of our area.

"Come here," Harrison said.

He lifted one arm and I hurried forward to help him off the bed. Instead, he hugged me close and kissed the top of my head.

"Don't you worry," he said. "My cabbage is as hard as concrete. A little bump like this is nothing."

I wiped the tears off of my face and nodded. "Still, you're not to be alone for twenty-four hours. You're to go home and rest and I'll be checking on you every two hours to make sure your pupils haven't suddenly dilated or you've slipped into a coma because of a brain bleed or swelling or anything weird."

"Excellent bedside manner," he said. "I feel so much better."

"Is that sarcasm?" I asked.

"Yes, I believe it was."

"Well, that's a good sign at any rate."

We took a cab to his home in Pembridge Mews. It didn't take long, but I could see his head had to be hurting, as he rested it on the back of the seat and kept the cold pack they had given him firmly in place.

The cab let us off along a row of impressive white houses, the sort that were tall and imposing and inexplicably reminded me of wedding cake. Harrison fished in his pocket for his key. I took it from his hand and unlocked the door. The knob for the front door was set in the middle of the door, which I found charming and made me think I was entering a hobbit home.

Harrison wobbled on his feet and I quickly put his arm over my shoulder and my other arm around his waist as I helped him over the threshold. A door led to the first-floor apartment, but Harrison motioned to the stairs.

"My flat is on two," he said.

We maneuvered our way up the steps and he took his keys back to open his door. I'd be lying if I said I wasn't curious about his home. Was he as neat and tidy as he seemed or did a slob lurk beneath his starchy shirts and expensive suits?

He wobbled again and I led him to the big squashy couch in the middle of the main room. It was a mountain of cushy brown leather in front of a large-screen television. Exposed redbrick made up one wall while windows looking down on the street made up the opposite. A compact kitchen filled one side of the room while a door to the right opened to a hallway with several doors, which I assumed were the bedrooms and bathroom.

"Do you want to go lie in your bed?" I asked.

Harrison kicked off his shoes and reclined on the couch.

"No, I'm good here," he said. "I'm just going to keep the ice pack on for a bit. It's just a bump. Nothing to worry about."

He reached for the remote and switched on the television. A soccer match came on and he perked up with interest.

"If you get overexcited, I'm switching it to a cooking channel," I said.

"I'll be good," he said. "I promise. I'm fine. You don't have to stay, you know."

"Yes, I do."

I stood not knowing what to do with my hands. Why was that? I crossed my arms but that felt belligerent, so I put them on my hips, but that seemed angry. Finally, I clasped them behind my back, trying to look casual.

"Can I get you anything?" I asked. "Water? Tea?"

"You don't know how to make tea," he said.

"You could talk me through it," I said. I moved to the kitchenette and glanced in his cupboards. I didn't find fixings for tea or coffee or anything else. A glance in the fridge showed a few bottles of Britvic apple and raspberry juice and nothing—and I do mean nothing—else.

"Thanks, but I'm good," he said.

He watched me as I left the kitchen and began to prowl the room, looking for a distraction. A stack of *Financial Times* was on the coffee table, and I sifted through it, not really reading the headlines, just sort of skimming them.

"Scarlett, do I make you nervous?" he asked.

"No!" I jumped. Yeah, not exactly selling my answer, there, was I? "I'm just worried that you might black out again."

"I won't," he said. "It just rocked me a bit. I've been hit harder than that on the rugby pitch. It'll just take a while for the dizzies to pass."

"You play rugby?" I asked. I knew this. Viv had told me before, but it was hard for me to reconcile the buttoned-down Harrison Wentworth with a sport that I had always considered to be for knuckle draggers.

"You sound surprised," he said.

"I just thought of you as more of a cricket player," I said. "Or maybe chess."

He rolled his eyes and then closed them. "You're doing wonders for my manhood."

"Are you all right?" I asked as I hurried to him. "Are you dizzy? Faint? About to vomit? Where do you keep your bags?"

He cracked one eye open and looked at me. Our faces were just inches apart. I was struck by how long his eyelashes were and by the fullness of his lips. Definitely too pretty of a face for a rugby player.

"Ginger, you exhaust me," he said.

I gathered this was not a compliment, and I really couldn't blame him.

He closed his eye. In moments, he was snoring. So here I was alone with a sleeping man in his apartment. Hmm. I have to admit the possibilities were intriguing.

Chapter 24

Despite the temptation, I decided I would not snoop. Disappointing, I know.

The doctor had said to wake him up every two hours. I settled in on the floor in front of the couch and began my vigil. Thankfully, there was a *Doctor Who* marathon running, which helped to pass the time.

After my cursory sweep of his kitchen I realized I had nothing to feed him, and I didn't want to leave him on the off chance he took a bad turn. I called Viv and had her bring over soup and sandwiches.

Together we woke him. I checked his eyes and had Viv double-check them. She insisted on feeling the knot on his head, which was pretty impressive and made him wince when she touched it.

"I can design a hat to cover that if it doesn't go away," she offered.

"Thanks, I'll keep you posted," he said. I couldn't tell if he was being sincere or not. I suspected not.

Viv stayed and hunkered in to eat and watch television with us.

"So, who do you think attacked you?" she asked as we finished up the soup and I tossed the cartons in the garbage.

Harrison and I exchanged a look. We hadn't spoken of it, but I knew he was thinking the same thing I was: that it was too coincidental to have been a random robbery.

"I think it has something to do with the Grisbys," I said. I kept my gaze on Harrison's face. I wanted to see if he agreed with me.

Viv glanced at him and he gave a small nod. "It makes the most sense."

"Do you think it was the murderer?" she asked.

Harrison and I exchanged another glance. We both nodded. The realization made a shiver run down my spine. What if Harrison had been killed? Again I felt the sinking sensation in my chest. Guilt really is a heavy load, isn't it?

As if by mutual agreement, we didn't speak of it again. After a few hours, Harrison started to fade. Viv and I checked his pupils just as he was beginning to snore. They were okay.

"Are you going to stay the night?" Viv asked me. Her voice had a bit of innuendo in it, which I chose to ignore.

"I think I have to," I said. "The doctor said to wake him up every two hours for the first twenty-four. I'd feel awful if anything happened to him. Speaking of which, you're not walking home alone."

"I'll be fine," she said.

"No, if Harrison and I were followed from the funeral home and attacked, then they could be outside, lurking, waiting to strike again," I said.

Viv frowned at me. "Have you been watching the horror channel again?"

"No!" I lied.

I had watched it a few weeks ago by accident when I was flipping through channels, therefore it was unintentional and not my fault, so I wasn't going to cop to it. Besides I only watched the second half of Richard Kelly's *Donnie Darko*. Let's just say, giant creepy bunny and lesson learned.

Viv looked at me with a dubious expression so like Mim's, I almost confessed. Almost.

The doorbell rang, and I was relieved to lead her out. "There's your escort."

"What? You didn't call a cab, did you?" she asked. "That would be ridiculous."

She followed me down the stairs and I glanced out the window on the side of the door to be sure it was who I expected. It was. I opened the door and greeted Nick and Andre with hugs.

"Sweetie, what is happening?" Nick asked as he released me.

"Chaos," I said. "Viv will explain on the walk home."

I pushed Viv out the door. She glanced over her shoulder at me and I saw a frown crease her forehead.

"Lock up behind us. Call me immediately if you hear

any weird noises. Scratch that—call the police and then call me."

"Got it," I said.

"Scarlett?" Andre asked. He shouldered the umbrella I had insisted that he bring.

"No time to explain," I said. I made shooing motions with my hands. "Go quickly. Be careful. Call me when you get home."

The three of them hurried off the stoop and I locked the door behind them. I raced up the stairs to Harrison's apartment, which I also locked up tight and then hurried to the window to watch the three of them walk down the street until the trees obscured them from view.

Yes, we were probably all being a touch paranoid, but when I thought about Harrison's cement cabbage being whacked, I figured it was better to be defensive than dead.

Harrison stirred on the couch but didn't wake up. It was after eleven and finally fully dark outside. I flipped through a few channels, but I was televisioned out. My eyes were feeling heavy, so I decided to walk about the apartment and get the blood flowing. I did not intend to snoop. No, I didn't!

I'd already used his bathroom, so I knew the layout of that beige-tiled room and other than a towel dropped on the floor, it was pretty tidy for a bachelor pad. No spit stains on the faucet or anything. I wondered if he had a cleaning service.

The other two doors led to an office and a bedroom. The bedroom was neat, with bed made, dresser drawers pushed in, no clothes on the floor. I opened the closet door—don't judge, I was bored.

Suit jackets and shirts and slacks and ties all hung neatly on hangers. Shoes were lined up along the floor below. A wicker hamper sat at one end. A pair of undershorts—he was a boxer man—were on the floor beside it, obviously a missed shot into the basket.

I closed the closet door and surveyed the room. The one thing that struck me was that there were no pictures anywhere. No group shots of friends, no framed photo of his parents, no artwork, nothing. I glanced back out into the living room and noted there were no pictures there either.

Now I was curious. I thought about my own bedroom at Mim's. Granted it was trapped in adolescence with electric-pink walls and a Spice Girls poster, but I had also unpacked a picture of my folks and had photos of Mim and Viv sitting on the top of my bureau. I glanced at Harrison's large dresser. Nothing. Not even a comb.

This compelled me to look in the last room of the apartment, the office. A dark wood desk-bookshelf combination dominated the room and faced the windows. A closed laptop sat on a blotter. A crystal clock, which looked like something someone was given for ten years of service, sat on the right corner. The bookshelves were stuffed with titles like *Principles of Macroeconometric Modeling*. Yawn. But again, there was no indicator that a person actually lived here, no knickknacks, tchotchkes, sports team posters, nothing.

"Find anything of interest?" a voice asked from behind me.

I whirled around to see Harrison leaning against the doorjamb, watching me.

My heart was thumping hard in my chest, but I forced a laugh that came out as more of a squeak. "Sorry, looking for some reading material."

I gestured to the shelf behind me. "You seem to have cornered the market on the cure for insomnia, and I have to say your décor brings the word 'barren' to mind. I've seen cheap motel rooms that have more ambiance."

To my relief a smile tipped the corner of his mouth. "Sorry, when my girlfriend moved out, she took all of the good stuff with her."

He pushed off of the door frame and left the room. I was pretty sure my jaw had hit the floor with an audible smack. Harrison had lived with someone! When? Why didn't I know about this? Why hadn't he or Viv mentioned it? When did she leave? And most important, was she pretty? How pretty?

He disappeared into the bathroom and I waited in the hallway, pacing while trying to process this news. I was an idiot. He was twenty-nine years old. He was a handsome, successful economist who was gainfully employed and had an amazing flat. Of course he'd had a girlfriend.

The door opened and he came out smelling of mint toothpaste and wearing plaid pajama bottoms and a gray T-shirt.

"Let me check your eyes," I said. I pushed him under an overhead light.

"I'm fine, Scarlett," he said. "Really."

His pupils looked normal, but I followed him into his bedroom just to make sure he didn't keel over while climbing into the bed.

Naturally, I ignored him. "I'm going to crash on your couch. I'll be in to check on you every two hours just like the doc said. I've got the alarm on my phone set and everything."

He shook his head as he sank onto the mattress. "Look at you mothering me. Who'd have thought?"

"I have layers," I said.

I watched as he relaxed against his pillows. He gave a heavy sigh as his eyes shut. When he was halfway asleep, I leaned in close and whispered, "Why did you and your girl-friend break up?"

His eyes fluttered half open and he gestured me closer by crooking his finger at me. I leaned in, assuming it was a really good secret, since it had never been mentioned before.

He caught a hank of my hair in his hand and tugged me even closer. Our noses were practically touching when he said, "She didn't have big blue eyes or red hair. She didn't smell like sunshine and she didn't make me crazy."

Then he kissed me right on the mouth. It was swift and sweet, but it came with an electrical surge that I was pretty sure was going to leave scorch marks on the tips of my fingers. Holy wow!

I pulled back and so did he and then he gave me a slow smile and said, "I knew it."

Knew what? I stood gaping at him like a big idiot and what did he do? He fell asleep!

I backed out of the room as if he were a lion and I expected he might spring at me, which, judging by that kiss, if he touched me again, could cause a neighborhood black-out. Quietly, I closed the door and took his spot on the couch. The TV was off, but I stared at it anyway. Sleep seemed a very far way off, indeed.

I refused to dwell on what had just happened. He was loopy from taking a shot to the head. Surely, he couldn't be held accountable for his actions, and I had been caught by surprise, so I wasn't accountable either. These things happen and there was no reason to examine it further. Right? With any luck, we'd both forget all about it in the light of day.

To keep my mind off the sounds of the house settling, which bore an unnerving resemblance to the heavy tread of footsteps on stairs, and also to keep from scrutinizing the meaning behind accidental lip-locks, I forced myself to think about the Grisbys.

There was just no denying that the one with the most to gain from Geoffrey's death was Liam. If Tina was pregnant with a new heir, that would be a game changer for him. But would he actually try to murder a pregnant woman? The thought horrified.

When two hours had passed, and I'd begun to doze sitting up, I went back into the bedroom and roused Harrison. I don't think he was fully awake, but the nightstand light gave me enough illumination to see that his pupils were fine. It was now after one o'clock in the morning and I was pretty sure he was in the clear.

I scrounged a blanket and pillow from the closet in the office and made a nest for myself on his big squashy couch. I put my phone on the table so I would hear the alarm go off in two hours. I figured I only needed to check Harrison one more time and then I could go. Truth be told, I dreaded facing him in the light of day and planned to avoid it for as long as possible.

It took me a while to hear my alarm going off. I had to

fight the blanket off of me and when I sat up, I had no idea where I was. The citrusy bay rum man smell that was distinctly Harrison tickled my nose, and then it all came rushing back and I rested my head in my hand. I was officially exhausted.

I dragged myself off of the couch and went into the bedroom. Harrison was asleep on his side. I switched on the lamp and leaned over him.

"Harrison, wake up," I whispered.

He bolted awake with a gruff cry and before I could move he grabbed me by the arms and yanked me over him and onto the bed. I sank into the soft downy comforter with him looming over me.

"Hey!" I cried. "It's me, Scarlett. I'm just checking you for a concussion."

He frowned at me and then let out a sigh and rolled away. The bed was so soft, I was sure I could have melted right into it, becoming just another soft feather in the duvet. Sheer force of will made me drag myself upright.

"I was having the weirdest dream," he said and ran a hand through his hair. "Or was it?"

"Let me see your eyes," I said. I turned his head toward the light and leaned over him. "They look normal. How does your noggin feel?"

Harrison felt the bump and winced. "It only hurts when I touch it."

"Do you feel dizzy at all?" I asked.

His gaze moved over my face and lingered on my mouth. "Not because of my head injury."

I felt my face get hot and I began to scoot toward the edge

243

of the bed. Did he mean . . . ? No, it was best not to think on it, and it was definitely time to go.

"Here," he said. He took the extra pillows and put them in the middle of the bed. "You sleep on that side. The couch is comfortable, but there's nothing like a bed."

My eyes burned from sleep deprivation. Gritty and sore, all my lids wanted to do was close. I didn't have enough stamina to argue, but still I waffled.

"I promise you'll be safe here," he said. "Besides I don't like the idea of you being out there where I can't watch over you."

"All right," I said. "But if you put one toe over on my side, I will smack it back. Clear?"

"Crystal," he said. He looked like he was trying not to smile. It didn't matter. He could have busted out a belly laugh and I wouldn't have noticed. I was unconscious before my head even hit the pillow.

I awoke to the sound of rain peppering the windowpane and gray sunlight trying without much success to peer through the window. Again, it took me a moment to get my bearings.

This was not my bed. It was Harrison's. The thought brought me snap upright like a soldier to attention. I glanced at the other side of the bed only to find it empty. Over the sound of the rain, I heard water running and realized Harrison must be in the shower.

This filled me with such an adolescent sense of awkwardness that I bolted out of the bed and hurried into the living room to find my shoes. I could feel myself practically in a panic as I gathered my jacket and purse, debated scribbling a note, then rejected the idea in favor of sneaking out of his house before he came out of the bathroom.

What if he came out wearing only a towel? I did not think our acquaintanceship was ready for that. Then again, he had kissed me. What did that mean? Had he just been addled? Did he even remember?

The sound of water stopped and I went into a full-on anxiety attack. I unlocked his door and hurried out into the hall, looking no doubt like a woman who had just come from a one-night stand. *Oh, good grief! Do not let me run into any of his neighbors*, I prayed, or *I'll never be able to show my face over here again.*

Luck was with me as I hobbled down the stairs, trying to pull on my shoes while slinging my purse over my shoulder. In seconds, I was out the front door into the cold, wet morning without an umbrella. I had the feeling it was the perfect omen for how my day was going to go.

I trudged the five-minute walk home, knowing that by the time I got to the shop I was going to look like a drowned rat, which, given what awaited me, might have been my preferred outcome.

Chapter 25

When I arrived at the hat shop, it was to find Nick and Andre sitting in the back room with Viv. The shop hadn't opened yet, and they seemed to be enjoying a pot of tea and a pile of scones with clotted cream.

"A bit early in the day for a sweet tea, isn't it?" I asked.

"Not when there is gossip to be had," Nick said. "So tell us was it everything you'd hoped for?"

"Was what everything I'd hoped for?" I asked.

Viv pursed her lips and glanced at the window as if examining the pattern of the rain on the glass.

"You know," Andre said, and he wiggled his eyebrows at me. "You and Harrison?"

"He was injured!" I protested. "I was merely keeping an eye on him."

"Are you blushing?" Viv asked. She sounded as ridiculous as the other two.

"No!" I cried. Which was a total lie. I'm a redhead and I could feel how hot my face was. I figured on the mortification scale I was probably hovering around an eight or an eight point five. "Listen, Harrison could have died because he saved me from an attacker. There was nothing romantic about it. I merely stayed with him to repay the debt."

They all looked at me as if I was not fooling them, not even a little. Argh.

"Of course, you're right. We shouldn't tease," Nick said. He patted the empty chair beside him. "Would you like some tea?"

"Yes, please," I said. I was really going to have to get them all drinking coffee, at least in the morning.

"Then you can tell us all about your night's adventure," he said.

I rolled my eyes. With friends like these, who needed siblings?

My phone chirped in my purse. I thought about ignoring it but then thought it might give me the distraction I needed.

I retrieved it from my bag and opened up the screen to read the incoming text. It was from Harrison. It did not read happy. He wanted to know where I was immediately.

"Excuse me," I said. I quickly texted back that I was just fine and then redirected by asking how he was.

Viv handed me my tea and my phone chimed again.

Andre peeked over my shoulder and I glowered at him and shifted my seat.

"It's from him," he said to the others.

"He just wants to know that I got home okay," I said. "Okay?"

They all glanced away but I could see them exchanging smiles. Ugh, I felt like I was in middle school again.

Harrison ignored my question and texted that he had to go into the office but was planning to stop by the shop with Detective Inspector Finchley to talk about the attack, among other things. A surge of panic hit me. Among other things? That couldn't be good.

I texted back a sure-no-problem text in the hope that it would read casual and not freaked out. Then I put my phone away.

"Well, if you won't gossip about you and Harrison," Nick said, "you have to tell us what's happening with the Grisbys. Andre told me that was Tina Grisby you were with yesterday."

"It was," I said. "Poor thing. Her husband was murdered and now she's pregnant and she thinks someone is trying to kill her."

"Pregnant?" Nick asked. He looked perplexed. "Are you sure?"

"Quite sure," I said. "Well, at least that's what she told me."

"I was telling Andre last night that I know I've seen her before," Nick said. "In fact, I'm quite sure of it, and I must say I find it hard to believe that she's pregnant."

"Why?" I asked.

"Because when I saw her, she was with her lover—her *lady* lover," Nick said.

"What?" Viv asked. "And you didn't tell me before?"

"We were too busy gossiping about—" Nick's voice broke off when he glanced at me.

"Uh-huh," I said. I decided to let it pass. "Are you absolutely sure? Where and when did you see her?"

"In Hyde Park, having a picnic in the tall grass," he said. "And yes, I am quite sure."

I glanced at Viv. This certainly changed everything.

"Can you describe the woman she was with?" I asked.

"Yes, it struck me that she and Tina had a similar look, but where Tina is vivacious the other was reticent," Nick said. "She was pale and mousy-looking with long brown hair and glasses. Honestly, I never would have put them together if I hadn't seen it for myself."

Mousy. Hadn't I thought the same thing when I'd met Rose Grisby for the first time? Could it be?

I picked up my phone. There was another text message from Harrison. I ignored it and opened the Internet. The screen was small but I managed to bring up a picture of Rose Grisby from the newspaper report about her father's funeral. I enlarged the picture and held it out to Nick.

"That's her!" he cried.

I turned to Viv. "It all makes sense. If Tina and Rose are a couple, then I'm betting they killed off Geoffrey not only so they could be together, but if Tina is pregnant, they can be together and inherit the entire estate."

"You need to call Inspector Finchley," Viv said. "This could solve his case."

"You're right," I said. But it didn't feel right. I just couldn't reconcile the woman who had sought me out for help as a murderer. "Or I could go and talk to Tina myself and make sure we're not making any false accusations."

"Scarlett, no," Andre said. He sounded as bossy as Harrison and I found I didn't like that tone any more from him. "You and Harrison were attacked. It could have been Rose or Tina or some thug they hired. Now, you can't put yourself in harm's way again. There is a fortune at stake here and these people are playing dirty. They're obviously not above harming anyone who gets in their way."

"But it doesn't make sense," I protested. "Why would Tina ask me to get her a safe place in the States if she's in on the murder?"

"She's trying to throw you off by playing the victim," Andre said.

"He's right," Nick said. Andre gave him a grateful look.

"Please, Scarlett," Viv said. "I really must insist that you be sensible about this."

I sighed. My clothes were still damp; my hair was a tangled soppy mess. I took a long, bracing sip of tea.

"All right," I said. "I'm just going to dry off and change and then I'll call Finchley."

"That's my girl," Andre said.

Nick and Viv smiled at me. As I left the back room and headed into the shop, my gaze lingered on Ferd, the carved wooden bird that sat on the top of Mim's old armoire. He always reminded me of Mim—she loved that old wardrobe— and I wondered what she would do in my place.

Mim had been a force of nature. If Viv and I had impulse control issues, it was because it was stamped in our DNA right down the line from Mim. I did mean to go and dry off and call the inspector, really I did, but the more I thought about it, the more I wanted to see Tina for myself. I just couldn't believe she was a murderer, and if it wasn't her, then she could very well be in terrible danger.

"Don't tell," I whispered to Ferd and then I headed out the front door and back out into the rain.

Chapter 26

The gate at the Grisby mansion on Bishops Avenue was closed. This presented me with a variety of options. I could hit the buzzer on the gate and hope that Buckley would remember me and let me in. I could try to scale the fence and have them call the police on me. I could slip around the yard looking for an alternate entrance and risk being eaten by guard dogs. Yeah, none of these options held much promise.

I decided to use my natural charm and vivacity and see if I could work my magic on Buckley. If that failed, then I'd scale the fence.

I hit the buzzer. Buckley's voice answered within moments.

"Grisby Hall, how may I help you?"

"Good day, Buckley." I put a lot of pep in my greeting.

"This is Scarlett Parker, from Mim's Whims. I'm here to see Tina Grisby."

"Hello, Ms. Parker," he said. "One moment, please."

Well, at least he sounded like he remembered me. I waited.

"I'm sorry, Ms. Parker, but Mrs. Grisby isn't in," he said. He sounded regretful.

I noticed there was a camera over the buzzer. No doubt he could see me getting drenched. I decided to work it, and I sneezed and then shivered.

"Are you quite sure?" I asked. *Achoo!* "We had an appointment. Maybe she forgot."

"She has been rather . . . well, that could be," he said. "Here, come on in and dry off and we'll get this sorted."

"Oh, thank you, Buckley," I said. Yes, I was absolutely fine with pity being his motivation to help me.

As the gates swung open and I hurried down the drive toward the house, I didn't think I would have to do much to make myself even more pitiful than I already was. I even sneezed for real.

Buckley met me at the front door with two big fluffy towels.

"Here you are," he said. "Mrs. Eudora Grisby is in the drawing room if you'd like to join her while I track down Mrs. Tina Grisby."

"Oh, that would be nice," I said.

I followed Buckley down the hallway of family portraits into a cozy room that was exactly what you'd picture in an English mansion. It had two plush wing chairs in front of a crackling fire and a gorgeous Oriental rug on the floor. The walls were dark wood paneling with built-in lighted shelves to display artifacts from all over the world.

"What's this?" Dotty asked as I came into the room with Buckley. I had draped one towel around my neck and was using the other to dry my hair.

"Ms. Parker is here to see Mrs. Tina," he said. His voice was gentle. "I thought she might keep you company and warm up by the fire."

"Of course," Dotty said. She did not look as happy to see me as usual and I wondered if she recognized me without Viv beside me.

"I'll return shortly," Buckley said.

"Thank you, Buckley, for everything," I said.

I moved to stand before the fire and let its heat wash over me in pleasurable waves. I was cold all the way down to my bones and I had begun to think I would never be warm again.

"Thank you for inviting me in," I said.

"I didn't invite you," Dotty said. She arched one eyebrow at me and I got the distinct feeling she was very unhappy with my presence.

"I'm Viv's cousin," I said. "I mean Ginny's."

"I know who you are," she said. She didn't sound happy about it. "You're a redhead. It's been my observation that redheads are sly and untrustworthy."

I slowly lowered the towel from my hair. Okay, this was awkward. "I have to disagree."

"You're husband stealers, that's what you are," she snapped.

Oh! My mind flashed to the Wonderland tea and the

scene Cara Whittles had made about being Mr. Grisby's real wife and heir.

"Well, I can see how you might not like redheads," I said. "But we're not all like that."

It was then that I noticed the cross-stitch in her hands. She was gripping the round frame so tightly, she was pulling the fabric out of it.

"Why?" she snapped. "Why did you do it?"

I held the towel in front of me. You know, as if it could provide buffer from her rage.

"Do what?" I asked. I eyed the door that Buckley had shut behind him. I wasn't too keen on being in a closed room with Dotty just now.

"Why did you steal my husband?" she asked. Her eyes crackled with fire and I had a feeling if she were a few years younger, she'd have tried to snatch the hair right off of my head.

"Dotty, you have me mistaken with someone else," I said. "I'm not Cara Whittles. I'm Scarlett. I work at Mim's Whims. I'm Ginny's granddaughter."

"Oh." Dotty's eyes went wide.

She glanced down at her lap. She looked at her stitchery as if she'd never seen it before. Then she glanced up at me and her eyes became unfocused again. I felt my stomach drop. This was not going well.

"I bore his children," she said. "Four. Three girls and a boy, his heir."

"I know," I said. "I helped with the Wonderland tea—"

"Quiet!" she roared. She rose from her seat and threw her cross-stitch across the room. She was so angry she was

shaking. "You are nothing! Nothing! You bore him no children. You were just a plaything, a silly little plaything."

"Dotty, stop!" I cried. "I am not her. I did not steal your
husband."

"Don't you lie to me!" she cried.

"I'm not!"

She took a step forward and I ducked behind one of the
wing chairs.

"Well, I had the last laugh. Ha!" She barked as if to prove
she was laughing. It did not sound even remotely like a
humorous chuckle to me. "I killed him. I ended his miserable self-centered life."

I clutched the top of the chair to steady myself. It couldn't
be true. Her husband had died in Italy.

"What are you saying, Dotty?"

"His phobia about germs, his insistence on everything
being just so, it was maddening," she said. "He always
smelled like disinfectant." She wrinkled her nose. "He abandoned me! It was no more than he deserved!"

It felt as if time stopped and with it my ability to breathe.
It couldn't be true what she was saying. But then I thought
about how she believed Viv was Mim and I was Cara. Could
it be that she thought Geoffrey her son had been Geoffrey
her husband? And in her rage over his desertion from their
life, had she murdered him, not realizing she was actually
killing her own son?

"Who are you talking about, Dotty?" I asked.

She looked at me as if she thought I was as dumb as dirt.
Then she made an oh-poor-baby face.

"What's the matter?" she asked. "Do you miss your lover?"

"I am not nor was I ever Geoffrey Grisby's lover," I said. How could I convince her? How could I make her stop seeing me as a redhead?

I glanced at the towel around my neck and quickly lowered my head and wrapped the towel around it. If it was my red hair that was confusing her, I needed to hide it. "Look at me. I am Ginny, your friend the milliner. Ginny."

My resemblance to Mim was mostly in my large blue eyes. I had freckles, which Mim had never had, but we had the same fair complexion and heart-shaped face. In fact, when Viv and I were very young and wore hats covering our hair, we were frequently thought to be sisters.

Dotty frowned at me. Then her eyes cleared and she held out her hands.

"Oh, Ginny, you have to help me," she said. "I've done a horrible thing. I killed my Geoffrey."

I took her hands in mine and helped her into a seat. I sat across from her and said, "It's all right, Dotty; just tell me what happened."

Unfortunately, the towel slid off of my head and landed in a heap on the floor.

"You!" Dotty cried. She snatched her hands away from me and leapt from her seat.

I snatched the towel off of the floor and tried to wrap my hair back up, but a sharp whack on my shoulder made my arm go numb.

"Ouch!" I yelped.

I glanced up to see that Dotty had grabbed one of the iron pokers off of the stand by the hearth. For a lady of advanced years, she wielded it like she knew how to poke a fire or knock out an unsuspecting shopkeeper, who would be me.

I scurried back from her and she brought it down right where I'd been standing. It smacked into the carpet and left a nasty black mark that I knew was not going to endear either of us to Buckley.

"Dotty, you've got it wrong," I said. I danced backward, avoiding her wild swings. I yanked the towel up around my head as I went. "Look at me. Look at my eyes. Ginny. Remember?"

Dotty stopped and looked at me. Her eyes went fuzzy and she dropped the poker. I kicked it away. This time when I took her hands it was to make sure she didn't grab anything else to whack me with. My shoulder smarted and my arm still tingled.

I half dragged, half led her to the door. I didn't care if I had to scream the house down. I wanted backup and someone was going to bring it. My preference would have been Buckley, but about now I'd be just as happy to see a gardener or a postman. Anyone.

"I'm so confused," she said. She looked forlorn and I felt for her—truly, I did—but I had to know.

"You know, don't you," I said. "It wasn't your husband that was poisoned, Dotty; it was your son."

To my surprise, her eyes filled with tears and she hung her head and sobbed. Not delicate little sobs, but great big wrenching waves of grief that swept up from her epicenter and roared out like a tsunami of pain.

"I tried to tell him that it felt wrong," she cried. "I remembered that my Geoffrey wasn't the bad Geoffrey, but he told me that Geoffrey was going to take off with his lover to Italy again and that the evil redhead would make sure we lost everything. I thought we should just poison her, but he said Geoffrey would cut us off if we harmed his lover."

We paused by the closed door. I let go of one of her hands so that I could turn the knob. I patted her awkwardly on the shoulder as she continued to weep. Poor Dotty. Someone had used her own addled sense of time and person against her.

"Dotty, who is 'he'? Who told you that you were poisoning your husband?"

She glanced away from me as if afraid to answer.

"Did Tina have anything to do with it?"

"What?" Dotty asked. "Tina? No. She's going to have a baby, you know: the next heir."

"Actually, no, she's not," a voice said.

Chapter 27

"George!" I cried. "Am I glad to see you."

He ignored me and looked at Dotty.

"Gram, what are you doing with her?" he asked. He reached out and snatched the towel off of my head then he looked at me. "Gram doesn't like redheads, but I've always been rather partial to them."

He smiled at me and for the first time I noted that there was no warmth in his smile. In fact, it chilled me to the bone. I felt Dotty recoil from me as soon as my hair was revealed, but I refused to let go of her hand until I knew what was happening.

Abruptly, I remembered my conversation with Harrison and Viv, about how George had tried to keep Cara from being arrested, and George's comment when we first met about how he liked redheads. I had thought he was flattering me, but what if I wasn't the redhead to whom he'd been referring?

"You like redheads. You studied in Italy," I said. "You—"

I stumbled. I wasn't sure how to put into words what I suspected.

"Had an affair with my grandfather's mistress?" he asked. "Yes, yes, I did."

"George!" Dotty cried. "How could you?"

"What can I say, Gram?" he asked. He spread his hands wide. "I can see why Gramps left you for her. She is glorious."

Dotty sucked in a breath and I knew George had just scored a direct hit.

"We had a bond, you see," George said. "She knew that Gramps was going to leave her nothing, not even the villa that had been her home for thirty years, and I knew that Geoffrey was never going to be man enough to impregnate his pretty young wife. Turned out I was wrong about that."

He made a mock alarmed look that reminded me of the George I'd known before and would have made me laugh if I weren't scared out of my wits.

"So after Gramps died, we took care of Geoffrey. Gram helped." He reached forward and cupped her chin. "It felt good plotting the murder of the man who had done you wrong all those years ago, didn't it, Gram?"

She whimpered and tried to pull her chin out of his hold.

"Sadly, those shaky old hands of yours weren't much help loading up Uncle Geoffrey's bath products with poison, were they?" He clucked with disappointment and released her. "We had hoped to kill him slowly over time, but then Cara got impatient, so we decided to have him drink it on down. The tea party was an excellent opportunity."

"But how could you get him to drink it?" I asked. "It smells horrible and it burns."

"When you're a germ-phobic nutter, dousing yourself in disinfectant all day, you build up an immunity to the astringent smell," he said. "Besides, given the choice between being poisoned or shot, which would you choose?"

"Poison," I said. My mouth was so dry it was hard to speak. "Because you might be able to get help in time."

"Beautiful thing about formaldehyde," George said. "It was easily acquired—thank you, Busker and Sons—and it's corrosive. Poor Geoffrey thought he could call for help, but no, his throat swelled shut. After a few convulsions, his entire system shut down."

"So it was you," I said. "But why? You won't even inherit."

He shrugged.

"I've been managing Liam since the day I climbed out of the womb. He's good looking, but there's not much going on up here, if you know what I mean," he said and he tapped his temple. "I assured Cara that once Liam inherited the estate, it would really be me taking charge. Everything was going so well until Tina turned up pregnant and befriended *you*."

He said this as if it were inexplicable.

"You were the one who attacked me and my friend yesterday," I said.

"That's what snooping will get you," he said. "Why couldn't you just leave it alone?"

"Because Tina asked for my help," I said.

"Oh please," he scoffed. "She doesn't need anyone's help. She's a gold digger of the first order. Do you really think she married Geoffrey, twenty years her senior and as neurotic as a squirrel, for love?"

"It's been known to happen," I said. "You don't choose who you fall in love with."

He studied me for a moment. I didn't like the look in his hazel eyes. It was cold and predatory, and it made me shiver.

"Don't mistake me, Scarlett," he said. He reached forward and grabbed a lock of my hair. He twined it around his finger and pulled me close. My hand tightened on Dotty's as if she could anchor me from the evil that was pulling me forward. "I was really looking forward to getting to know you."

The innuendo in his words as he sniffed my hair made my stomach twist. I was so not letting him touch me. Ever.

I stomped on his foot. Hard. He yelped and I hit him in the chest with my elbow. Thankfully, he let go of my hair, but I wouldn't have cared if he'd ripped it out by the roots. I was not staying here another second.

"Buckley!" I screamed. "Buckley, help!"

I began to run, dragging Dotty with me, and to my surprise, she came.

"He won't be of any use to you," George called as he hobbled after us.

It was ominous the way he said it, and now I was terrified for Buckley as well. I yanked Dotty out the door and down the hallway. We stepped into the ornate foyer when Cara Whittles rushed out from the hallway across from ours. In her well-manicured hand, which sparkled with jewel-encrusted rings, she held a lethal-looking gun, and it was pointed right at me.

"You!" Dotty cried. She yanked her hand out of mine and charged forward, heedless of the gun, looking like she was going to smack down the redheaded tart.

"Dotty!" I grabbed her hand and held her back. "She has a gun."

"I'll stuff it down her throat," Dotty said.

Cara frowned as if she hadn't quite expected Dotty to be so feisty. Her hand shook and I wondered how comfortable she was with this whole situation.

"Don't shoot them here," George said as he joined us. He sounded very matter-of-fact about us being shot. This did not give me the warm fuzzies, as you can imagine.

"If you shoot us at all, you'll go to jail," I said. I looked over the voluptuous woman in her skinny jeans and wedge sandals with a man's dress shirt half buttoned over her purple bra. It appeared she and George had been enjoying a little alone time before I came along. "There are no beauty parlors in jail. No makeup, no jewelry, no spas."

She visibly paled with every word I spoke. Oh yeah, I was getting her where she lived.

"George, make her stop!" Cara demanded. "I don't want to hear her speak."

George made a fist and tapped my jaw with it. I flinched and he smiled.

"Next time, I won't be so gentle," he said.

Cara gave me a triumphant look and I studied her face. Her age was beginning to show in little wrinkles by her eyes and the sag behind her jawline. Her beauty was fading. She had to know it. It was very clear why she'd leeched on to George. If she could get him to take care of her, all of her problems would be solved.

"Why did you make such a scene at the tea?" I asked.

George lurched at me as if he'd hit me, but I held up my hand to ward him off.

"No, I really want to know," I said. "Weren't you worried that the police would be onto Cara as a murderess if she threatened Geoffrey?"

"No," George said. Then he grinned and again I was struck by how his mirth lacked any discernible warmth. How had I missed that?

"For the very simple reason that we knew Geoffrey was going to die while she was in police custody," George explained. "Liam insisted she be arrested, and I gave a token protest to seem to be the caring sort. It gave her the ultimate alibi. And, of course, who would suspect me? I'm the lesser brother, the younger one, who wasn't going to inherit—the throwaway child, if you will."

It was then that I noticed Dotty sidling around the foyer moving oh-so-slowly behind Cara. She had the same manic glint in her eye that I'd been on the receiving end of when she couldn't see past my hair color.

"George, that's not true!" Cara protested. "You're the strong one, the smart one, the one who will take control of the Grisby fortune."

"Well, you should know, Cara," I said. "I'm sure you tried on all of the other Grisby men. Did Liam and Geoffrey Junior reject you flat-out? Was George really the best fit or was he the only one interested in sloppy seconds?"

This time the back of George's hand connected hard with my mouth. My upper lip was smashed against my teeth and my cheek felt like it had been hit with a hammer. The blow staggered me, knocking me off my feet.

When George would have followed it with a kick, a horrific crash followed by a shriek that was cut off in midpitch interrupted his momentum and he spun around just in time to see Dotty stagger back from where she had smashed a large crystal vase over Cara's head.

Cara lay unconscious in a puddle of water and glass shards with pink and white roses scattered all around her.

Dotty and George glared at each other over the body.

"Gram, you daft old bag, what the hell are you doing?" he roared.

I scrambled forward to get the gun. George stopped me by stepping on my arm and pinning it to the floor.

"Think again, love," he snapped.

I wondered if I could take him, and I thought about punching him in the back of the leg to see if I could bring him down, but just then the front door burst open and Inspector Finchley appeared with a pack of uniforms behind him.

"Step off the lady, Mr. Mercer," Finchley ordered.

George lifted his foot off and gave the detective a bland look. "I'm sure this looks out of sorts, but I can explain."

"Mother!" From behind the officers Daphne, Lily and Rose charged into the house. "Are you all right? What's happened?"

"George killed Geoffrey," Dotty said. "And I think I helped."

She promptly burst into tears and threw herself into Daphne's arms. Daphne looked over her mother's head at her son and I saw it in her face: the singular lack of surprise. It was then that I realized Daphne knew. She knew what her son was capable of and had probably always known.

"Detective Inspector Finchley, you're going to want to arrest my son for the murder of my brother," she said.

"Oh, that's right," George snapped. "Come in here and let me take the fall. What? Are you hoping your precious Liam still has a chance to inherit?"

"No, I'm hoping Tina has a healthy baby boy, who inherits," Daphne said.

"How can you say that?" George cried. "Don't you see? This way we would have had it all. Isn't that what you wanted? Haven't you been yelling about how it is rightfully yours because you are the oldest and how your dear brother was screwing you out of what should have gone to your sons?"

"No, not my sons," she said.

"Oh, of course!" George barked with bitter laughter. "Just your *son*, your one precious shining golden son, Liam. Liam the perfect. Liam the glorious. Does the sun even know how to rise without Liam?"

Daphne gave him a sad look. "My one mentally healthy son, yes."

"I'm not crazy," George protested. "Just because Gram is daft, does not mean I am. You have to stop saying that. Cara didn't think I was crazy. She thought I was strong and handsome and brave."

"You murdered your uncle!" Daphne's composure

cracked and she shrieked at him. Lily and Rose gave her shocked looks, but Daphne's gaze never left her son. "If that's not sick, what is? Your father is on his way here from the States. We'll do whatever we can for you, George."

"But don't you see I did it for you?" George's voice grew soft and childlike. "I did it for you, Mommy."

"Oh God," Daphne cried. She pushed Dotty into Rose's arms and spun away. Lily caught her and held her and Daphne began to sob on Lily's shoulder.

Lily gestured for the police to take George away and they snatched him by the arms and led him down the hall. I watched from my spot on the floor, riveted by the unfolding family drama.

The front door opened wider and Tina pushed her way into the room. She saw me on the floor and she hurried over to help me up.

"Scarlett, I was just at the shop and Viv told me that she thought you'd come here to see me—what were you thinking? You could have been killed. Oh heavens, it would have been all my fault," she wailed.

She steadied me on my feet and behind her I saw a flash of long blonde hair, and then Viv was hugging me, shaking me, and then hugging me again.

"You are such an idiot," she said.

Given the situation, I knew better than to argue, and instead I hugged my dear cousin back in a grip that I was pretty sure strangled.

An ambulance was called for Cara. I mentioned that I was worried about Buckley and another uniform went looking for him and found him unconscious in the kitchen. He had a knot on his head that needed to be looked at, but otherwise he appeared okay.

We took up residence in one of the back rooms. I held an ice pack to my swollen lip while Dotty told her rather scattered version of events to the police and I tried to fill in where I could. Finchley looked supremely unhappy with me, but he was so busy taking down the facts that he didn't pause to lecture me.

Through the open door, I saw Liam arrive. He led Viv to the side of the room to talk. He was visibly rattled, and I saw her give him a bracing hug before he joined his mother.

When she joined me, I asked, "All right, Viv?"

"I will be," she said. "Poor Liam. He knew his brother resented being the second born, but he had no idea that it had festered so."

I gave her a sympathetic half hug. "Probably, it wouldn't have if he hadn't had the misfortune to hook up with Cara the master manipulator."

"Maybe." Viv shrugged. "Or maybe the demon was inside of him all along. His mother certainly seems to think so."

"Or did his mother contribute to it by always favoring her older son?" I asked.

"What a mess," Viv said.

"Agreed." I glanced at her. She hadn't yelled at me for ditching and coming here, and she certainly had every reason to do so. "I'm sorry I left the shop without telling you. I just knew that I had to see Tina, and you all seemed determined to stop me."

"Impulse control," Viv sighed. "Harrison says we have none."

"Harrison?" I asked. I felt my heart thump hard in my chest. "When did you speak to Harrison?"

"I called him while you were holed up with Finchley."

I swallowed hard. "Did he sound mad?"

"After he stopped yelling, no, not so much," she said. "He said he'll be over later to speak to you."

"Did he say anything else?" I asked, trying to sound casual.

Viv turned and looked at me. She was studying my face intently. "Should he have?"

"No!" I said. "Not at all."

"Hmm." Viv hummed but said nothing more.

Tina approached us hesitantly and I noted that Rose followed closely behind her as if not wanting to let her out of her sight.

"Is it sorted?" Tina asked.

"As much as it can be," I said. "Apparently, George was in cahoots with Cara to murder Geoffrey and take over the estate. He was convinced he could manage his brother, but he didn't expect you to be pregnant."

"Yes, I imagine that was a surprise," Tina said. "Among other things."

I gestured between her and Rose. "So, how long have you two been a couple?" They gave each other a wary glance and looked like they would deny it.

"My friend Nick, the one in the orange jogging suit, saw you two picnicking in Hyde Park," I said.

Tina took a deep breath and then sighed. "We . . . It just sort of happened over the past few months."

"We didn't mean to fall in love," Rose said. "We didn't want to hurt anyone, but there it is."

I studied Rose. When she looked at Tina, her face lost its submissive pallor and became flushed with affection. It was a good look on her.

"Geoffrey became increasingly difficult over the past few months, always pressuring me to have a baby," she said. "I was so sad and lonely and Rose was so kind and helpful and then one day I realized that I was in love with her."

"We planned to tell Geoffrey and leave together to go live on the continent, but then I discovered I was pregnant," Tina said.

"Geoffrey would have fought us if he'd known," Rose said. "So we kept it quiet, trying to plan what to do and then the tea happened and he was murdered. We never wanted that. Never."

Rose looked miserable and I couldn't help but feel for her. Falling in love with her brother's wife had to have been horrifying but then to have him murdered on top of it. What a mess.

"Ms. Parker," Inspector Finchley said as he approached. "You are free to go—for now."

"Thank you, Inspector," I said. I glanced at the wreckage in the foyer and had to ask, "What will happen to Dotty?"

Finchley gave me a hard look. "That's for the Crown Prosecutor to decide."

"But she's not all there, is she?" I asked. Finchley continued to stare at me. "And she did save my life."

Finchley did not look as if he thought this was as big of a deal as I did.

"I'm sure you'll get an opportunity to speak on her behalf," he said. With a nod, he left us.

"Thank you," Rose said. "I'm sure George played on Mother's confusion and manipulated her into helping him."

"It's the least I can do," I said, "since I thought you two were Geoffrey's killers."

"No!" Tina looked aghast.

"I'm so sorry," I said. "But when Nick said you were a couple, I thought—"

Rose put her arm around Tina and hugged her close. "We do look to have motive."

"I suppose we do," Tina said. Still, the look she gave me was reproachful.

"Well, I did come here to talk to you first," I said. "I didn't call the police."

"Why not?" Tina asked.

"I just couldn't believe it," I said. "I didn't believe that you could kill anyone."

At that, she stepped forward and hugged me. "All is forgiven, then."

I hugged her back. Now I could only hope that the rest of the people in my life were as generous as Tina Grisby.

Chapter 28

They were not. It started with Fee, who was outraged that I had gone off half-cocked, as she put it, and nearly gotten myself killed.

"You scared us to death, yeah?" she cried.

"I'm sorry," I said. I leaned over toward Viv, who was sitting beside me on the floor in front of the fireplace in our flat above the shop. "Was I this hard on you when you disappeared to Africa a few months ago?"

"Worse," she said.

"I'm sorry," I said. I felt like my vocabulary had been whittled down to just those two words.

"You can stop saying that now," she said. "To me, anyway. I forgive you. I understand the impulse thing. The others, I'm not so sure."

"Thank you," I said.

Down below the shop was closed. The rain was pouring outside, making the evening sky dark and gray. Viv, Fee and I had escaped upstairs to enjoy a glass of wine by the fire.

Andre and Nick showed up shortly after that, bearing a box of raspberry and pear tarts. The raspberry was my favorite, as it had a thick layer of cream beneath the raspberries that tasted just heavenly with the crunchy, buttery pie crust.

When I reached inside the box, Andre smacked my hand away. "Those are for after dinner, assuming we let you have any dessert. I am still very unhappy with you, Scarlett."

"I'm sorry," I said. I glanced at Nick and puffed out my lower lip just slightly and batted my eyes. "You forgive me, don't you?"

"Oh no, you don't," he said. "Puppy eyes do not work on me. I am immune. What were you thinking? You could have been killed. No, don't speak. Save it for dinner, when we're all here."

I glanced over my shoulder at Viv. "All here? We're expecting more company?"

"Harrison is coming over with food," she said.

A flare of alarm coursed through me. "Cooking with his head injury? Is that wise?"

"I think he's picking up takeaway," Viv said. "He said something about braised pork, black pudding and apple three ways."

Okay, I can admit it. If he brought food, I was absolutely letting him in, damn the consequences, which I expected would be significant.

Nick poured wine for us all and I sipped from my glass while the others chattered about the day's events. Shortly after, the door to the apartment opened and in came Harrison bearing several bags of carryout food.

Nick and Andre popped up to help him. Viv and Fee joined them, but I stayed by the fire. I watched Viv kiss Harrison's cheek and check his bump. He winced. Fee kissed his cheek, too. They exchanged a smile and I felt a tiny spurt of jealousy ignite in my chest. What was going on between them, anyway? They made goo-goo eyes at each other, but then he kissed me. What was that about?

Maybe he didn't remember kissing me. Maybe he had been loopy from the bump on his head. Oh, horror! Maybe he thought I was Fee and the kiss hadn't even been meant for me!

"So, how is our reigning hero?" Nick asked Harrison.

"Yes, how is the noggin?" Andre asked. "Did Scarlett nurse you back to health?"

It was then that Harrison's gaze sought me out. His green eyes were positively magnetic, and I couldn't look away even when I tried. I felt my mouth go dry. Did he remember?

"Yes, yes, she did," he said.

"Well, since you were so gallant in saving her life, I suppose it was the least she could do," Nick said.

"Oh, I brought those pictures you bought at the opening," Andre said. "They're all wrapped up over there."

He gestured at three brown-wrapped packages leaning against the far wall.

"Brilliant," Harrison said. "It's been pointed out to me that my flat has less warmth than a low-budget hotel room."

He moved into the kitchen area and began to help Viv gather plates and silverware. The table only sat four, so it seemed by mutual agreement that we would all eat picnic style in front of the fire.

Viv spread a large tablecloth on the floor and Andre opened up more wine. The boxes of takeaway were placed in the center, and everyone helped themselves.

Fee sliced up a loaf of fresh bread that Viv and I had picked up at Saturday's market. Nick scrounged in our refrigerator until he found the fixings for a salad. It was mostly made of sliced cucumbers and tomatoes with crumbled feta cheese on top, but no one seemed to mind.

"Well, now that we're all here, Scarlett, you have to tell us everything from the very beginning," Nick said. "Do not skip out on any details."

"Fine," I said. I put my fork back down on my plate. I glanced around to find everyone watching me. I realized I had to make this good but also much less life-threatening if I wanted their forgiveness.

So I launched into what one might call the Disney version of the events that transpired, starting with my need to see Tina, then George admitting he had attacked Harrison and me, and wrapping up with Dotty bashing Cara on the head after George had admitted that he and Cara were in cahoots to take over the Grisby fortune.

My audience was rapt and when I finished, Nick refilled my wineglass, this telling me more than anything else that all was forgiven, at least by him.

Theories flew around the room as to who had instigated the relationship between Cara and George. Andre and Nick thought Cara had corrupted the young man, while Viv speculated that George's own mother issues had caused him to seek out his grandfather's mistress and lure her into a relationship.

"Well, it could have been a business relationship," Fee said. "Like me and Harrison, yeah?"

"Business relationship?" I asked. I was trying to look casual but I could feel Harrison's gaze on my face while I waited for Fee to explain.

"Didn't I tell you? Harrison is teaching me how to invest my money so that when the time comes, I have enough capital to open my own shop."

"I tried to tell you," Viv whispered in my ear.

"So you did," I said. I tried to ignore the silly burble of happy that was bubbling inside of me. There was no point. I was not going to date anyone for at least another ten months, and Harrison was our business manager. It would be positively stupid to be interested in him. Right?

"Well, it was very apparent that there was more going on with Cara and George than business," I said. "I think he was in love with her and I think she was using him to maintain the lifestyle to which she had become accustomed."

"And Daphne called *us* a pair of oxpecker birds on a hippopotamus?" Viv asked.

"She did not!" Andre cried.

"She did," Viv said.

"Rude!" Nick huffed.

"A show of hands for tea," I cried. They all raised a hand and immediately resumed their discussion of the Grisby family dynamic, which to my mind could easily be called dysfunction junction.

My legs were cramping, so I rose from my seat and took

a stack of dirty dishes to the kitchen. I left the plates in the sink and took up the kettle. That raspberry tart simply demanded hot tea to wash it down.

I had just put the kettle on the stove when I heard someone move behind me. I turned to find Harrison standing by the sink with his arms crossed over his chest, watching me.

"You're looking positively domestic, Ginger," he said.

"Boiling water is a big step for me, Harry," I said.

"It's Harrison," he grumbled. He stepped forward and brushed my swollen lip with his thumb. "Does it hurt?"

"No worse than your head," I said.

He reached around me for the teapot and canister of tea. He made the cramped space seem even smaller and as I caught the scent of his particular cologne my mind immediately flashed to that moment in his room. Yes, that moment. I shook my head. It was best not to go there.

"So, how is your head, anyway?" I asked.

"It's good," he said. He filled the infuser with loose tea leaves and dropped it into the pot. "Or it was until I got a call that a certain someone had gone out to Grisby Hall even though she'd promised me she wouldn't."

He turned and faced me as he spoke and when he finished, he was looming over me, a habit of his I did not appreciate.

"The promise was broken once Tina asked me to help her get to the States," I protested. I tried to put more space between us, but I was wedged between him and the counter. There was no place to run, because believe you me, I would have.

"No, it wasn't," he said. "Another person's cry for help doesn't invalidate a promise you made to someone else."

"Yes, it does," I said. "It's called an extenuating circumstance."

He leaned back and shook his head at me as if he didn't know what to do with me. Well, that was mutual.

"Speaking of circumstances, why did you leave so abruptly this morning?"

"Oh, well, I heard you in the shower, so I figured you were fine," I said. Maintaining eye contact was suddenly uncomfortable, so I glanced over at the paper-wrapped pictures Andre had propped against the wall. As a diversionary tactic, I said, "That was very nice of you to support Andre by buying some of his work. Which pieces did you choose?"

He didn't answer right away, so I glanced back at him to see if he'd heard me. He was studying me intently and I felt that traitorous fluttery feeling that liked to surface whenever he was around. I tried to tamp it down, but his bright-green gaze was wreaking havoc with my ability to concentrate.

"I bought the pictures of you," he said. "Well, you and Viv, actually, but mostly, it was the one of you that I wanted."

I stopped breathing and had to force the air out of the bottom of my lungs to ask, "Why?"

"At the time of the opening, it was because I liked them," he said. "Andre really captured the essence of you in that shot, but now . . ."

He paused and I held my breath.

"Well, after last night—" he began, but I interrupted. I had to know.

"What do you remember about last night?" I asked.

A slow smile spread across his lips and he answered, "Everything."

"Oh." My voice was little more than a puff of breath, and I was a bit afraid I was going to pass out. I forced myself to inhale.

"Well, now I guess your picture will have to keep me company, until I get the chance to kiss you again," he said. He looked at me from under his lashes. "Still determined not to date anyone?"

Okay, this was too much. He was too handsome, too charming, too much to resist. A girl could only take so much, after all.

"I—"

The kettle chose that exact moment to emit an ear-piercing whistle. It interrupted what I had been about to say, and I took it as a sign from the universe that the answer I had been about to give had been wrong.

"Tea time!" I cried and bustled around him to retrieve the kettle. As I was pouring the water into the teapot, I could have sworn I smelled the faint, very faint scent of lily of the valley. Mim.

I got the distinct feeling that Mim was a-okay with my decision not to date for a year and that she didn't want me to give in to the first handsome man who came along.

Harrison stepped up behind me and leaned close to whisper in my ear, "It's quite all right. I'll wait for you."

Well, if that didn't make my eyesight go fuzzy and reduce my innards to jelly. I couldn't even draw a breath until he walked away and joined the others.

To think I could have dated him when we were ten and twelve and he would be completely out of my system. In fact, the old me probably would have dated and broken up with him twice by now. The floral scent grew just a little bit stronger and suddenly it made sense.

"All right, Mim," I muttered as I arranged cups and saucers on the tray with the teapot, cream and sugar on it. "I'll take my time with this, but if I lose out on a good one because I waited, I'm blaming you."

The scent flared a teeny bit stronger and then disappeared. Mim approved. Great. It looked like I was going to learn impulse control whether I liked it or not. Ten more months until I was datable again; surely if Harrison could wait so could I. Right?

Dear Reader,

Traveling to London is always a delightful getaway for me. I just love spending time on Portobello Road in the hat shop with the girls. I never know what's going to happen next. Can Scarlett really go ten more months without dating, especially with someone as dishy as Harrison hanging about? Is Mim really haunting the hat shop, or is it just wishful thinking for Scarlett and Viv? Only the next book in the series will tell.

Writing about a locale like London requires me to flex my librarian muscles, which is another reason I so enjoy the series. I can spend days studying everything from London funeral homes to hat shops to afternoon tea both in person (amazing) but also through books and articles. If you're a research junkie like me, I want to invite you to check out my mystery series for library lovers.

Featuring Lindsey Norris, a small town library director on the Connecticut shore, this series is full of the quirks and eccentricities, as well as the warmth and comfort, that come from living in a tight-knit community. The crafternooners, for example, are Lindsey's closest friends. These ladies meet every week to discuss a book, work on a craft and nosh on delicious food. They also like to debate Lindsey's love life, but she's very good at keeping the conversation on the book at hand.

In their upcoming adventure, holiday cheer fills the town of Briar Creek, making even the grumpiest public servant almost chipper. Things take a somber turn, however, when Lindsey finds her brother Jack hiding in one of the library's meeting rooms. Jack tells her that he's on the run from someone who wants to kill him and that he'll explain later. When later comes, Lindsey opens the door to the meeting room to find her brother missing, leaving a dead body in his place. Now Lindsey is in on borrowed time, trying to find her brother before the police or the killer do.

Keep reading for a preview of On Borrowed Time, *available November 2014 from Berkley Prime Crime. You can preorder it now from all major retailers at jennmckinlay.com*

Happy Reading!
Jenn

Lindsey Norris, director of the Briar Creek Public Library, strode across the library with her keys in hand. It was lunch hour on Thursday, which meant book talk, crafts and snacks, as their weekly crafternoon book club gathered in a meeting room on the far side of the building.

Out of all the activities the library hosted, this was by far Lindsey's favorite. She figured it was the book nerd in her that loved it so, but truthfully, these ladies had become her dearest friends since she'd moved to Briar Creek a few years ago and any moments she shared with them was time well spent.

"Lindsey, wait up!" a voice called to her from the children's department. She spun around to see an old-fashioned aviator charging toward her.

Lindsey squinted. Beneath the leather cap and goggles,

well, she couldn't make out much, but she was pretty sure she recognized the upturned nose and stubborn chin as belonging to her children's librarian, Beth Stanley. But it was hard to say, as the rest of her was dressed in a white scarf, leather bomber jacket, black pants and boots. Not the typical wardrobe for a woman who spent most of her time doing finger plays, felt boards and story times.

"What do you think?" the aviator asked. She planted her hands on her hips and stood like she was posing for a photo.

"I'm not sure," Lindsey said. "Who are you?"

"What? Oh!" The woman wrestled her goggles up onto her head. "It's me— Beth. What do you think of my steam-punk outfit?"

"It's the bomb," Lindsey said with a laugh. Beth looked positively delighted with herself and with good reason. "You look like you could have stepped right out of Scott Wester-feld's *Leviathan*."

"Yes!" Beth pumped a fist in the air. "That's exactly what I was going for. My teen group worked on these at our meeting last night. You should see some of the stuff they made. We're all getting together at the Blue Anchor tonight to have our holiday blowout and show off our outfits."

"I love it," Lindsey said. Not for the first time, she thought how lucky the community was to have Beth, who truly brought reading to life for kids and teens.

"I think you look ridiculous," a voice said from the circulation desk. "Mr. Tupper never let his staff run around in costume, and certainly not out in public."

"No one asked you—" Beth began, but Lindsey cut her off.

"That will do, Ms. Cole," she said. "Beth has done amazing things to get our teens reading."

Ms. Cole sniffed but didn't argue, which Lindsey felt was a big improvement. Known as the lemon to the rest of the staff, Ms. Cole was an old-school librarian who longed for the days of shushing loud patrons and shunning late borrowers.

"Walk and talk," Lindsey said to Beth. "Crafternoon is starting soon, and I need to set up the meeting room."

"Who's bringing the food this week?" Beth asked.

"Nancy."

"Oh, I hope she baked cookies," Beth said. Nancy Peyton, who was also Lindsey's landlord, was known throughout Briar Creek for her exceptional cookie-baking skills. Since it was December and the holidays were just weeks away, Lindsey knew that Nancy had been giving her oven a workout.

"I think that's a safe bet," Lindsey said.

She glanced out the window as they turned down the short hallway that led to the crafternoon room. The town maintenance crew had been decorating the old-fashioned lampposts that lined Main Street with garlands of silver and gold tinsel, and hanging green wreaths with red ribbons just below the lamps.

The decorations added just the right amount of festive energy to the air and helped ward off the gloom that seemed to be descending upon them in the form of menacing, steel-gray clouds, which were reflected by the water in the bay, giving everything a cold, hard and unforgiving appearance.

The crafternoon room had a small gas fireplace and

287

Lindsey had a feeling that they were going to need it today to fight off the wintery chill in the air.

"So, I was thinking you should come and meet up with me and the teens at the Blue Anchor tonight," Beth said. "It'll be fun. I even have enough steampunk gear for you to wear."

Lindsey glanced at her friend. She could not picture herself looking like a souped-up Amelia Earhart, still Beth had spray-painted the goggles copper and stuck all sorts of knobs and gear and even a dragonfly on them. They were pretty cool.

"I don't like to leave Heathcliff alone for that long," she said.

"What alone?" Beth asked. "He's been mooching cookies off of Nancy all day."

"No doubt," Lindsey said. Nancy liked to have Lindsey's dog, Heathcliff, with her during the day. "Which is why he's going to need an even longer walk than usual tonight."

"Aw, come on," Beth said. "It'll be fun. Charlie's band is playing, and who knows? You might run into one of your admirers."

Lindsey gave her a bland look. "I have no idea to whom you could be referring."

"Sully or Robbie," Beth said. "You know they're both hovering around waiting for you to give any hint of encouragement."

"Did you finish the book for this week?" Lindsey asked.

"Nice conversational segue—not," Beth said. "Yes, I finished *The Woman in White*, but you didn't answer—"

"Did you know that the novel was so popular that Wilkie

Collins had "Author of *The Woman in White*" inscribed on his tombstone?"

"Fascinating, but you might want to save that tidbit for when the other crafternooners start to grill you about your love life," Beth said.

Lindsey turned the key in the lock and pushed it open. The room was dark, and she flipped the switch to the left of the door before stepping into the room.

Her gaze moved past the door to where she saw a man standing perfectly still. She felt a thrill of recognition surge through her, but the man shook his head from side to side and then put his finger to his lips. Lindsey knew immediately that he didn't want anyone to know he was here.

She quickly stepped back out of the room, bumping into Beth as she went.

"What's the matter?" Beth asked.

"It's freezing in there," Lindsey said. She shivered as if to prove it. "Even with the fireplace, there's no way this room will be warm enough to meet in. The heat must have been turned off or maybe a window was left open. I'll check it out. In the meantime, could you set up one of the other meeting rooms for us?"

"On it," Beth said and she hustled back down the hallway in the direction of the main library.

As soon as she was gone, Lindsey opened the door and hurried inside. She quickly shut and locked it behind her.

"Jack!" she cried.

"Linds!" he said in return.

The ruggedly handsome man met her halfway across the

289

room with his arms open wide. Lindsey leapt at him, and he caught her in a hug that almost, but not quite, crushed her.

When he released her, Lindsey stepped back and stared at the face so similar to her own. She had many people in her life whom she considered close friends, but the bond between siblings was one that could not be surpassed.

"Okay, brother of mine," she said as she crossed her arms over her chest in a fair imitation of their mother when she was irritated. "Start explaining."

From *New York Times* Bestselling Author

Jenn McKinlay

Cloche and Dagger

THE FIRST IN THE BRAND-NEW HAT SHOP MYSTERIES

Not only is Scarlett Parker's love life in the loo—as her British cousin Vivian Tremont would say—it's also gone viral with an embarrassing video. So when Viv suggests Scarlett leave Florida to lay low in London, she hops on the next plane across the pond to work at Viv's ladies' hat shop, Mim's Whims, and forget her troubles.

But a few surprises await Scarlett in London. First, she is met at the airport not by Viv, but by her handsome business manager, Harrison Wentworth. Second, Viv seems to be missing. No one is too concerned about it until one of her posh clients is found dead wearing the cloche hat Viv made for her—and nothing else. Is Scarlett's cousin in trouble? Or is she in hiding?

"A delightful new heroine!"
—Deborah Crombie, *New York Times* bestselling author

jennmckinlay.com
facebook.com/TheCrimeSceneBooks
penguin.com

M1340T0613

"[McKinlay] continues to deliver well-crafted
mysteries full of fun and plot twists."
—*Booklist*

FROM *NEW YORK TIMES* BESTSELLING AUTHOR

Jenn McKinlay

Going,
Going,
Ganache

A Cupcake Bakery Mystery

After a cupcake-flinging fiasco at a photo shoot for a local
magazine, Melanie Cooper and Angie DeLaura agree to make
amends by hosting a weeklong corporate boot camp at Fairy
Tale Cupcakes. The idea is the brainchild of Ian Hannigan, new
owner of *Southwest Style*, a lifestyle magazine that chronicles the
lives of Scottsdale's rich and famous. He's assigned his staff to a
team-building week of making cupcakes for charity.

It's clear that the staff would rather be doing just about
anything other than frosting baked goods. But when the
magazine's features director is found murdered outside the
bakery, Mel and Angie have a new team-building exercise—find
the killer before their business goes AWOL.

INCLUDES SCRUMPTIOUS RECIPES

jennmckinlay.com
facebook.com/jennmckinlay
facebook.com/TheCrimeSceneBooks
penguin.com

FROM *NEW YORK TIMES* BESTSELLING AUTHOR

JENN MCKINLAY

-The Library Lover's Mysteries-

BOOKS CAN BE DECEIVING
DUE OR DIE
BOOK, LINE, AND SINKER
READ IT AND WEEP

Praise for the Library Lover's Mysteries

"[An] appealing new mystery series."

—Kate Carlisle, *New York Times* bestselling author

"A sparkling setting, lovely characters, books, knitting, and chowder! What more could any reader ask?"

—Lorna Barrett, *New York Times* bestselling author

"Sure to charm cozy readers everywhere."

—Ellery Adams, author of the Books by the Bay Mysteries

jennmckinlay.com
facebook.com/TheCrimeSceneBooks
penguin.com

M1145AS0613